A Place
Near Eden

Nell Pierce holds a Master of Fine Art in Fiction from The New School. She has worked at a literary agency in New York City and at the Family Court of Australia. *A Place Near Eden* is her debut novel.

A Place Near Eden

Nell Pierce

ALLEN&UNWIN
SYDNEY•MELBOURNE•AUCKLAND•LONDON

First published in 2022

Allen & Unwin
83 Alexander Street
Crows Nest NSW 2065
Australia
Phone: (61 2) 8425 0100
Email: info@allenandunwin.com
Web: www.allenandunwin.com

 A catalogue record for this book is available from the National Library of Australia

ISBN 978 1 76106 617 7

Set in 13.25/18.75 pt Adobe Jenson Pro by Bookhouse, Sydney
Printed and bound in Australia by Griffin Press, part of Ovato

10 9 8 7 6 5 4 3 2 1

The paper in this book is FSC® certified. FSC® promotes environmentally responsible, socially beneficial and economically viable management of the world's forests.

For Mark Bo Chu

Prologue

A STRANGE CONNECTION BOUND THE three of us, Celeste and Sem and me. When I think of them now, they are at the houses where we used to live. At the big house on Angel Street, sitting on the faded red couch out front, their bare feet resting next to dirty cups and plates from dinners weeks past, globs of tomato sauce sun-baked into the crockery. Or at the beach house near Eden, out on the squeaky fibro deck, the calls of bellbirds dissolving into the hot air. Or right back at the beginning, at the house on Carlisle Road, lying on blankets on the front lawn. Sometimes I wish I could go back to those houses. Ask them what happened in their rooms and under their ceilings and have them whisper my old words back to me, retell my conversations, and show me how their windows opened and their floorboards creaked as we moved about.

I remember the local swimming pool. The insects we called flying saucers because they hovered over the water and zipped away. The sun blinking onto the grass through the shifting leaves overhead. Babies, held under their arms and dipped into the pool like cookies into milk. My bathers hanging around my crotch, the material thinned from summers of chlorine, Sem pinching the fabric and whispering, 'Elephant butt.' Acne by the corner of his mouth. That feeling when I plunged beneath the water, the world muffled, like I'd made myself disappear. All those things come back to me easily.

I remember sitting on the lip of the wading pool, just turned thirteen, waiting for Sem and Celeste, the prickle of the concrete beneath my thighs. Little kids staggering about with floaties on their arms. Old women resting in the shallows, lifting their toes into the fountain spray. I remember the flesh on the bodies of those women, the skin that hung from their arms and under their necks. Blushing when I realised I'd been looking too long. This moment, sitting on the lip of the pool, I remember. It would be one of the days when my brother, Sem, vanished. I just didn't know it yet.

I remember the anticipation. Even now, when I go to my local swimming pool, a shadow of that feeling remains, soaked into the concrete, in the damp shapes where swimmers have lain to dry off. Expectation. We all felt it. Waiting for Sem and Celeste to come back from behind the changing shed, waiting for the girls to take off their shorts and lie down in the sun, waiting for the spray of the cannonball to reach our cheeks, waiting for the swimmer to feel the hand around her ankle tugging her beneath the surface.

I can still picture the way they came back across the grass, Celeste and Sem, almost holding hands, the tips of their fingers touching, knuckles brushing.

'Can you smell it on me?' Celeste asked, leaning in, the ends of her hair tickling my face.

I shook my head, not even knowing what I was meant to smell, and Sem smiled at me affectionately.

'She's just a kid,' he said. Sem and Celeste were fourteen, almost fifteen.

'But you do know what it is?' Celeste pressed, looking at me with her flat grey eyes.

'Of course,' I said, though back then I hardly knew what pot was, let alone what it was supposed to smell like. To cover my ignorance, I pushed myself over the lip of the pool and charged off among the toddlers.

'Watch it, Tilly,' Sem called after me.

Celeste was laughing. I heard the splash of her following me across the shallow pool. I think she laughed even harder when the little kid went down. I remember looking at him. He had colourful swimming shorts on. Red, maybe. Or blue. He got up and was quiet for a moment before he began to cry. Blood started to run from his head, where he must have hit it on the pale blue tiles beneath the water.

One of the women who had been sitting in the shallows chatting now stood. She had grey hair gathered up in a ponytail and was wearing red lipstick. 'What's going on?' she asked, looking first at Celeste and then at me. 'Who's supervising this child?' She was intimidating, this woman who wore bright red lipstick even in the pool.

Before we could answer, the mum arrived, holding a baby wearing a sodden nappy and a rashie. 'What's happened?' she asked the woman with the lipstick. Then she kneeled down beside the boy in the water, taking his chin in her hand and turning his face to examine his head.

When I look back on it now, I think I can remember bumping the boy. The soft pressure of his body against my knee. The give of him. How he looked when he fell. The blood coming from his head. I was scared of getting into trouble. That's why, although I was the one who knocked the boy down, I turned and pointed to Celeste and said, 'It was her. She pushed him.'

So maybe that's what happened. I pointed at Celeste to save myself. If it had not been Celeste standing there, but Sem, or a girl from school, I would have done the same.

But then I remember Celeste walking back across the grass, her fingers grazing Sem's. The way she had leaned in, almost mocking me, asking me if I knew. The heat of anger rippling through my shoulders as she laughed. I can remember it that way too. I turned and pointed at Celeste because I wanted to punish her.

And then there's another memory, one that comes just as easily: Celeste was the one who knocked down the boy. I turned to look back and saw her standing over him, laughter dying on her lips at the sight of the blood coming from his head. I pointed to Celeste because she was the guilty one.

4

The more I think on things, one way or the other, the more real they seem. That I was afraid of getting in trouble. Or that I wanted to punish Celeste. That it was her fault, or mine. I can believe it either way.

I think I must have gone to fetch my mum and Celeste's mother Christina from the lap pool. By the time we'd returned to the wading pool, Sem was gone.

———

There is a swimming pool in the town near where I'm staying now, and I like to go there and sit in the bleachers by the lap pool. Watch the kids climb up to the diving board and walk out along its wobbling length. Sometimes, when I see a girl about the right age, fourteen or so, with even just one or two qualities your mother used to have—her hair, maybe, or her attitude, strutting along the board—I like to imagine it's you standing up there, about to plummet into the water below.

You'd be a year old by now, but I've seen a hundred versions of you at all different ages. Sometimes you're a child, a little girl running into the ocean and gasping at the coldness of the water. Other times you'll be a teenager, walking to school or sunbathing with your friends in the park. I see you as a young woman with messy hair getting out of a car. At the pool, you're always the age of your mother that day when the boy was knocked down. And there really is a moment when I think I've seen you. A glimpse into your future. But then it passes, time snaps back and I remember you're still just a baby. I realise that the girl I'm looking at is a stranger, and I can turn away.

It's funny. I see you everywhere. But I never see Sem. In the end, he really did disappear completely.

Sometimes, I imagine you are all together again, living in a nowhere place, and if I crawled into a dark cupboard, or opened my eyes underwater at the pool, I might catch a glimpse of you all there.

Part I

Part I

Chapter One

I HAD PLANNED TO TELL you everything that happened to Sem
and Celeste and me when we were older. What happened out
at Eden, and the events that followed. But I can see now that
the story starts earlier, at least as early as the day Sem moved
out. The day they took him away. Maybe even earlier. With
the accident on the bridge, perhaps. Or maybe the story really
began when my parents decided to foster Sem.

The fact that my parents had chosen Sem made him even
dearer to me. He arrived fully formed, thirteen years old, with
a flop of dark hair and a pointed chin. I felt lucky to have him.
But for my parents it wasn't a matter of luck. Mum talked about
the drawn-out bureaucracy of the foster system with such frustration, it was as if she deserved Sem, as though every hurdle
was preventing her from claiming the son she was owed.

We were the Holmans, our name written in cursive script
across our letterbox. We lived in Canberra, in a suburb of

long streets of single-storey houses with low front hedges and yellowed lawns. The air got so cold in winter that it hurt to breathe in. Summers were so hot that your skin burned just walking to the car and the sky was an eerie, saturated blue.

Almost as soon as he arrived at our house, Sem started running away from it. When he wasn't running away, he was angry. Most nights he got home from school and stormed straight to his bedroom, shutting his door with a bang, and wouldn't come out until long after dinner was over, when he would eat the plate of now-cold food Mum had left out for him. But sometimes he didn't come home at all, and Mum and I would sit in the car out the front of school for ten minutes, twenty minutes, half an hour, until Mum let out an anxious sigh and went in to see if any of the teachers could find him.

Each time Sem disappeared was a fresh worry for my parents. Usually, he didn't venture too far. Once a friend's mother called up to say that he was at her house, and there was the night Dad found him down by the lake, shivering beneath a picnic table. But sometimes he travelled further. He took a bus out of town and the police had to be called. One time it was three days before they found him and brought him home.

My mother, I think, felt humiliated. It was as if her love was not enough. And my dad, well, I don't think Dad had been too keen on fostering Sem in the first place. In the days before he arrived, Dad kept bringing up all the ways in which Mum wasn't prepared to care for a teenage boy.

'What will you do when he comes home drunk, or smelling of weed?' Dad asked one night over dinner.

'I'll have a mature conversation with him,' Mum said, spooning more carrots onto her plate.

'Good luck with that.' Dad smiled mockingly.

Or, driving past a group of boys standing around out the front of the newsagency, Dad announced, 'He'll be destructive. He'll break things. Make a mess. That's what boys are like.'

Mum just shrugged and said, 'We'll deal with that when we come to it. Material things really aren't that important anyway.'

So when Sem arrived only to keep trying to leave, Dad probably felt vindicated, in a way. He liked to say that Sem was 'trouble' and 'troubled'. When he found a pack of cigarettes under Sem's bed. When Sem helped with garden work and tore the end of the drainpipe away from the roof. When Sem swore at the dinner table, didn't do his homework, tagged his name on his desk in white-out, touched all the expensive and breakable things when we were shopping. Dad had a special tired voice that he used when he talked about Sem. It was a tone of accusation too. Directed not at Sem but at my mother, who had brought Sem into our lives.

When I think about it now, I'm surprised it didn't occur to me at the time that Sem was running from my dad and his disapproval, his obvious reluctance to have Sem in the house. But then I think of Mum. Maybe it was her he was trying to escape. The moment she met him, Mum already loved Sem like she'd had him for all of his thirteen years. Maybe that was what he wanted to get away from: the great weight of her love and the expectation that went with it. Like she'd given so much to him—carefully packed lunches and home-cooked dinners, freshly washed clothes and lifts home from school—now she was waiting for him to give something back.

But then I think maybe he wasn't running away from my parents at all. Maybe he was running towards something. Looking for a certain place or person, or trying to get back to family or friends that he loved.

Or maybe those were the things he was running from. Something that happened with his mother, or later, at one of the other foster homes. Running away from things in his past. Now, I can understand that kind of running. To escape your history, you have to escape yourself. Whether it's under a picnic table or on a bus out of town or plunged into the alien silence underwater, you have to find a way to somehow, even if just for a moment, make yourself disappear.

Maybe, I think now, Sem was running away from me.

Mum and Sem and I moved to the house on Carlisle Road the week after the big storm. I guess this was when my parents officially separated, though I'm not sure I was entirely aware of that at the time. I thought we were moving to the Carlisle Road house because it was close to the hills, and Mum needed a break from the city. Like we were on a kind of retreat, while Dad stayed back in the city to work, and soon we'd go back to our real life.

The storm was so bad it was in the news. When we got to Carlisle Road, we saw the evidence of its destructive power. Part of the downstairs sitting room had been reduced to rubble by a thick, bleached-blue eucalyptus and, around the back, the orchard was a wreck of fruit and broken trees.

When I think of those first days at that house, I think of Celeste. The pale skin on the underside of her foot, her leg extended as she read in bed, the first time I saw her, glimpsed through an open door.

A family of five had once lived there—a doctor and his wife, their two daughters and a son—but by the time we moved in the doctor was dead, his wife in a nursing home, and it was the grown son who was renting the top floor of the place to us and the bottom floor to Christina and her daughter Celeste, with whom we shared a kitchen. It was only going to be for six months or so before the sale went through and the new owners came to demolish and redevelop the lot. I suppose Mum was in such a hurry to find somewhere for us to stay after we left Dad's house that this was probably the best she could find. Somewhere to hide Sem away and protect him from what she feared was coming down the line.

Mum had met Christina at the library where she taught her evening community English class. Christina was the children's librarian, though really she wanted to be an artist. She used to work on her sculptures in the back garden, standing barefoot in the grass in clay-stained jeans and an old T-shirt, frowning in concentration. Mum and Christina were already friends, so moving in together was pretty easy. It made sense.

In our first few days at Carlisle Road, we helped Christina collect the fruit from the peach trees on the property that had been destroyed in the storm. The peaches were small and so thickly fuzzed that after a while they started to hurt my hands. We sorted them into baskets by their quality and size. Now when I see peaches in the supermarket, fat and ever-ripe, it's hard to believe they are the same fruit.

———

Looking back at that time, I find it difficult to trust my memories. It was a long time ago, and there was so much happening all at once. Sem lived with us for two years, but so much occurred in those last few months, after we moved to Carlisle Road, that it's hard now to keep track. For example, which came first: Sem's accident, or my visits to the counsellor? I think it must have been Sem's accident at the bridge.

The bridge spanned the creek that ran by our school, swelling when it rained and drying to a trickle when it was hot. On the day of his accident, Sem and I were walking home from school. It must have been a Friday, because Monday through Thursday Mum usually picked us up, but on Friday she taught her class at the library and Sem and I made our own way home.

It was raining hard, and we'd missed the bus because I wanted to go back for my maths book, which I had left in my locker. That year, I was enamoured with maths. My teacher was new to the school, and he was young. Early twenties. Just out of uni. There was a nerviness to him, standing in front of the class, that would make his voice suddenly go soft in the middle of explaining an equation and a slight flush would rise up in his pale cheeks. He was so sincere. Easy for a thirteen-year-old to fall in love with.

By the time I splashed back through the rain with my text-book, the bus had gone and Sem was in a mood, because my delay had meant we would get cold and wet. We'd have to trudge in the rain to the next stop to catch a different bus.

We walked in the gutter, because there weren't any foot-paths along the first few blocks. Sem was in front and I trailed behind. I was annoyed with myself for going back for the textbook. I should have left it. Now Sem was angry with me, and the book was probably getting ruined anyway in my wet backpack.

But then Sem turned and looked at me over his shoulder and smiled. 'I never knew you were so keen on maths,' he said. 'But then again, it is a handsome subject. Romantic, even.' He was teasing me. I'd been forgiven. Of course, Sem knew all about my maths teacher. When Mr Rood wasn't fumbling with a whiteboard marker in the classroom, he was serving as the school counsellor. My brother met with him weekly, on account of his behavioural issues. Mum called it 'acting out'.

Later, after everything that happened, I tried to find Mr Rood. I thought he'd be able to clarify some things. Tell me about Sem. What he had been through. But the school wouldn't share his forwarding address. I think they knew what I was after. They cited confidentiality.

Now that I felt I'd been forgiven, I came up beside Sem, so we were walking side by side.

I can't remember why we started talking about the bridge. But we were talking about it, and about how some of the other kids—boys, mainly—would climb over the low concrete wall that ran along the side of the bridge to stand on the narrow ledge below and graffiti their names.

Sem had a paint marker in his coat pocket that he'd pinched from the art room at school. As we neared the bridge, he took it out and showed it to me, then he leaped up onto the bridge wall. The next step would be to lower himself down carefully until he found his footing on the ledge that stuck out several feet below. But a car had come up behind us and stopped. I turned to see Mr Rood, my beautiful maths teacher, running towards us. For one wild moment I thought he was running to me, but he went past without stopping and I realised he was heading for my brother. 'No!' he called.

Sem looked back at Mr Rood and his expression was strangely resentful. And then—and it did look almost like a jump—he disappeared over the edge.

Sem was lucky to have survived with as few injuries as he did. Everyone agreed on that. We were lucky it was so unseasonably rainy, and the creek wasn't too shallow. Lucky he had fallen at just the right angle, with the right amount of tension in his body as he hit the water.

Mr Rood made it down to the creek before I did, and he must have pulled Sem out of the water. When I reached them, Sem was lying on the bank among all this garbage—old cans of soft drink and bottles and chip packets—and Mr Rood was kneeling beside him, pushing Sem's wet hair off his face. Mr Rood took off his grey woollen jumper, folded it, and put it under Sem's head on the muddy bank. I was struck by that: Mr Rood putting his beautiful grey jumper in the mud seemingly without a second thought. I almost said something, but Mr Rood looked up at me, and the expression on his face, the unfiltered panic, made me realise that I should have been worried about my brother, not the jumper. Until that moment I hadn't understood how seriously Sem had been injured. I can't quite describe the feeling that came over me then. I think the closest word is ashamed. Ashamed for my concern about the jumper, but also ashamed that Sem was hurt. As if it was my fault. I should have stopped him. I should have tried to hold him back.

Sem had a concussion and a fractured wrist. The wrist was a bad break. It was complex. That was the term the doctors liked to use. A complex fracture. A complex wound.

—

I think it must have been after Sem's accident when Dad took me to the counsellor for the first time; I still had regular visits with Dad at the beginning, when we were living at Carlisle Road. But he didn't take me to Mr Rood, the school counsellor. Dad had found a woman named Mrs Rose. I think I saw her twice. Maybe three times. Dad drove me to her office, which was in a shopping centre. Glass walls, with a view over the car park. I've thought back on those sessions with the counsellor many times, trying to remember what kind of questions she asked me and in what order. I know now that this is very important: the type of questions and the order of them. Questions that demand a certain kind of answer, or questions that open the door to a room in your mind and let you discover for yourself what might be there.

Mrs Rose asked me about Sem. About how he was with me. The way I remember it, she started innocently. We talked about how Sem helped me with my homework sometimes, and how sometimes I had to help him, because he hadn't had a consistent education before he came to us. I'm sure we talked about that, because I remember feeling a little guilty, or embarrassed, talking about Sem and his schoolwork. I guess I thought I sounded like a bit of a snob.

And Sem really loved some parts of school. Like English. He loved English. So I felt bad telling Mrs Rose that sometimes he used words in the wrong way, and I would have to tell him what they really meant. He'd have some new word he'd just discovered, like 'exuberant', but then he'd go around saying things like, 'This pie is exuberant,' and I would have to tell him that he wasn't using the word the right way.

It's funny thinking back to the young me who corrected Sem like that. As if I knew better than him. After all, why shouldn't a pie be exuberant? It's kind of poetic. But I was a different person when I first met Sem. More dominant and confident. Maybe it was because I was still just a kid, only on the very edge of puberty. Or maybe it was because nothing bad had happened yet. I was still going happily about my way in the world. I'm embarrassed to think about it now, but Sem was never bothered by my correcting him. He'd just say that I hadn't spoken to enough people.

'No one really talks the way you say they do, Till,' he'd tell me.

So, all that's to say I'm sure I spoke with Mrs Rose about Sem and English. But at some point the tone changed. I didn't realise that until we were already talking about it. Talking about if Sem ever came into my room, and did I close the door when I was getting changed, and what was our routine in the bathroom, and did he have a girlfriend, and did I have a boyfriend.

I try to remember what I said, and how I felt about Sem back then. And, if I'm honest—and I am trying to be honest with you here, that is the whole point of this thing—I think I was attracted to him. Sem seemed so cool. And grown up. There was part of me at thirteen years old, in that counsellor's office, that wanted Sem to be my boyfriend, even if I didn't really understand what that meant. I don't think I knew how dangerous it was to want that. How destructive it might be to suggest such a relationship to this bespectacled middle-aged woman in her office above the car park in the shopping centre.

But I must have said something concerning to Mrs Rose during those sessions. I must have implied that something had happened between Sem and me. Maybe I thought it wouldn't be such a big deal. Maybe I thought it was okay to exaggerate a little. Like how the girls at school did sometimes, to show each other how grown up they were.

I have a memory from around this time of overhearing a group of popular girls at school gossiping, and one girl, who lived on my street, boasting that she had a boyfriend and had kissed him. I didn't say anything, because I wasn't part of their circle, but I knew the boy in question, who lived on our block, and he was definitely not her boyfriend, in fact he barely even said hello to her.

Maybe that's why I said what I did to Mrs Rose. Maybe I was just talking myself up. I do know that whenever people talked about boyfriends or sex or anything like that it made me uncomfortable. I think it was because I felt like I was behind. No one was really interested in being friends with me, let alone anything more, and it was embarrassing to have to admit that. Maybe all Mrs Rose's questioning about showering and bedroom doors and boyfriends and girlfriends had me feeling like I needed to defend myself, to pretend that I was on the same page as everyone else, that I hadn't been left behind or cast out.

Now, in retrospect, I wonder whether maybe the whole arrangement with Sem really wasn't appropriate, even if nothing had happened. If I was thinking about him like that, then perhaps we needed to be separated. It wasn't fair that he had to go and I got to stay, but I guess the foster system isn't fair.

So, I think I must have said that something happened between Sem and me. Because I remember the social workers. It was the day after Mum and Dad's big fight. Mum was out the front, gardening, and Dad came around. I heard them yelling and looked out from the window upstairs to see them shouting at each other on the lawn. It was difficult to make out what they were saying, but the next day, the social workers arrived.

Mum showed them into our living room upstairs and asked me to bring biscuits. At the time, I thought they were there because they were worried about how Sem had gone over the bridge. Neither Sem nor I had ever mentioned that he had been planning to tag his name that day. I'd thought he'd get in trouble. But when the social workers arrived, I realised that I needed to come clean, so that they understood it was just an accident, nothing more.

'There's something I have to tell you,' I said, handing Mum the biscuits. 'Sem was climbing the side of the bridge that day because he'd been planning to tag his name. He slipped and fell.' I pulled a face, as if to acknowledge that it had been a pretty stupid thing to want to do.

But Mum just furrowed her brow. 'Go to your room, Tilly,' she said. 'I don't have time for this right now.'

I went and sat on my bed. The interaction hadn't gone the way I'd thought. I started to question why the social workers had come after all. If it wasn't because of the bridge, was it because of Sem's running away, or my parents' separation? Or was it—as I now suspect—because of what I'd said to Mrs Rose?

I sometimes wonder about the timing of Sem's accident. Did he go over the bridge before Mrs Rose or after? Perhaps it was after. Maybe he jumped because they told him what I said and he was angry that I'd lied and he'd have to leave us. And then I feel confused, and I think that I'm forgetting and getting things mixed up. Because wasn't Sem just planning to tag his name when he slipped and fell? Wasn't it all just an accident?

Now, I blame those sessions with Mrs Rose, whether they happened before the bridge or afterwards. Because I think that it was in those sessions that my sense of what was true was shaken. Maybe that's when I changed. I was no longer that kid who so confidently told her foster brother that he was using words in the wrong way, who sat in the counsellor's office and spoke and did not think about the consequences.

But if I'm really honest, when I look back at those sessions with Mrs Rose and everything that happened after, right up until today, I know that I'm to blame. And maybe that's what changed me: the knowledge that I could hurt someone so badly without even meaning to. Maybe that is the truth I'm not able to believe.

Chapter Two

THE DAY SEM LEFT STARTED like any other day at Carlisle Road. We went to the pool, which we often did back then, though summer was drawing to a close. Mum had wrapped a plastic bag around Sem's cast, but still, he wasn't allowed to go in the water, so he and Celeste spent most of their time behind the changing sheds, or hanging out under the trees. In the early afternoon we came home and lay around on the front lawn, drinking cordial and eating sandwiches. We were waiting for the car to come for Sem. Mum must have discussed it with me, though I can't remember the conversation. I think it was one of those things that gradually became evident, in the way things often did back then, like Mum and Dad's separation, the move to Carlisle Road. Everyone just started acting as though it had already been announced, and eventually I caught on.

So, the day Sem left, I was expecting it, but I wasn't prepared for what it would mean. We were all out on the lawn. Mum was wearing one of her own creations—a sleeveless brown sack. By then, those sacks were all she wore. When we left the old house where we'd lived with Dad, Mum stuffed all her clothes into the donation bin that stood outside the post office at the local shops. Then, at Carlisle Road, she set up her sewing machine on the kitchen table and began to whirr out new clothes from off-cuts she'd got on sale at fabric stores and recycled op shop finds. I loved that sewing machine. One of my strongest memories from those early days at the Carlisle Road house is the calming rhythm of Mum's Singer, her foot beneath the table pressing down on the pedal like she was playing an instrument.

When she was with Dad, my mum had seemed just like all the other mums I knew. Unremarkable. We weren't particularly close—not like those mums and daughters who went shopping and gossiped together—but we didn't fight either. Mum was reliable back then. Dinner was always on time, and I knew how I was getting to and from school. She bought my clothes and books and other things I wanted, like toys and colourful pens and packets of collectable stamps that I kept in an album in my desk drawer. And she did the same for Sem when he arrived. I didn't really appreciate it at the time. I took for granted that she would always be there, making my life work.

But after the separation Mum changed. At the house on Carlisle Road, and even more when we moved down to Melbourne, to the house on Angel Street. She started going out into the bush—'connecting with nature', she called it. Once she even burned a box of her old things in the back garden at

Carlisle Road while Sem and I watched from the window, half laughing and half afraid. It was 'a spiritual cleansing', she said. We stopped eating meat and Mum started giving me these huge vitamin pills that I hated swallowing and which I hid under my mattress and flushed down the toilet.

I felt shocked, I think, when Mum first started to change. But because it coincided with the move to Carlisle Road, I linked the two in my mind, and saw it as a sort of life experiment Mum was trying on for size. It was just temporary. Things would go back to normal, I thought. And besides, Sem seemed to find the whole thing funny, so I pretended to find it funny too. By the time Sem left, and we moved to the Angel Street house, Mum's new way of being had become normal. Life had somehow moved along, and everything had changed, without me ever really stopping to realise it.

Looking back, I wonder if those changes in Mum might have been part of the reason that she and Dad split up. Maybe she needed space to be herself. Perhaps the separation was more about Mum than anything to do with Sem. I mean, it makes sense. Isn't that what separations are usually about: the people who are separating? But then I remember how Dad had never really wanted Sem in the house. I think of Mr Rood and Mrs Rose. How Mum was when they took Sem away. And how Dad came over the next day.

'Gone then, has he?' Dad said, standing in the driveway almost in the same place where the car had parked to take Sem. He was standing out there because Mum wouldn't let him come inside. 'I thought I might need to come and collect her,' he said, looking at me. I was behind Mum, up on the porch. Celeste and Christina were watching from inside, behind the flywire door.

'You got what you wanted, Andrew,' Mum said, her voice wobbling. 'Now you can leave us alone.'

Dad raised his hands. 'You're getting worked up,' he said. 'Please try to stay calm.'

'You need to leave,' said Mum.

'This was for the best,' Dad said. 'I hope eventually you'll be able to see that.'

Now, I wish I'd gone down to Dad that day instead of hanging back on the porch. The idea did cross my mind, because of what he said, about coming to collect me. That challenged an idea I'd developed, that Dad didn't want to spend time with me anymore. You see, after my sessions with Mrs Rose, I hadn't seen my dad at all. So I'd decided that what I said about me and Sem must have disgusted him. When I thought about it, I felt sick with shame. Even before I went to see Mrs Rose, when we were still living at Dad's house, Dad had told me I couldn't wear my bikini to the pool anymore, only my daggy old one-piece, and he never let me go out with my midriff showing. The kind of stuff I'd told Mrs Rose, about Sem and me, I should only have talked about with kids at school; it was meant for secret chats in the playground or at the bus stop after school, not adults. Of course, I didn't know what was happening between Mum and Dad behind the scenes, how things were more complicated than I knew. But still, it does seem to me now, looking back, that I was at least partly right, and that what I'd said to Mrs Rose did affect my relationship with my father, putting a distance between us.

So, I do wonder what would have happened if, instead of hanging back on the porch, I'd gone down and talked to my dad. I almost did. I think it was loyalty to Mum that held me back. And also fear. I was worried that he would reject me right there in front of Mum, with Christina and Celeste watching through the flywire door. I couldn't face that.

———

The day Sem left, Mum was lying on her back on a blanket in the grass, hand over her eyes, long grey-brown hair spread out like a veil. We all smelled of spice and chlorine but there was a special sourness to Mum, like milk just starting to spoil. The smell of worry. Nervous anticipation.

Celeste's mum, Christina, was reading a paperback, sitting with her knees drawn up as if she were a teenager and not a middle-aged woman, the cuffs of her white linen pants hitched up to reveal her narrow ankles. From time to time she lifted her eyes and glanced around as if she were monitoring us all, quietly keeping watch.

I was lying on my stomach, half on the blanket, watching my brother through the grass. He was walking awkwardly from his accident at the bridge as he picked his way among the debris still scattered from the storm.

Celeste lay by my side wearing big white headphones. She was resting on her elbows, her shoulders milky with sunscreen.

'Your brother's cute,' she said.

'Huh?'

'Don't pretend you don't know what I mean. I see the way you look at him.'

I had been watching Sem limping among the bricks. But now, face hot, I flipped onto my back. 'Gross.'

I'd helped Sem pack his bags that morning. Of course, he had left it to the last minute. I emptied the drawers of his t-shirts and jeans and underwear, the smell of him mixed with the laundry detergent Mum used. When I took the shirts from the wardrobe, I saw that he had stuck up pictures on the back wall. One was a photograph of a labrador, with its tongue stuck out, standing in the dirt with a ball. A second photograph showed some playground equipment, in the evening, with long shadows. There was big soccer poster: a guy, running, poised to strike the ball. And, finally, a poem, printed out in large text with the author's name in italics. A poem about gardening, and about writing too.

It might not seem like much. A few things in a cupboard. But when we lived with my father, Sem and I weren't allowed to decorate our rooms. In fact, it was one of the things that Dad and Mum fought about.

'It isn't right,' Mum said. 'We need to welcome Sem into the family. It should be: *What's mine is yours.*'

Dad disagreed. 'I will treat him the same way I treat my own child,' he said. 'When he's saved up for a house of his own, he can treat it however he likes. Until then, he'll play by my rules. Besides, it's one thing to welcome a stranger into your home, it's another to let him take over the place. There must be a reason he was being bounced around before we took him in.'

I remember Mum telling Sem he had to take down all the posters and photographs he'd brought with him from the last house, and the next day he ran away again. But, when we left Dad's house and moved to Carlisle Road, Mum said we were free to do whatever we liked with our rooms. So why had Sem decorated the back of his wardrobe? A secret place, that was only his?

Sometimes, when I dream of you, you're grown up, a teenager already, yelling at your mother the way Celeste used to yell at Christina, defending herself when she was caught smoking down the side of the house on Carlisle Road. Even when Celeste was in trouble, she was always the one doing the yelling. Her angry voice reaching my room on the first floor or our small lounge room, where Mum would raise her eyebrows and say, 'At it again.' Or, like Sem, you're slamming doors, keeping secrets in your room, running away. That fiery spirit they shared. I can't imagine that you won't be like that too. I imagine that perhaps your grandmother will teach you to be an artist. Maybe, like your father, you'll love words. There are so many different ways I imagine you.

On the lawn, I rolled over. Mum had also turned onto her stomach and had lifted a corner of the blanket up to her face.

Christina put down her book and came over and moved her hand over Mum's back in small circles, rubbing the coarse brown fabric of her dress. Mum lifted her head and I saw that she was crying.

'Celeste,' Christina called.

Celeste and my brother were standing together among the bricks, backs to us. Now, Celeste half-turned.

'Time for you girls to take a shower. Sem, come keep Nancy company while I find them some towels.'

Nancy was my mum. I didn't go to comfort her as she cried. I just followed Christina and Celeste across the dry lawn, picking my way carefully to avoid bindies.

Inside was a long sunroom, the blinds drawn so that only slender fingers of light reached into the cool gloom. Next, the kitchen, slate-blue tiles up the walls, a plastic jug of cordial on the bench. Then the small dining room, table covered with a white cloth. Down the long corridor, past the room where I had first glimpsed Celeste, and into the bathroom. Sunlight softened by the mottled glass illuminated bright green tiles with clean white grouting and brass faucets.

I remember that bathroom so clearly, Celeste lifting her yellow sundress over her head and dropping it onto the green-tiled floor. She was wearing a black bikini exploding with sunflowers. I was very jealous of that bikini. She reached around to undo the ties holding the top in place. And then the bottoms, shimmied over her thighs to the cool green floor. Naked, her body pale where her bathers had been, she walked around the shower cubicle to the toilet and the sound of her wee filled the room, bouncing off all the polished surfaces, so that she was everywhere at once, urinating.

'Here you go.' Christina came in and placed two deep green towels on the edge of the bath.

Celeste got into the shower. The heavy sound of the water coming down.

'Jump in too,' Christina said to me. 'The hot water doesn't last long.'

I took off my shorts and tank top, stripped off my swimsuit and stepped into the shower, the cubicle already full of Celeste. She was washing her hair. The suds were running over her breasts. Her sparse pubic hair was dark, pulled long and straight by the water. Quickly and silently, I washed my own body, running an old yellow bar of soap over my limbs. I was thirteen, but a late developer, and my own chest was only just beginning to form. As the scent of Celeste's shampoo dispersed, a new smell rose around us, deep and warm. I understood the smell instinctively. Sweet. Fertile. I looked down to see the water around our feet was tinged with pink.

'Sorry,' Celeste said. 'I'm on my period.'

She passed me the shampoo and stepped out of the shower, her body disappearing into a dark green towel. I lathered my hair, closing my eyes against the stinging suds. When I opened them, Celeste was gone and all I could smell was the chemical tang of shampoo.

And when I came back outside, dressed again in my shorts and top, a white car was idling in the dusty driveway.

———

I think the old house on Carlisle Road is townhouses now. I looked it up, once. All those big dark buildings knocked down to make way for something new, fresh and bright.

———

A social worker was standing beside the white car. She was wearing a navy t-shirt that was stretched out around her bust. Sem was throwing his bags into the boot.

He came over to say goodbye. The air felt cool against my shower-wet hair. There was a smell to Sem when he gently pulled me in, a new man smell. He was in the middle of a growth spurt—'shooting up', Mum called it—and his body had become long: long shins, long forearms; even his face, greasy and starting to fuzz, had a new length to it.

'See ya, Till,' he said. I could feel his cast pressed awkwardly against my back. He let me go, and then he lifted his hands in front of his face, like a camera, and took an invisible photo of me. 'Miss ya,' he said.

At that moment, after Sem had said goodbye to Christina and Celeste and, finally, Mum, when the car was pulling away down the drive, I thought I would never see him again. That he was free of our family. Perhaps he was. We were all free after that. No longer the Holmans. Our old identities and lives gone.

Over the next couple of months, as we packed up our belongings, I felt like I was floating way out in the ocean. Out where it was too deep to stand. All I could see around me was water.

The old rules—the rules of land—didn't apply anymore. Now I had to learn to swim. But I was lucky, because I wasn't entirely alone in the deep. I still had Mum, floating beside me, learning to swim too, as we put all our things in the car and Mum drove us down to Melbourne. Seven hours, through flat, dry paddocks to a new state and a new city, and the house on Angel Street.

Chapter Three

IT'S FUNNY HOW IMPORTANT A decision can seem in hindsight, when at the time things just as easily could have gone another way. That's how I feel about the party. I can only wonder who I would be now if things had followed a different path.

I admit, I probably spend more time than is healthy engaged in pointless thoughts of that nature. How doing one thing differently might have changed everything else. If I never went to the party, then maybe I never would have met up with Celeste or Sem again. Perhaps our paths would have kept winding further and further away from each other. But then I think maybe we were already set on paths that were converging and, if not at the party, then at some other time we would have found ourselves together again.

It was Liam's brother's party. Liam was Mum's new boyfriend. A quiet type who knew how to crack a charming smile and who lived with us at the Angel Street house. Liam invited me, along with everyone else who was living there then. The house at Angel Street had six bedrooms, three upstairs and three downstairs, and the empty rooms were always being sublet to different tenants. There were often party invitations floating around. If one person was invited, usually everyone was. And by then I was almost nineteen, and about to finish high school. I was a little old for my year level. I'd stayed down a grade when we moved to Angel Street, because the system was slightly different, and I had a bit of a hard time socially adjusting to the new school. The day of the party, it was only a few months before my final exams.

It was the weekend, and I had come back from the pool late. It was evening but still bright, one of the first long hot days of that spring. I was cycling home. The movement of the bike through the still day created the idea of a breeze, my bathers drying underneath my dress leaving watermarks around my breasts, my hair like straw, face pulled tight with chlorine. People were starting to come out into the street, now that the heat was softening, doors propped open and people on the grassy nature strip in the middle of the road, eating and drinking and lying on blankets, music playing. I was on the final stretch, my legs pumping as I climbed the hill, when I saw them. Liam, out front, smoking. Mum, unchaining her bike. And a new couple who were visiting from France, leaning against the fence. They were all about to cycle off to the party. If I had been a few minutes later I would have missed them. But instead, I met them at the gate, and they told me about the party, and the evening felt long and promising, and so I let myself be swept along with them, the five of us cycling in a group back down the hill.

The party was at a big ramshackle house with a sloping lawn out back and trees lit up with fairy lights. I got drunk very quickly. Probably a combination of my inexperience with alcohol, the heat, and having had so little to eat all day. Maybe it was also because I was embarrassed to be around Liam's younger brother, Noah. Noah was considerably younger than Liam—I think perhaps he was a half-brother or maybe a stepbrother—and he was handsome. He kissed my hand when I arrived, a joke that caught me off guard. It was confusing, and it embarrassed me. I thought he was teasing me, but I wasn't quite sure how. And I felt I might have betrayed something about myself— seemed pathetic or clueless. Especially during the months around the time of the party, when I realised I was about to finish school without a single romantic encounter, I was very sensitive about seeming naive. If someone mentioned something from the adult world that I didn't know much about—especially anything to do with sex—I would pretend that I already knew all about it, even if I didn't. And I was nervous of showing that I was interested in someone in case they weren't interested in me, and then I would look stupid for ever thinking they could be attracted to me.

Maybe it had something to do with Mum and Liam, who were forever kissing, holding hands, disappearing into the bedroom in the middle of the day. I felt like they were showing me how much I didn't understand. Perhaps, if you're eighteen or nineteen yourself when you read this for the first time, you will be surprised by this. But although I was living in the Angel Street house with all sorts of people, I wasn't a social person. I didn't really have friends, let alone a boyfriend. I liked to spend my days by myself, at the pool or reading in the park.

That time seems distant now. So much has happened since, I almost feel like a different person. But in truth it wasn't that long ago, and I probably haven't changed very much. I've had some experience with sex, so don't think I'm quite as awkward. But, if anything, I'm even less social today than I was back then, and still don't really know much about relationships.

Anyway, I wandered, dazed and alone, around Noah's garden for a while, smoking cigarettes when they were offered to me, catching glimpses of Liam and my mum across the lawn, enjoying being around lots of people and being drunk.

I must have talked to a few people at the party that night, but the only one I really remember is Peter. Peter was one of those people who saw nothing embarrassing about unrequited desires. He wasn't at all shy of expressing his intentions. Peter must have been drifting around on his own too, but he seemed so assured when he came up to me that I thought he knew everyone, and I was the only odd one out. He came over and launched into a long description of a documentary he'd watched over the weekend. I couldn't tell you now what it was about, but we were getting on well, the two of us, and I could tell that he was feeling quite hopeful about me and about the evening, so it must have been a surprise when I suddenly leaped up and took off across the lawn without a word of explanation.

Celeste had probably been at the party for some time already, moving through the different areas of the garden, or inside the house, talking with people, smoking, drinking beers. Maybe if I hadn't got drunk, I would have seen her earlier, and perhaps without the alcohol I would have avoided her altogether, maybe even gone home. But as it happened, I was sitting with Peter on a low rock wall that separated the lawn from the garden bed, and I looked up and there she was, softly lit by the fairy lights strung around, holding a beer, her hair long and loose.

'Celeste!' I called, weaving my way between the people standing around on the lawn. 'Celeste!'

I was already quite close to her when she turned, almost close enough to reach out and touch her, but when she looked into my face it brought me up short. I suddenly felt very foolish, running across the lawn to greet her like an old friend, when it was entirely possible that she'd forgotten me altogether, or had never thought anything of me in the first place. I realised that I must have been drunk, to go making a public scene like that.

Maybe Celeste saw some of these emotions pass across my face, because, after a second, she produced a big smile and stepped away from the group she was standing with to greet me.

It must have been five or six years since we had last seen each other, back at the house on Carlisle Road, but Celeste started filling me in on what she had been up to as if it were the natural thing to do, as if this were the way we always used to talk.

Later, she said she'd thought it was funny, the way I came stomping across the grass to her, and how wild and wonky I looked, smelling of pool water, my hair a weird, dry mess. One night when we were out at the house near Eden, sitting across from each other over the Scrabble board, she said there was something endearing about me that night, that it seemed like I'd changed from the kid she'd known before—cold and quiet, standoffish—but now she knew it was just that I was drunk. And I thought to myself that was typical of Celeste, always marrying a compliment with something undermining, so that I would feel grateful for her friendship, and keep on needing her.

So it was at the party, standing on the lawn, that I heard about Sem again. Celeste didn't bring him up right away. At first, she told me about the place where she was living, with her mum, out on the edge of town, and how she'd met Liam's brother Noah through another friend, and they had been together for a bit. And I think that reinforced an image I already had of Celeste: that she was much more mature and worldly than me, even though there were only two years between us.

'That's all over now, though,' she said. 'Me and Noah. He turned out to be a real bore in the end. We're still friends though.'

I shrugged when she said that, and gave a little laugh. I wanted to seem as worldly as she was, not like some dumb kid. And I think she saw this, because she sighed and took my hand and led me down to the back of the garden, where there was more privacy. Celeste pulled me over to the low stone wall—a continuation of the wall where I had been sitting with Peter—and we sat, knees touching. Celeste's face, her big wet eyes and long nose and her parted lips, were all made more dramatic by the deep shadows.

'I'm so glad to run into you, actually,' she said. 'I've been thinking about you.' She reached over and put her hand on my knee. 'God, it's funny seeing you again. You look almost exactly the same. But taller, of course.'

'You sound like my aunt or something,' I said.

Celeste didn't laugh, or even acknowledge what I'd said. She seemed distracted. I feel almost certain now that she was planning to tell me about Sem, and how they were a couple. But she must have changed her mind, at least a little, because she didn't come right out and say that. Instead, she took her hand off my knee and said, 'Nothing has been easy for Sem, you know.'

This was unexpected, and I tried, through the fuzz of the alcohol and the excitement of seeing Celeste again, to understand what she was implying, why she'd brought up Sem so abruptly. And I wasn't sure what she knew about why he'd left our house all those years ago. I imagined that maybe Sem had told her about what I did, that it was my fault he had been taken away. Suddenly the party seemed sinister, as if everyone was looking at me with judgement in their eyes.

'You still see Sem?' I asked.

'We kept in touch,' she said. 'I mean, we'd been going out. We kept emailing for years. You know Sem, he's good with words.'

So they'd been together when we were younger. I hadn't known. When Celeste told me, it immediately seemed obvious. The looks they used to shoot each other. The way he'd casually touch her leg. Perhaps their relationship was something I just hadn't wanted to see back then. Maybe I'd been jealous. But I didn't share any of these thoughts with Celeste. I just nodded and smiled as if I had known all along.

—

I should explain that I hadn't seen or heard from Sem since the day he'd left. I didn't know where he was living, or how to find him. I didn't know what happened to him after he left us, and I'm ashamed to admit that I didn't ask either.

I remember one evening, when we were packing our things for the move to Angel Street, I dropped a porcelain lamb that my mum's mother had given her and its little head snapped off.

'Another thing you've destroyed,' Mum said. She picked up the pieces and held the head against the body, but chips were missing at the join. 'Goddamn it,' she said quietly. 'What have I done?'

I spent the rest of the evening turning Mum's words over in my head. Another thing I'd destroyed. I thought about how Sem had been taken away, and how we didn't live with Dad anymore. The destruction of our family. I considered what role I'd played in all that. But then I made myself stop. It was too difficult. It's only recently that the memory of the lamb has come back to me, now that I'm reopening that chapter of my life.

—

When Celeste told me that she'd kept in touch with Sem after we'd left, I felt self-conscious, seeing myself through Celeste's eyes, aware of how easily I'd given up the boy I'd called my brother. I think I had imagined Sem living an entirely new life after he left us. I'd never thought about what it must have been like for him to be sent away. Maybe that's what Celeste meant when she said things hadn't been easy for him. Maybe she could see that I hadn't ever really thought about Sem, about what his life had been, or how things were from his perspective. I was too caught up inside myself. The realisation started a swirling unsteadiness in my head and my stomach.

'He's not here,' Celeste said. I must have been casting my eyes around the party, looking for Sem. 'It's good timing actually, because he's been away, but just got back. You should come and visit. It'd be the right thing to do.'

'Now?' I asked, and she smiled.

'Not now, Tilly. You're drunk.'

I walked home with Celeste that night. The sky seemed to swing right round into the earth, the stars shooting through the dark. Bright white streaks.

Next day I woke up late. It was already early afternoon. Celeste was sprawled at the end of my bed, looking up at the ceiling. She must have stayed the night. I had a dim memory of her saying I was too drunk to be left alone, and she was too tired to get home. When I moved my legs, she reached her arms up over her head so they rested across my calves. 'Fuck, it's hot,' she said. Her long hair had fanned out, tickling my knees. 'It's hot, but I'm hungry. Do you feel like sausages?'

We walked down the street to buy them and brought them back to the kitchen. Celeste cooked while I sat at the table, watching.

'Did you see my mum last night?' I asked.

'Huh?' Celeste had her back to me, pricking the sausages in the pan with a fork.

'She was at the party. I'm not sure where she is right now, but she might be around, if you want to say hi.'

Celeste looked over her shoulder at me. 'I saw her last night. My mum was there too. They had a good time catching up.'

'Oh, great,' I said, wondering what their conversation had been like, and what my mum would think if she walked in and found Celeste in her kitchen. Mum had never been the biggest fan of Celeste.

'Sem will be around today,' Celeste said, turning away from the stove and leaning back against the counter. 'Just got back from up north.'

'Oh yeah?' I said.

'Come see him,' Celeste said. 'He's good. Different, though.'

Liam came into the kitchen then, and Celeste turned to smile at him.

'Want a sausage?' she asked, and he shrugged.

'Here you go,' she said, sliding one onto a piece of bread. She brought it over to him, plate in one hand, spatula in the other. Liam took it from her and had a bite.

'Good?' Celeste asked. 'Let me try some.' And she leaned forward, as if asking him to feed her.

Liam blushed, and looked away. 'I'd better get going,' he said, heading out the back door, his feet heavy in his boots. Celeste shot me a look, like we were conspirators. I remembered that day on the lawn, years earlier. *Your brother's cute.*

We went back to my room to eat, and Celeste stayed, lying across my bed, talking. The heat was unrelenting, even as the sky outside my window slowly darkened, into dusk. The consistency of the heat made me feel like day and night had no meaning after all. Just one continuous moment, hanging out and chatting, with nothing much to do, in the hot air.

Celeste talked about her mum's art studio, and told me she was planning to study art herself. She was putting together a portfolio of self-portraits. She explained about Noah and how they'd met at a farm out in the bush. She told me about Sem. How they'd broken up after he left Carlisle Road but kept in touch, and got back together recently when he moved down to Melbourne. How he was working in construction but she wanted him to switch to restaurants. He was a great cook, she said. Even desserts. Especially desserts. She said they hosted dinner parties together, at Sem's place, and Sem was such a perfectionist that he wouldn't serve a dish until he was completely satisfied with it, even if it meant the final course wasn't served until one in the morning. 'Maybe if there's one thing he could work on, it's his timing,' she said with a smile. 'His housemates are probably sick of me because I'm there twenty-four seven. I've basically moved in.'

Eventually we fell asleep again, sprawled across my bed, and when we woke early the next morning it was still just as hot, and we cycled to the pool, Celeste on Mum's bike.

The pool was only just open, calm and quiet, a few bodies tracing laps back and forth. We threw our towels down and went straight for the water. Later, we lay on the concrete and read books we'd brought with us from home as the pool slowly got busy around us. Celeste was reading a gothic romance, a slight smile appearing and disappearing on her face as she turned the pages. I wasn't really into fiction back then. But there was this encyclopedia set I'd found on the shelves at Angel Street, and it quickly became one of my favourite things to read. So, I had probably taken a volume with me to the pool that day. It must have been a funny sight, me lying on my towel with that heavy tome open in front of me. I liked to open the encyclopedia at random and discover something new about the world. I thought that if I understood that potatoes were from the Americas, that they caused the Irish to starve, that their tubers may be edible but their berries could poison you, then the next time I held a potato in my hand, or ate a chip, I would understand the potato in a way that I hadn't before. I thought that if I could understand the history and the facts of a thing, then I would know the truth of it and the world would lay itself open to me.

It must have been nearly lunchtime when we went back into the water, bobbing among all the bodies, the sun glinting where it could find an open patch between us all. When our fingers began to prune, we returned to our towels. Celeste fell asleep. My stomach was starting to growl when an orange cheese puff suddenly appeared on the concrete beside my book. And then another. Three more in quick succession, one landing in Celeste's hair, another bouncing off her forehead. She opened her eyes.

'Hello,' she said, and I looked up to see a man standing over us, a bag of cheese puffs in his hand. Celeste opened her mouth wide and he tossed one inside.

'How long have you lazybones been here?' he asked. 'You've cooked yourselves.'

If that wasn't true for Celeste, it was for me, my skin flushed all over with a pink burn that would only intensify when the sun went down.

'We're bored,' Celeste said. 'There's nothing to do but burn.'

'I have a suggestion,' the man said. Then he looked at me. 'Hello,' he said. He was smiling, but there was something behind it—tension, maybe, or some kind of reluctance. I couldn't tell. Honestly, he could have even been amused. It wasn't an expression I found easy to read at the time, and now I don't trust myself well enough to describe it.

'Hello,' I said, shading my eyes with my hand to get a better look at him. And that's when it hit me. It was Sem. He looked different. He was still thin, but he'd grown into his body, not so gangly anymore, but sinewy and tall. I can picture him now, standing with those cheese puffs, a little dimple in the centre of his chest, between his ribs. It seemed important not to let on that I hadn't recognised him immediately. But I couldn't think of the right words to convey this. So I think I said something like, 'Celeste's been filling me in on you.'

I wonder what he thought Celeste had told me. Or maybe it was just that he saw through my casual pretence to the strange emotions underneath, the messiness of it. Because his face closed up and he shrugged and sat down on the concrete by Celeste's feet. He put his hand on her ankle. 'We're having people over tonight, if you're interested?' he said, looking at Celeste. He popped a cheese puff into his mouth. 'What do you think?' he asked me.

I felt like I might burst into tears at any moment. I didn't want to go to Sem's. I was sunburned and thirsty. We hadn't eaten since breakfast, and I wanted to go home and take a cool shower and lie under damp towels. I didn't want my first hours back with Sem to be spent drinking with people I didn't know, head spinning, trying to talk over all the noise. I wanted to sit down in a quiet place with him. To eat a meal with him. To have him to myself. But when I started to say that I should be getting home, Celeste sat up on her elbows and gave me a look of such meaning that I felt I had no choice.

'You just have to come,' she said as we rinsed off under the showers in the concrete changing room. I gingerly inspected the extent of my burn, pressing my fingers into my upper arms and watching the white fingerprints dissolve back into red.

'I'm sunburned,' I said.

'You're too tanned to really burn,' Celeste said. 'If you don't come it'll be awkward. He only came to the pool because I texted and told him you'd be here. Don't you want to hang out with him? You probably don't think so now, but it'll be better with a few people around, take the edge off things. You'll see.'

Was that the first time that Celeste, with her pale grey eyes and her penetrating gaze, convinced me to do something I didn't want to do? There was such an energy to Celeste.

Cycling through the heat, following Sem, she turned to look at me, lifting her fingers from the handlebar and reaching for my hand, so we were flying along, side by side, linked. Her desires were infectious. My burn seemed more like a tan, Sem so miraculous, his house the inevitable place for us to be. We stirred up a breeze as we cycled along, the world endlessly hot and still around us.

When we arrived at Sem's place, one of his housemates was still asleep, the other watching TV, hardly glancing at us as we came in. Sem took us through to the kitchen and said he'd make us some drinks.

The house had a big front room with a kitchen at the back, and the bedrooms were upstairs. It was actually not that far from Angel Street, and I remember thinking that it must've been fate that we'd all moved to Melbourne and met up again.

The first thing that struck me about Sem's place was the utter absence of decorations—or, really, anything at all. It looked like a house that was being readied for sale, or one that had been emptied just before the new owners moved in. In fact, one of the only non-utilitarian objects in the whole of the downstairs area was a little white Buddha, small enough to fit in the palm of your hand, sitting in the corner of the kitchen countertop.

The second thing I was aware of was the atmosphere between Celeste and Sem. Celeste had implied that she and Sem were in a relationship. The way she'd described his dinner parties, how much time she spent at his house, it had sounded like they were a couple. But now they moved around each other like strangers, and Celeste seemed almost nervous. At my house, she hadn't hesitated to rummage through the cupboards looking for salt, opening and closing drawers searching for the cutlery, but here she stood with her arms crossed over her body while Sem looked around helplessly for something to drink. Finally she said stiffly, 'Is it okay if I take a proper shower? I need to wash my hair.'

'Sure,' Sem said. 'You staying here tonight?' And I was surprised that he asked, that it wasn't assumed. She had told me they basically lived together.

Sem seemed erratic. I was soaking in the details of him as he made the drinks—the bones of his wrists, the angle of his jaw—trying to match them to my memories of him. I was struck by how differently he held his body from how I remembered him as a teen. Maybe that was a result of the fall from the bridge. He'd lost that easy athleticism he'd had in his youth, and perhaps some of the confidence that went with it.

He pulled out bottles and glasses and mixed drinks. And he drank a lot, very quickly. I sensed that underneath his awkward exterior, there was anger lurking. Or perhaps I was expecting to find anger there. So I was surprised when, as I stood to leave even before Celeste returned from the bathroom, he came over and put his arms around me, his drink sloshing down my side, cold, his chest warm and hard against mine, his damp breath in my ear.

'Come around again on Friday,' he said. 'We'll be having a proper party. Please, Till. You have to come. I really want you to.'

I could feel my face flushing with emotion as he let me go, and I had to look away. For some reason, I didn't want him to see the happiness and excitement there. Didn't want him to know how I treasured his words. *You have to come. I really want you to.* Sem probably spoke like that with everyone, I told myself. It didn't mean anything. But deep down I couldn't help but wonder hopefully, *Maybe those words are just for you.*

Chapter Four

I DID GO BACK TO Sem's house for the party. Celeste couldn't make it—she had gone to see a painting exhibition, out of town—so I was on my own.

I didn't want to arrive too early, and so on Friday evening I played things very cool with myself. I went to the pool around four o'clock and lay reading my encyclopedia as the crowd thinned around me and the evening insects began to come out. I cycled home and, as if I had no plans for the evening, I sat around in the kitchen while Liam cooked a stew, which dragged on as the meat refused to become tender and instead boiled into lumps of rubber in the pot. It was almost ten o'clock by the time it was ready to eat. As I took out bowls, Mum came into the kitchen and poured herself a glass of red wine, and said that she'd spent the afternoon with Celeste's mum, Christina.

'Her art practice is really coming along,' Mum said. 'She's in a group show next month at this really great little gallery in the city. We all have to go.'

'Okay,' I said.

'And her studio—it has these beautiful big windows that look out at the mountains. I said she should knock the whole wall down and let in the fresh air, but she said that wouldn't be so conducive to art-making. We should go out there and do menstrual paintings together. Apparently it's very cathartic.'

I hadn't told my mother that I'd seen Sem again. In part, it was that I wanted to avoid a conversation about the past, and what we had done to him. But also, I wanted to make my own decisions, without her input on what I should do or how I should act. Maybe I was worried that she'd take over, making Sem's return all about herself. And so I ate quietly, deliberately casual, taking second helpings, lingering to help wash up at the end. And even then, after the meal, which was lengthened with wine, I went back to my room and lay on the bed and read some more of the encyclopedia, entries on sweet and savoury pudding, haggis and blood sausage and Henry VIII.

The encyclopedias were decades out of date, but that was part of their appeal. When they described pudding, for example, they were telling me other things too, about the writers and the way they saw the world. It made me feel like the truth was something that hissed out, under pressure, around the edges of sentences. Even when people tried to tell the truth about something as mundane as a tomato, they still couldn't help but betray other things about themselves.

So, I read the encyclopedia as if I had nothing else to do that night, and only in the early hours of the morning did I finally peel myself from the sweaty sheets and get on my bicycle to ride to Sem's house, where the party was by then well underway.

When I arrived, the house was packed, the front room and kitchen crammed full, people standing shoulder to shoulder and chest to chest, spilling through to the back garden. I angled myself between them, looking for Sem. I must have spent an hour searching before I found not Sem but his housemate, who I'd met earlier that week.

'Do you know where Sem is?' I yelled over the din.

'Sem? He's gone already.'

'Gone?'

'Up north. Left this afternoon.'

Up north—that was what they all called it. What they really meant was that they were going out into the desert, to a little tourist spot known as Welcome Well that sat awkwardly among the mining towns and Indigenous communities, oblivious to both. The town had been established on the back of a discredited UFO theory in the seventies, and enjoyed a brief moment of popularity before it quickly passed out of relevance. Going up north meant going to Welcome Well, but it also connoted a mindset. Up north was away from the city. It was about being spiritual, connecting with the desert and the sky.

Months later, Peter and I would make the drive ourselves, out along the endless highway to the tiny town—a boarded-up pub, a few dilapidated houses surrounded by dead lawns, and a hotel that had been built in 1976 when the government confirmed a UFO sighting there. The hotel now sat empty, save for the few squatters and campers who occasionally took up residence in the old rooms. The government had retracted its statement about the UFO within days and put the whole thing down to an administrative error. The people who went up north went there with a heavy dose of sincerity or a heavy dose of irony, and I think for everyone, sincere or not, a big part of the draw of the place was the spectacle of the old hotel.

I remember when Peter and I drove there, the land was so flat you could see the low buildings from miles away. The front of the hotel was brick, painted a pale grey, with a mural of aliens with dark almonds for eyes and flying saucers with antennas protruding out the top, like old TVs. The place was falling apart, but you could go in and walk around, look at the bedrooms, stars painted on the ceilings, with novelty beds shaped like cheesy UFOs. When we went there, the hotel was empty, but there was some evidence of recent inhabitants: plastic bottles and food wrappers and a bathroom that smelled too bad to enter.

Beyond the hotel, just a short drive down another dusty road, was a campground, where hippies lived in tents and trailers, a couple of big rusty telescopes pointed at the sky. You could go out to the hotel and the campground and the last forty or fifty years would blur away, and in that sense the place did have a supernatural effect. It sounds silly, but you have to understand that the place took on much more significance after everything that happened out at Eden, when we were trying to understand Sem and what his life had been like.

———

It was later that spring, after Sem went up north, that Peter took me on our first date. I wore a pink velvet dress of Celeste's. For about a month, or maybe six weeks, after I saw Celeste at Noah's party, Celeste and I hung out a lot. Most often she came to my house, though from time to time I made the long bike ride out to hers, and we'd sit in the back garden among Christina's sculptures—lots of female figures, made of everything from clay to plastic bottles.

When Celeste was younger, at the house on Carlisle Road, she'd been dismissive of Christina's art. Christina had made great plaster-cast moulds of her breasts and displayed them in the garden at the front of the house. I can picture Celeste now, standing by the newly erected breasts, with her arms folded across her own chest, scowling.

'It isn't even original. It's like a sad copy of something from a museum twenty years ago. Gross.' Just like Celeste, to be so critical of her mother, only to turn around and decide she wanted to be an artist herself.

I think Celeste had found it embarrassing, all that focus on the naked female form, especially around that time when she was just discovering her own body. I stumbled on her once, in the garden at Carlisle Road, examining one of Christina's statues: a female figure, cast in fiberglass. Celeste was looking at it carefully, and there was something about her facial expression, and the way that she was holding her own body, that let me know she was comparing herself to the sculpture. When she saw me, she immediately adjusted her expression to one of derision.

'Can you believe this junk my mum makes?'

Now that Celeste was interested in art herself, she was no less critical of Christina, but her arguments had taken on more of a philosophical tone. She'd criticise each work for its technique, its originality or its place in her mother's body of work. And when, occasionally, she said, 'Actually, I think this one's quite good,' the faint praise felt precious, hard-earned. I felt glad for Christina, and that sculpture took on a new significance in my eyes. I'd look at it and try to discern how it was special, better than all the rest.

Christina usually stayed in her studio working, but sometimes she'd come and sit with us when she was taking a break. 'What do you think?' she'd ask about her new work. 'Tell me honestly.' And then she'd drop her chin a little and close her eyes, as if preparing herself. I'd always say that I thought it was great, and then Celeste would give her unsparing feedback.

'It's a sign of my respect,' Celeste said, when I asked her why she was so harsh. 'If I'm not honest about what I think, then how will she ever improve? I wish you'd say what you really think. She'd benefit from it, you know. You shouldn't just say what you think other people want to hear.' And when I huffed and turned away from her, she put her hand on my knee and said, 'I mean that as a compliment. Your ideas are always so great when you share them. You're too selfish with your thoughts.'

So it was during that period back when we were still getting to know each other again that we found the pink velvet dress. I was meant to be studying for my final exams, but Celeste convinced me to go to the op shop instead. It was about a week after Sem's party, and I mentioned how his housemate said he'd left town. I was surprised by Celeste's reaction to the news. Instead of nodding as if she already knew, Celeste swore and said she'd been calling Sem for days, but he'd been dodging her. I wouldn't have thought she'd admit that to me, even if it was true. And perhaps it was an unintentional slip on her part, because she didn't bring it up again.

I was glad for an excuse to go out that day, because the atmosphere in the Angel Street house was tense. Mum and Liam were fighting, and hearing their raised voices reminded me of how things had been with Mum and Dad when they were separating. I found it hard to concentrate on my studies.

Before I left, I finally told Mum that Sem was around—or had been around—but that he'd gone up north. I'd been so nervous about telling her, but she merely laughed.

'He came around to see me on Friday,' she said, 'while you were out at the pool.'

'What?'

'Yes, he came around and we had a cup of tea before he left for the desert.'

'Why didn't you say anything?' I asked indignantly.

'Probably for the same reason you didn't tell me you'd seen him,' she said, raising her eyebrows at me.

I was flummoxed. 'How long have you been in touch?' I asked.

'You know, I tried to talk to Liam about Sem,' Mum said. 'That was a mistake. He said it was typical of me. That if I'd only thought things through, I wouldn't have fostered Sem in the first place. He compared it to my bush excursions. Said I'm always putting myself first. He doesn't understand the good those trips do me; he didn't know me before. But you see it, don't you, darling? I mean, I was a shell of myself.'

After we moved to the house on Angel Street, Mum spent a lot of her time out in the bush. She'd fallen in with a crowd of New Age hippies, and was discovering something of herself that she'd lost when she married my father.

'And Liam said it was like the state of the house, and how we leave things here in such a mess. That we don't take enough responsibility. You know, Matilda, I'm always asking if you could pitch in a little instead of leaving your things around all the time. It affects other people too, you know.' She sighed and looked me up and down. 'Exams to study for but instead you're going out shopping with your friend. Liam would say the apple doesn't fall far from the tree. Just a pair of . . .' She didn't finish the sentence, but the unspoken words were written in the twisted lines of her mouth: *irresponsible women*. She shifted her gaze to look out the window, and I stood up to leave.

'I blame myself, you know,' she said, still not looking at me. 'Of course, I do.'

And I didn't know what to say, so I just left her there. I walked out the front door to meet Celeste, who was waiting by the gate.

The op shop was a little place down at the junction with a bright blue-painted exterior. Inside it smelled like mothballs, and everything I touched seemed misshapen and sweat-stained, while everything that Celeste pulled from the hangers was full of magical promise. I can picture Celeste now, coming out of the change room in the pink dress, pale velvet with thin spaghetti straps. She posed for me, turning this way and that, then looked at herself in the mirror. 'What do you think, Tilly?'

A girl who worked in the shop came past and said, 'That looks so good on you,' and Celeste said, 'Yeah, doesn't it!'

I'd been reluctant to tell Celeste about Peter. Maybe I was worried that she would think Peter was boring—he *was* boring, I thought—and that if she encouraged me to see him it would only be because she was feeling kind, and it would be condescending.

Despite my leaving him abruptly at Noah's party, Peter had been persistent. He'd asked Noah for my number and sent me daily messages. Twice, he'd called just to chat, and I found myself anxiously hanging on my end of the phone, unsure what to say, trying to discern the purpose of the call. He talked about films, and he asked me about the exams coming up and did I have any plans for what I would do next? I remember thinking that he was very vocationally focused, always asking me what my goals were and what I was working towards. Now

I think it was probably Peter's way of making himself appear mature. And he did actually seem quite grown up to me. He was older than me by a couple of years, and he'd already worked on at least one project before we met—a short documentary about aged care homes that he'd helped write and produce and which had been commended in a film festival. His dad was a cinematographer who had worked on some pretty well-regarded films, so Peter inherited some of his reputation. And, in the end, Peter really did turn out to be focused on his vocation. He's probably the most successful person I know. I think Peter's stability was one of the things that drew me to him, in those early days. There was something quite dependable about him, when everything else felt slippery and unsure.

So, as we were unchaining our bikes outside the op shop, I told Celeste that Peter had asked me on a date, and her first question was what I was going to wear. We went home and went through my closet together and, of course, Celeste said I had nothing appropriate. So, she offered to lend me the pink dress.

Peter took me out to a Moroccan restaurant. He made a great show of his hunger, ordering way more than we needed, more than I could comfortably afford, and I felt anxious, thinking about the bill and who would pay it even before the food had arrived. When the dishes were brought to the table, steaming gently in terracotta bowls, Peter waved a hand magnanimously.

'Please, tuck in,' he said, and I could tell he was happy, enjoying himself, that he felt he'd brought me somewhere really special.

As Peter talked about documentaries, I ran my fingers up and down the pink dress where it lay against my thigh, feeling the soft grain of it.

'The legal system is up its own arse,' Peter said. 'It's actually shocking.'

Up and down, I ran my fingers against the dress.

'People are turning to their televisions to discover the real truth.'

I was thinking about Celeste in the op shop, posing in front of the mirror. The pink dress catching the light. I wondered what she was up to, while I was there with Peter, who was still going on and on about his documentaries and never asking me what I wanted to talk about. But maybe that was what made Peter and me a good fit, in a way. Because if he had asked me what I wanted to discuss, I don't think I would have known.

Now, when I think back on that first date, it's hard not to think of everything that happened later, with Sem and the documentary. But I don't want to get ahead of myself. I was telling you about the date, and Celeste's pink velvet dress.

That dress. I remember months later, down near Eden, throwing our bags in the back of the car, Celeste and Sem and me. Celeste was wearing the dress over her swimsuit, the velvet shimmering in the sun. It was a hot car ride, Celeste in the front, me in the back, music playing, windows down. She must have taken the dress off when we went into the water, sparkling, bracingly cold, so that we screamed with the shock of it, splashing wildly and leaping out, goosebumps sprung up on our arms and legs, hopping from stone to stone with the cool clear water running beneath us, then pulling on big jumpers as night came on. A goanna turned up and we fed it boiled eggs, whole, watching them slide down its gullet.

Of course, we drank. Beers mainly. We camped out overnight. Celeste and Sem shared his swag, and I slept in the car. In the morning we woke, hungover, splayed out around the place, dusty and cold, no eggs left for breakfast. I saw it as we were packing up, the pink dress, all twisted in the dirt. I took it back to the beach house, but no amount of washing could make it right again. Celeste hardly seemed to care.

'It's just a dress,' she said. 'It's not the end of the world.'

I kept that pink dress for a long time. I even took it when I left the coast house. I think I had this idea in my head that one day I'd give it to you. Which is ridiculous. As if a dirty old dress would mean anything to you at all. But it had something to do with reparation, which was a concept I thought about a lot after everything that happened out at Eden. I knew that I owed you, but it was difficult to see what I could possibly give you that would be enough. I think that's why I'm writing this account for you. So you can see how complex things were, and that some of the stories you hear may not really be true. You're much too young for it now, of course. But I hope maybe later it will help you understand everything that happened before you were born—events you never witnessed but which nevertheless shaped your life.

Chapter Five

THESE DAYS, IT'S THE MOST difficult memories of Celeste and Sem that first come to mind. It's hard to remember the happy moments, but perhaps that will change with time. Two years really isn't that long, despite everything that has changed.

In truth, we had many happy days. Before I saw Celeste again at Noah's party, I'd been spending a lot of time by myself. But when Celeste came back into my life I was no longer so alone.

Maybe one reason I don't so readily remember the happy days is that good times are often unremarkable. For example, there's one day I do remember having a great time with Celeste, but not because anything really special happened. It was more just a good feeling that I think we shared.

Celeste arrived at my house in the morning. 'I've found a new place I want to show you,' she said, standing over the crossbar of her bike. I unchained mine and we cycled off down the empty morning streets.

We stopped on the way at a supermarket, to get stuff to make sandwiches. Once inside, we split up. Celeste went to get the bread and I went for peanut butter in the next aisle. There was pop music playing; I didn't know the name of the song, but I recognised it, and when I came around the corner with the peanut butter, Celeste started doing this funny dance at the other end of the aisle. There were a few other shoppers around, but after a moment I joined in. We were standing at opposite ends of the aisle, dancing, with peanut butter and bread. It felt really good.

The place that Celeste wanted to show me was a garden, down by the river. It was attached to a university, but also open to the public. We were there on the weekend, so no students were around. The place was packed with hundreds of species of plants and flowers, a rambling rose garden, bristling banksia, a pond with broad lily pads, and paths winding through it all.

'Can you believe this has always been here and we just didn't know?' Celeste said. 'We should apply to come here so we can study the plants. I could learn how to draw them all.'

There were greenhouses and we looked through the windows at the long work tables and plant samples. I tried to imagine myself inside, scribbling notes with a pencil in a little notebook, measuring green shoots and prodding the damp, dark soil.

We made our sandwiches and ate them under a willow tree. Celeste stripped off one of the long tendrils and wove it into a circle that she wore on her head while we ate. Then she took it off and held it out, and I bowed my head and she placed it on top.

While Celeste finished her sandwich I stood and looked out over the pond. From where we were sitting, we couldn't see any other people. The garden was all ours. I wanted to keep it forever. That feeling of togetherness. That incredible feeling of not being lonely at all.

So I felt betrayed when Celeste went up north later that month, like she owed me an apology, for stepping in and out of my life so carelessly. I think I was especially shocked that she wasn't even going to say goodbye. Maybe the truth is that I was distracted with Peter and with finishing my exams. It seemed to me that Celeste was the one who became distant, not me, but of course that's only my perspective.

It was only by chance that I bumped into Celeste on her last day in town, at the supermarket, filling her trolley with provisions for the drive.

'Oh, hello,' she said. 'I'm going up north to see Sem.' She glanced away for a moment, looking uncomfortable, but when she returned her gaze to me her expression was confident. She gestured to her trolley. 'Peanut butter sandwiches for the car,' she said.

And I smiled and pretended like this was no big deal to me either. 'Well, have fun,' I said. 'See you round, I guess.'

It was an awkward encounter. At the time, I thought she was feeling a bit guilty, because she hadn't told me she was leaving and she knew I'd be upset. But now I'm not so sure that's right. She didn't owe me anything, after all. Now, I think maybe she was uncomfortable because of Sem. She was taking a risk going out there after him. She was chasing him across the country, and maybe she was worried that the reason she had to chase was because he was running away. And perhaps she thought—wrongly, as it turned out—that as his one-time sort-of sister I would be able to discern something of this. That I'd see her with her shopping cart of bread and spreads and think she was desperate and sad.

———

Mum broke up with Liam at the end of that spring, not long after Celeste left, just before my final exams. They had a huge fight in the kitchen and Liam left that same day, driving out to the coast to work as a berry picker. After Liam left, Mum was in a real temper, stomping around, and I allowed myself to share a little of her anger, because first Celeste and now Liam had left without really saying goodbye.

The morning of my final exam, Mum fried sheep's brains for my breakfast, the rich smell filling the kitchen, the flesh beneath the fried exterior soft between my tongue and the top of my mouth. 'My mum always used to make them for me,' Mum said. 'Brains for the brain.'

'Sheep for the sheep,' I said, and she swatted me with a tea towel, playful, and for a moment Liam was forgotten. It was just me and Mum and the significance of my final exam that day.

My class sat our exam in the school gym, where the staff had set up rows of desks, the smell of basketballs and old sweat meeting the sweet woodiness of pencil shavings and the musk of damp socks. They made us take off our shoes as we came in, so that we didn't mark the court, and at the end of the three hours our footsteps were like rain, hushed, almost cosy, on the way out.

When I arrived home after the exam, the house was hot and quiet. I had been expecting Mum to be waiting for me, ready to cook whatever her mum had cooked for her after she finished school. But instead the kitchen was still and empty, light falling through the windows across the warm table and illuminating the air. There was a note for me on the bench. She'd gone out into the bush again.

I shouldn't have been surprised that Mum was gone—she'd been so shaken by the breakup with Liam, and whenever things got tough for Mum she took refuge in the bush—but I thought she might have stuck around long enough to hear about my exam. Still, this was typical Mum. Predictably unpredictable.

When I went into my bedroom, I saw an old pasta jar full of fresh flowers on the bedside table. Beside it was a slip of paper that said: *Congratulations!* It was from Peter. One of the other Angel Street residents must have let him in. And it was Peter who called me minutes later, wanting to hear how it had all gone, wanting to take me out to celebrate. He came to pick me up in his dinky blue car and we drove to an Italian restaurant in the city. I wore my own clothes this time, jeans and a shirt, and we ate spaghetti vongole and drank wine, like adults, with a little candle in the middle of the table.

Later, he came back to the house with me. I don't think another person had ever felt so real to me before. The vulnerability of the pulse in his neck. The pale expanse of his torso. The hard bones beneath his skin. It was spooky to think that he was there, inside his skin, behind his eyes, travelling through his veins with each beating pulse. I lay on the bed, my head against his sweat-dampened chest, unable to sleep with his new body there. Cars hummed far away.

Next morning, after Peter left to go to work at the studio—to subsidise his own filmmaking, he was working as an assistant for an indie production company—I cycled to the garden Celeste had shown me, lay in the grass and read my encyclopedia, high clouds rolling slowly through the blue sky. I went back to that garden every day that week, alone, lying in the shade of the evergreen trees. In the mornings, sprinklers turned, misting the grass with rainbows.

———

Mum stayed out in the bush for a few weeks after my exams. Without Liam or Mum around, the house lost some of its warmth. I felt I didn't know anyone who was living there anymore—people came and left so rapidly, staying just a few days. The upstairs bedrooms were often vacant, just a few people passing through, and some nights I was the only one in the whole house. I spent as much time as I could in the park, or at the pool, just letting the time fall away.

Peter was the one who suggested I should get a job. 'How else will you have any independence?' he said. 'It'd be good to make some money while you figure out what you're really passionate about doing next.' I'd applied to study arts at university, because I didn't know what else to put down, but if I got in, I was planning to defer. Peter thought that was a good idea.

He said I shouldn't study something without a clear purpose to it. He helped me polish up a résumé—if you could even call it that; it was basically just a list of the schools I'd attended—and came with me as I dropped it off at all the restaurants in the neighbourhood.

I was offered a waitressing job at an Italian restaurant on the main street managed by the owner's son, a big guy in a waistcoat who sat at the payment counter in the centre of the room, playing games on his phone. The chefs were always yelling at me for being too slow, or bringing back a plate that wasn't quite right, or standing in the wrong place. The closest thing I had to a friend was another waitress, Paula, who was a little older than me and on a working holiday from Spain. 'Just try to *think!*' she would exclaim whenever I set a table with the wrong cutlery or forgot the bread plates. Still, Peter was right. It was good to have some money, and a routine. Free time in the park, lunches or evenings at the restaurant, and, more often than not, nights with Peter, who shared a townhouse with an older guy who was studying physics and told me the first time we met that he saw psychedelic drugs as key to exploring some of the higher concepts.

But just as I had settled into my new routine, I came back from the park one lunchtime to find the house busy again. I could hear voices in the kitchen, the squeak of hinges and the rattling flap of the flywire door bouncing against the frame. Outside my bedroom were a few old cardboard boxes filled with an assortment of my things: school books, clothes, my backpack lying to one side. Inside my room, I found a stranger, a woman, asleep in my bed, her boots still on. She was lying diagonally across the mattress with her arms curled around her head, her fingernails rimmed with black. I felt something tightening in my chest as I turned and went down the narrow corridor to the kitchen.

Mum was sitting at the table eating a steaming plate of broccoli. She was dirty, her ankles caked in mud, her hair like floss, wild eyes staring out of a sunburned face. Another stranger sat beside her, a man, smoking clove cigarettes, a collection of butts already crumpled in an empty jar in front of him. Behind them, on the stove, dirty pots and pans rested on the unlit burners. The sink was full of dishes.

'You're back,' I said, opening the fridge, the lights winking on to reveal rows of empty shelves, all my food gone: mince and bacon, milk and eggs. 'Looks like you were hungry.'

'Tilly, darling,' Mum said. 'Don't be rude. Put on the kettle. Let's all have some tea.'

⸻

They didn't leave, Mum's guests from the bush. Mum had rented my room to the woman on my bed, and there were three others in the upstairs bedrooms. Their numbers often swelled with friends and lovers who came to participate in meditation sessions, bringing with them collections of crystals, sage smudge sticks, books of affirmations and tarot cards, sometimes staying a few nights.

We needed the rent money, Mum said; she had blown her latest library job by disappearing off to the bush. The new residents and their guests hung around the house, cooking up giant pots of vegetables and leaving them to sweat on the stove and smoking hundreds of cigarettes, so that the air was always thick and fetid.

No one seemed to care for the house. They were happy to let the kitchen sink clog up with old vegetable peelings and the rubbish bin overflow. In the downstairs bathroom, the toilet bowl turned brown and the mirrors became speckled with old toothpaste and spit. It was everybody's house and no one's responsibility.

Ejected from my room, I slept on the couch, waiting with bleary eyes as our new housemates sat up late talking and smoking, only to be jerked awake again at dawn when another lot came in for their morning meditation.

Some nights, Mum would come and sit on the floor beside the couch, her head resting against my side. She'd talk about Dad and how he'd left us high and dry, how difficult things were.

'Never give up your life for a man,' she said into the gloom.

My eyelids were heavy against my cheeks. Her hair was soft, like feathers against my arm. The room was hot, and the creases of my limbs, my elbows and knees, felt damp and sticky. I shifted and rolled over, trying to find a comfortable position.

'You have to keep something for yourself,' Mum said. 'Always keep something back just for you.'

Eventually I fell asleep, and when I woke, the sky outside the high windows was so pale, just a sleepy yawn of pink, and Mum was lying on the carpet beside the couch, fast asleep.

I climbed over her and went to the kitchen, where her friends were already clunking around making tea.

I was so tired.

I cycled to the gardens and slept on the damp lawn, waking up disorientated. I hurried back to the house to change for my lunchtime shift.

When I got home I found Mum in the kitchen, sipping one of her innumerable cups of tea. I went to the fridge to get my yogurt, but, of course, it was gone. Eaten by one of Mum's new friends, no doubt.

'This house is impossible to live in,' I said to Mum.

She looked at me, sharply. 'You think I'm the one who makes places inhospitable? Darling, pot calling the kettle and all that.'

'What do you mean?' I asked.

Mum just smiled. 'You don't have to stay here, you know, darling. Aren't you grown up now? Feel free to find a place for yourself if you don't like what I'm offering.'

'I have a job,' I said. By this stage my voice was trembling. I was standing by the kitchen door, and I could feel my muscles tensing.

'We'll see how long that lasts,' Mum said.

'Why do you always make me feel like crap?' I was afraid I was going to cry.

'God, Tilly, darling,' Mum said, 'don't take yourself so seriously. Can't I poke a little fun without you blowing up in my face?'

I sat down opposite her at the kitchen table, but she wouldn't look me in the eye.

She stood up and went to the sink to tip out her cup of tea. 'It's gone cold,' she said with her back to me. 'Put the kettle on for me, will you, darling? Let's not fight today.'

———

It was a blisteringly hot day when Celeste returned at the start of summer. I was out the front, curled up on the sun-bleached red couch reading my encyclopedia, when the white ute pulled up. Celeste got out and went around to the tray, extracting her bag and a big bunch of yellow flowers wrapped in paper. Her denim shorts cut into her tanned thighs, and her hair was all gathered on top of her head. I leaned forwards, trying to see who was driving, but she came back around and leaned in through the front passenger window, blocking my view. Then she turned and came up the path towards me, her familiar face full of warmth, as the ute drove away.

'Hello, Tilly,' she said, throwing the flowers at me. 'Scooch.'

She dropped her bag and then plopped herself down beside me on the couch, wriggling her bottom in next to my feet. She smelled like mud, like salty plants. 'Congratulations,' she said, nodding to the flowers on my lap. 'They're for finishing your exams.' The flowers were scentless and filled with a brilliant orange-yellow dust that spilled across my arms and legs in jaundiced, sweaty streaks.

Behind Celeste, the front door swung open, held ajar while someone yelled back into the house, 'What?' and then two of Mum's friends spilled out onto the porch, barefoot men with a pervasive body odour. A woman stuck her head out my bedroom window. 'Wait for us,' she yelled, and then disappeared back inside.

'I see things have changed a bit around here,' Celeste said, shooting me a look of such amused sympathy that I couldn't help but smile. She reached over and grabbed my hand, pulling me into her, half crushing the flowers. 'You need me here to look after you,' she said.

———

I was meant to work that evening, but Celeste convinced me to call in sick. We put on our bathers and cycled to the pool, where the concrete was still packed with bodies at 4 pm. The summer felt endless that day, the two of us lying on towels, our wet shadows drying around us, limitless sky above.

We slept on the front porch that night, me on the sofa, cramped and hot, Celeste on the bare boards, her bag under her head. Celeste smoked her cigarettes and I tried to talk to her about Sem and what had happened up north. He hadn't come back with her, I learned that much. But our conversation felt like a dance, side-stepping around facts and events that were invisible to me, until finally Celeste said, 'Look, he's just taking some space, alright,' and it was clear I should leave it at that.

———

It was in those early days of summer, while Celeste was saving me from the chaos of the Angel Street house, that I felt her really begin to close in on me, twisting my arm in that clever, almost loving way she had. We went to the pool and, for the first time, Peter joined us. So, it was the three of us. And there was something off-kilter about the day, right from the moment we arrived at the pool to find Peter waiting there, leaning against the side of his car, wearing navy shorts and a polo shirt, with a green-and-blue towel thrown over his shoulder and ugly plastic sunglasses on.

'Hello, hello,' he said, kissing us both on the cheek.

When he pulled off his polo shirt by the pool to reveal that expanse of pale chest, his small brown freckles, his big pink nipples, I felt suddenly embarrassed by him.

'Well, this is the thing,' Peter said, lying back on his towel. His voice seemed too loud, somehow, and I regretted that Celeste and I wouldn't be able to hang out as we usually did, just the two of us, and that our routine of swimming, reading and napping wouldn't be natural to Peter, and I would have to make a special effort now that he was there. And beneath that there was a feeling of worry, that maybe this strain spoke to a deeper incompatibility. That it meant Peter wasn't right for me. And then, of course, there was Celeste.

Since she had come back from up north, Celeste had a new interest. She'd ordered a bunch of books online, many of them from America, about how we weren't all as free as we thought we were, that the government had more power over us than we realised, and some crazy stuff about aliens and UFOs. She carried these books around wherever she went, reading them on the couch on my front porch, or when we went to the pool, occasionally heaving dramatic sighs, as if inviting me to ask what was bothering her, but something—my confusion, or perhaps my timidity—held me back, which only seemed to encourage her performance. She would often bring it up unprovoked, and always when I least expected it. Coming into the house one day after we'd been at the pool, I stopped to look in the mirror in the hall and pulled wryly at my dry hair, saying, 'All that chlorine!'

Celeste came to stand behind me and pulled her fingers rather roughly through my curls. 'They put all sorts of stuff in the water, you know,' she said. 'The government. Who knows what it is? No one. They could be controlling our minds.'

I was too surprised to roll my eyes. Did Celeste really take that stuff seriously? It was so annoying to me, though at the time I couldn't have explained why. Even now, it's hard to pin down. Perhaps, in part, it was that I found it unsettling. All these facts I'd taken for granted were suddenly called into question, and there didn't seem to be a way to argue against it, because any source I called upon as authority could just as easily be dismissed by Celeste. But maybe, more than the craziness of the conspiracies themselves, what annoyed me was that Celeste's belief in them felt as if it were a performance. Aside from reading the books and making the occasional comment, she lived her life basically as she had before. It wasn't until one evening in the kitchen, when she scolded me for not reading the ingredient lists on the food I bought more carefully, that I finally turned to her and said, 'You don't really believe all that stupid stuff, do you?'

'Sem said you wouldn't understand,' she retorted.

And then I realised that all this—the books and the conspiracy theories—was Celeste's way of demonstrating the bond she had with Sem, even if he was still up north and she was back here. I think that, for Celeste, it represented something she and Sem shared that excluded me. It mystified me at the time, because I never questioned that there was something special between them. They'd dated. They kept in touch even after Sem had left Carlisle Road and I had moved away. They'd rekindled something of their relationship. Even if Sem was 'taking some space', they'd still shared something real. But now I can see that everything wasn't as simple as it seemed to me then. I wasn't thinking about how Celeste was always chasing after Sem, and he often seemed to be moving away from her.

So that day at the pool, I was in a bad mood already because of my worries about Peter, when Celeste pulled out her book about alien sightings on Earth and began to read, letting out one of her great theatrical sighs. I felt irritation flare up inside me. I flipped onto my back and closed my eyes and felt the sun come through bright and red and almost painful. I willed the light to flood through my eyes and scorch my brain.

'How about a round of ice creams?' Peter asked.

I didn't even open my eyes, but I could hear Celeste murmuring assent, and then the sound of rustling as Peter stood and found his wallet.

When he had gone, there was a thick silence between Celeste and me. And then I felt her hot hand on my arm. I still didn't open my eyes.

'What's up, crumb bum?' she said. 'You've gone all stiff, like a mummy in a coffin.' She laughed. 'You're going to get a terrible burn if you don't turn over.'

'Sarcophagus,' I said.

'What?'

'A mummy in a *sarcophagus*.'

Celeste was quiet for a moment. 'Whatever,' she said. Her hand was still on my arm. She walked her fingers up to my elbow. 'I wanted to talk to you about something, actually,' she said. I couldn't see her, I was looking up at the sky through closed eyes, but I could hear her, her heavy voice.

'About Peter,' she added.

When Celeste mentioned Peter, a kind of warmth blossomed in my gut, spreading up into my chest and then suddenly turning cold. Crazily, I felt like getting up and running to the pool, plunging beneath the water's surface. Anything to stop her saying whatever she was going to say next.

'I want to be honest with you,' Celeste said. 'These things aren't easy to say.' She took her fingers off my arm.

Beneath my back the concrete felt hard, pressing against my bones.

'I just don't think he's a good guy. Or, not that he's not good, but he's not good enough for you,' Celeste said. 'He's just so uptight, a bit controlling. It makes me worry for you, Tilly. I didn't think that was what you wanted.'

'Okay,' I said, opening my eyes and looking out into the big empty sky. I felt dizzy, almost shaky. 'Yeah, I didn't really like him that much anyway. It was just a thing.'

And I felt her hand suddenly on mine, warm, squeezing my fingers. 'That's what I thought,' she said.

I could have ignored Celeste's warning. Really, what would she have done? Now, looking back, I don't think she would have done anything at all. But her ideas were so infectious, and I was so easily infected, that I couldn't get her words out of my head. She squeezed my hand that day by the pool and it was as if the contract was signed and Peter was out. So when Peter called the next day, I didn't answer my phone. Nor did I reply to his texts asking did I want to come over to his mother's house for dinner, or what about spending a weekend out at the coast?

My phone buzzed in my pocket as Celeste and I lay in the hot grass at the park, looking up at the sky, feeling the curve of the Earth in the hollows of our backs. And part of me thought it was true that I didn't care that much about Peter. And part of me was heartbroken, desperate to pick up the phone.

Celeste rolled towards me and I turned to look at her, feeling the blades of grass against my cheek.

'I've got a house for us,' she said. 'So you can get away from this madness, have some space, your own room.'

'Where?' I asked.

'On the coast. It's a housesitting thing for the summer. An artist friend of my mum's who's gone to Europe.'

I was quiet for a moment. 'I'll have to quit my job,' I said.

'So quit,' said Celeste. 'You have to come. It will be great. Just the two of us.' She said it like it was a promise.

Chapter Six

THE CAR WAS HUGE AND old and red, a four-wheel drive. It had
a dull silver bull bar across its nose and tyres with teeth worn
down from chewing up miles of gravel and bitumen. Celeste
found it in the classifieds, and it took us all morning to cycle
out to the edge of town, where the factories and dealerships
were, to see it.

It's almost unbearable now, to think about that car. How
innocuous it all was. How innocent. How close we were to
making a different decision. Because, you see, as we cycled out
to see the car, I had already decided that we wouldn't buy it.
I would find a fault with it, something that couldn't be over-
looked. My phone felt heavy with Peter's unanswered calls and
messages, my bed empty of his warm body among the sheets.
I knew Peter would think that spending summer at the coast
was a waste of time and say that I should be focusing on the
first stage of my adult life, not idling away my days at the beach.

And just as Celeste didn't approve of Peter, I had the sense that he didn't think very highly of Celeste. Not that he had ever said as much aloud. In fact, I read his attitude in his quietness. The way, when I brought up Celeste's name, he paused before responding. Or a slight, condescending smile would pass over his face, as if it amused him that we were so close. And I knew he thought I was too influenced by her. That my deference to her was a sign of my immaturity. And perhaps he was right. At any rate, cycling out to see the car, it seemed to me that this was my last chance to escape. If we didn't buy the car, then we would have no way of getting to the coast, and the idea would be dropped. The plan was so vague, one of dozens of plans that blew up and then drifted away into the hot summer sky. If we hadn't bought the car, the trip to the coast would have probably been forgotten within a week.

The red car didn't come from one of the dealerships with their rows of bright flags snapping in the wind. We had to turn off the main road, winding our way around the factories and warehouses, over broken bitumen. It was parked in front of an old warehouse, a low brick building with an overflowing rubbish skip beside a corrugated electric door. The owner, who was waiting for us out front, was older, maybe in his seventies, with thick grey hair and a beard. He took us over to the car and slapped his hand against the bonnet, and we opened the doors and looked inside. And it was a funny thing. Because as we looked inside the car—the seats upholstered in a beige fabric, stained grey from wear, a ceiling of the same material that had come unstuck from the centre of the roof, so that it hung down, like gathered curtains—Celeste was very quiet. And when we closed the doors, Celeste said, 'Well, thank you very much,' without making eye contact, and it seemed like she was ready to leave, as if *she* had decided not to buy the car. It occurred to me that maybe she'd gone cold on the idea too.

But then the man told us that this had been his daughter's car. He'd bought it for her.

'She's seen some miles, but she's sound. Safe.' The car was, the man stressed, the type of car that a caring father buys for a child. 'My daughter is away working for the government now,' he said. 'I couldn't be prouder. Doesn't need her old man anymore, and that's the way it should be. But she always flies back in the holidays to visit me. She's her own person, you know, and when you're a parent you have to respect that. Got to let her do her own thing.'

I found myself thinking about my own father, Andrew. Since we'd left the house at Carlisle Road, I had seen him only sporadically at first, and later hardly at all. Mum certainly didn't encourage it. Early on, I'd been once or twice to visit Dad with his new wife, a woman named Sue, and meet their son and then their daughter when they were born. But when I was there, I felt in the way. Like an embarrassing memory of something Dad would rather have forgotten. And I couldn't help comparing how he was with them to how he had been with me. How he let the boy put up dinosaur posters in his room, or how his daughter danced around the house in sparkly pink hot shorts. So after a while, I told Mum I'd prefer to stop going. We did phone calls for a time, but as I got older they decreased in frequency too.

In the years since, I've thought a lot about my parents' separation. Tried to understand what was at the heart of it. Sometimes it seems to me that it was all Mum. It's true, I think, that there were signs she had grown tired of her suburban life. The most striking example was, of course, her insistence that our family foster a child, despite my father's opposition. It's as if there was some void in her life, and she was hoping that Sem would be the right shape to fill it. And, in a way, he was. Like a key, he slid into a difficult lock and, click, everything came undone. I can see my mother now as someone who was desperately seeking change, something new. The way she threw out all her old clothes before we left my father's house. How she grew her hair long and went out into the bush. She was searching. I can see that as the cause of my parents' divorce.

But then there's my father. He didn't want to be a foster parent. He was against it from the start but my mother forced Sem into our lives. And while it might not have been charitable of him to resist it, I also don't think it was so unreasonable. I imagine that this was just the last in a long list of ways in which Mum frustrated him. She never quite fit into the mould he imagined for her, never quite played the part. For example, not long before Sem arrived, Mum flat out refused to wear a dress to Dad's office Christmas party, which was meant to be quite formal, and insisted on wearing some old pants and a linen shirt instead. Dad just couldn't understand it.

'I'm asking you to dress up as a personal favour to me,' he said. 'I think you'll feel better when you're there and everyone else is in cocktail attire.' But Mum wouldn't budge. Another time she brought home a pregnant stray cat, even though she knew Dad was allergic. Dad won that battle: he took the cat and the litter of kittens born under the couch to a local vet clinic and we never spoke about them again. It's almost like Mum was provoking him, and when Sem arrived, turning his life on its head, that might have been the last straw.

That day we went to see the red car, I found myself thinking particularly of Dad, and the visits to the counsellor, Mrs Rose.

'And the bathroom,' she said. 'What happens in the bathroom? Does Sem ever come in with you?'

As I stood there, looking at the red car, I could hear Mrs Rose's voice in my ear, soft and persuasive, and I could hear my mum telling me I was the one who made places inhospitable. The way she'd turned from me and couldn't meet my eye. How Dad had let us go. Let *me* go. And I thought that maybe Mum was right. Maybe I was the one who ruined things, the one who could not be trusted, who made it hard for others to live.

And thinking of this, the car suddenly seemed like an opportunity. A means of getting away from everything and escaping for a while. Maybe if I went to the beach with Celeste, I wouldn't have to face all the questions that Sem had brought up. I could leave the voices and the memories behind. I'd be leaving Mum and leaving Sem. I could start afresh. I could be free.

So I was the one who said to the man, 'Just give us a moment, please.' I was the one full of excitement, persuading Celeste to love the car, with all its quirks and idiosyncrasies. It would be ours, I said, our key to freedom. I was the one who went back over to the man and said, 'It's perfect, thanks. Will cash be okay?'

Driving home from the warehouse—four thousand dollars poorer—the car's interior smelled musty, salty and warm, like old chips and dog breath. Celeste paid for most of the car with money Christina had given her as an early twenty-first birthday present, and I chipped in with what I'd saved from working at the restaurant. Our bikes were loaded in the back with their front wheels off—the guy had helped us. As we drove I had to hold my hands up the whole way to keep the fabric from the ceiling out of Celeste's face so she could see through the windscreen. From time to time I would catch her eye and dissolve into giggles, and she would say, 'Don't drop your hands, I need to see!' but not in a truly angry way. She found it funny and exciting too.

Maybe your grandmother, Christina, will keep that car. It never showed any signs of giving up. Maybe she will drive you around in it, batting the fabric away from the sides of her face, the windows open to let in the breeze, and you in the back, absent-mindedly finding out seams of grit between the seats. I like to imagine that sometimes. The pair of you, in the car.

I wonder if you will find Christina's art as challenging as Celeste did when she was young. Somehow, I don't think so. When I imagine it, the relationship will be different between the two of you. I think Celeste didn't like having a mum who pushed the boundaries. That was meant to be Celeste's job. It was probably painful to have a mother who was provocative, when Celeste was trying to be the rebellious one. I can sympathise, in a way. It was hard for me seeing my mum change from someone who had been so unremarkable and dependable into a woman who was unpredictable, who threw away her clothes and took off for the bush. We both wanted mothers who would just mother us, not mothers who wanted to be people of their own.

Now that I really think about it, of course Christina won't keep the car. What kind of person would hold on to a thing like that?

———

We left early, the sky a pale grey. Christina came around with paper maps in case our phones stopped working, bottles of vitamins, Tupperware containers of soup and foil-wrapped parcels of pies and eggs.

Celeste inspected them critically. 'These will stink up the whole car,' she said ungraciously.

But Christina was used to Celeste's prickly ways. Before we drove off, Christina gently poked Celeste's cheek with her knuckle. 'I'm losing my muse,' she said, and Celeste stuck out her tongue and smiled.

Christina stood in the road and waved until we rounded the bend. My own mum was not around to see us off. We didn't see much of each other; she was busy with her new friends and I didn't want anything to do with them. But I do have one clear memory of her at the Angel Street house around that time. It was about a week before Celeste and I left. I came home from the park to find her sitting on the back steps with Sem. I should have mentioned earlier that Sem had returned from up north before Celeste and I left for the beach; it's important to note details like that.

I came home that afternoon to find Mum and Sem talking on the back steps. They hadn't heard me come in, so for a few minutes I stood by the sink in the kitchen while they talked on the other side of the flywire door, unaware of my presence. I didn't turn on the tap to pour a glass of water because I didn't want to interrupt them. I was eavesdropping, I guess.

They were talking about Sem's work. Sem was telling Mum about a job he'd just got, constructing sandstone steps in someone's garden, and how easily the stone would stain.

'Have you thought about going to university?' Mum asked.

'Thought about it, yeah,' he said. 'Decided it's not for me.'

'Okay,' Mum said.

'Before she died, I asked Mum about it,' he began, and then broke off. 'I mean, I asked Janine about it and she said she'd support my decision either way, but I just don't think it's for me. Or not for me right now.'

Janine was Sem's birth mother.

'Okay,' Mum said again. 'Whatever makes you happy, love.'

And they sat for a moment together in silence.

'I'm so sorry,' Mum said then. 'I thought I knew what I was doing.'

And Sem reached over and put his hand on top of hers, on her knee.

'I do trust you,' Mum said. 'I know you, Sem.'

And then I must have made some sound, because Mum looked over her shoulder and said, 'Oh, hello, darling,' and Sem was standing up and making his excuses to go.

'Come see me some time,' he said to me before he left. 'Let's catch up properly.'

And I nodded and said I would, knowing of course that we'd already bought the car and were about to leave town. Hoping, perhaps, that by the time I returned from the beach with Celeste he'd be gone again, and I wouldn't have to think about our history anymore.

But in the end I did see Sem before we left. I'd gone around to Celeste's house one afternoon to start packing the car and I thought she was expecting me, but when I knocked on the door, it was Sem who answered.

'Hey there, kiddo,' he said. 'Come out back—we're having a barbecue.'

I went out to the back garden and found Celeste there putting hamburger patties on the grill.

'Want one?' she said. 'We have enough.' She didn't mention the reason I was there.

That afternoon, as Celeste and Sem sat with their legs touching, I could tell that she was reconsidering our trip, that there was a part of her that wanted to stay with Sem, now that he was back. Instead of packing the car with me, she was hanging out with Sem. And watching them, I was angry. Why should Celeste be allowed to drive this wedge between me and Peter, only to turn around and put her own romance first?

So I said to Sem, 'I suppose Celeste has told you that we're leaving in a couple of days?' And I felt a surge of satisfaction when he looked surprised. 'Just the two of us,' I said. 'We're going to the coast. We've got a place near Eden.'

⸺

To save on petrol, Celeste and I drove with the air-conditioning off and the windows down. Before we left, we'd spent the better part of an afternoon with a glue gun and nails, sticking the cloth ceiling back up as best we could. Still, on the long drive out to the coast it hung down between and around us. I hadn't got my licence, and so Celeste was going to drive us the whole way. We left just after lunch.

Eventually, the city gave way to farmland, dry and flat. Yellow grass. Outcrops of boulders. A few scraggly trees standing around in lonely circles. And the sky, seemingly stretched out to cover it all. Long, thin clouds.

'Sem would love this view,' Celeste said. 'It's almost super-natural, you know.'

'Yes,' I said, even though I didn't know.

'Do you remember,' Celeste said, 'how when he was younger he would stroke his top lip, that bum fluff just coming in that he was so proud of?'

I laughed. I did remember that, him stroking his lip as he talked.

When I think now about that drive to the beach, I picture Celeste with her hair all stirred up by the wind coming in through the windows, the great thump of air through the car, even the towels in the back seat whipped into life. She would have to drive for more than seven hours that day for us to reach the house near Eden by nightfall.

We were more than halfway there, barrelling along between the flat yellow fields, when we met the other car. It was a little white thing, and it came beetling along from the right, at an intersection that was otherwise just like all the other intersections we had flown through, unthinking. I didn't even make a sound. Instead of screaming, or yelling, I sucked in, hard, and grabbed the edges of the seat, as if I thought I could hold on to the previous moment, or hold myself back somehow from what was coming. But there was no collision. Celeste slammed her foot on the brake and we lurched forwards against our seatbelts and the white car went on its way with a long, angry blast of its horn.

'Sorry,' Celeste said, not looking at me, instead keeping her eyes fixed on the windscreen. She eased her foot off the brake and back onto the accelerator, and we began moving again. 'Glad you put your life in my hands?' she asked, and there was a real edge to her voice.

'Maybe we should pull over, take a break?' I suggested, knowing that what she really needed was for me to offer to take over for a bit. But, of course, I didn't know how to drive.

'We don't have time.' She pressed her foot down harder on the accelerator, as if to prove the point. 'We've still got so far to go, we're already pushing it. Don't worry, I'm fine.'

But the atmosphere in the car was changed then, and we hardly spoke for the rest of the day. Instead, we sat, sweating, the only noise the relentless thudding of air rushing through the windows and into the car.

We stopped for dinner where the landscape changed to fernery, just before the road dropped down to the sea. Amid the sudden green we found a shack selling meat pies and cartons of coffee-flavoured milk. I was bursting to go to the toilet. I'd been holding for miles. The outhouse was detached from the main building, standing alone at the end of a short path, and inside the air was thick with flies and heavy with stink, so I had to put my hand across my nose and mouth against the assault. When I came out, Celeste was standing by the car, having a smoke.

'I'm tired,' she said. 'I can't make it the rest of the way today.'

We didn't have much money, and there was nowhere really to stay, so we ate our pies and then decided we would sleep in the car, Celeste in the front passenger seat and me in the back, lying across three seats, windows cracked to let in some air. Celeste's mood was still frosty as we climbed into the car, and she barely said a word to me. As night came, the sky a spectacular purple and pink behind the trees, all the heat dropped away. The inside of the car, which had been sweaty for the whole drive, now turned so cold I had to rummage through my bag for the few warm clothes I'd brought. Even so, the cold got into my bones, waking me again and again, and I tucked my body into itself, my hands into my armpits or between my thighs, my chin pressed into my chest, knees drawn up, desperate to find enough warmth to fall back to sleep. One time when I woke, Celeste was shifting around in the front seat and I sensed she was awake too. But my memory of her frostiness from the day kept me from saying anything to her. I didn't want to provoke her again.

Next morning, the wave of heat came as a relief. Groggy, we peeled off our layers of clothes and ate scallop pies, Celeste sitting in the car with the doors open and her legs dangling out, and me sitting on the grass with my legs folded underneath me. Celeste put on the car radio and, catching my eye, smiled wryly. The tension of the day before seemed to have dissolved overnight and, if anything, the uncomfortable sleep had only improved our mood. There was something bracing about it. Reckless and carefree. Suddenly, we were back in it together again.

After we had eaten, I got back in the car and Celeste drove the rest of the treacherous, winding road down to the sea. The trees grew very thickly here, letting the sunlight through in swift bursts, like camera flashes, and it felt like we were celebrities driving through a paparazzi storm. Celeste turned the radio up even louder, so we could hear it over the air thudding in through the windows.

The wind really picked up when we got down to the water. It smelled salty and fishy, blowing in from the harbour and filling the car. We stopped at the first town we came to, a little place with ice-cream parlours and fish-and-chip shops, pharmacies with inflatable lilos and racks of swimwear out the front, fishing tackle and boating shops. People were sitting out at cafes down by the water, crossing the street in bathers and thongs, peering into the windows of quaint craft shops. A group of two men and a woman, pale-faced and straw-haired, stood around by the faded yellow public toilet blocks. We pulled into the supermarket's half-empty car park and went in for supplies—meat and bread and milk—the checkout girl greeting us with matter-of-fact friendliness.

Back in the car, Celeste checked the route, and then we were on the road once more, driving out past the mini-golf course, the lawn bowls club, onto a dirt road that cut straight through the bush, dense gums and craggy orange anthills on either side. We slid through another smaller town, little more than a camping ground and a few shops, and up into dense bush, so that now on our left was a sharp drop down to some distant, glinting body of water, the view screened by the tall straight white trunks of gum trees.

We reached a crossroad, where a cluster of eccentric letterboxes sprouted from the ground. Here we took a right onto a narrow dirt track which rose and fell so steeply that I was concerned the car might not make it. And then the road flattened out and there before us, in the centre of a clearing of short green grass and sand, was the house. It stood on stilts, the exterior walls painted the same dusty green as the gum leaves. At the rear, where we drove in, a water tank nestled, and next to it a lemon tree grew, its branches heavy with fat yellow fruit.

Celeste pulled the car up next to a set of wooden steps that ran up the side of the house to the balcony. In front of the house was thick bush, split by the opening of a walking track that quickly turned and disappeared from view. The pings of bellbirds echoed in the hot, dusty air.

I got out of the car, tugged my bag out of the boot and followed Celeste up the wooden stairs. The balcony was made of fibro board that creaked beneath our feet and was hemmed in with orange plastic netting. I went to the edge and looked out, trees stretching beyond and then brilliant blue water. Across the inlet, on the far bank, were sand and rocks and gums. To the right, I could see only trees, but I could hear the distant rhythm of the surf.

Behind me, Celeste was unlocking the sliding door to the house, and as I turned she let out a shriek, stumbling back, almost knocking me into the plastic fencing. A huntsman came scuttling over the deck towards us, just four legs, the others severed by the motion of the door. It disappeared under the tattered netting.

Inside, the house was small, with an open-plan kitchen and living area, and a narrow corridor with two bedrooms off it, one facing the water, the other looking out the back. The bathroom had a shallow square bath and a mottled-glass window above the sink, cracked open to let in the air. A plastic cup sat on the windowsill, with someone's old toothbrush, a razor, and a half-squeezed tube of toothpaste. The toilet was separate.

Celeste offered me the larger bedroom at the front of the house, and she took the back room, cool and dark, with the lemon tree rustling outside. While she unpacked in her room, I went to my window and looked out across the water. Two tall white gums stood on the opposite bank, gleaming in the sunlight. The city was far away now. It did seem, in that moment, as if I might have escaped. I felt like I had come to the edge of my old life and was looking ahead, into something bright and new.

Part II

Part II

Chapter Seven

THE HOUSE SAT BETWEEN TWO beaches. Out front, a narrow path had been hewn through the undergrowth down to an inlet, where the river met the sea. Looking out from the beach across the estuary, the water was flat and shallow over the sandy bottom and you could hardly tell that further out it dropped into a deep channel. There was only a slight darkening in the colour of the water there—hard to see against the glare of the sun—and, if you looked very keenly, a strange flatness on the water's surface where the wind could not stir up its usual ripples because of the current in the deep channel pulling out to sea. To the right, where the inlet met the ocean, the water was choppy and broke against the rocks. Further still in that direction, around the curve of the head, lay a second beach, a surf beach. At night, with the windows open, the sound of the waves sent me off to sleep.

We went swimming in the inlet most days. We came to know the tides, the water icy and clean when it came in from the sea, warm and cloudy when it was flowing out from the river.

At night we went down with torches, walking through the shallows, the water lapping at our calves, our darting beams of light illuminating hundreds of pale stingrays, hardly bigger than the size of my spread hand, the same colour as the sand, so they had only to settle to the bottom and they would disappear from sight.

Usually, we had the inlet beach to ourselves. Occasionally men came to fish from the rocks, or a family would come to swim, spreading their towels over the sand and sometimes setting up a beach tent, or an umbrella. From time to time, these families might picnic at the wooden tables by the public parking area—a short loop of road only half a kilometre or so from our house— attracting curious goannas in search of something to eat.

Celeste liked it when people came to the inlet beach. She liked to watch the families and speculate about their lives. Usually, she decided they were tourists, and the stories she told about them were invariably depressing. The mothers were either 'uptight bitches' or 'timid sad sacks', the children hadn't been brought up right, and the men were either deserving of more freedom and too spineless to claim it or entitled and lame. The occasional single was dismissed as a depressed loner.

On the morning of my birthday, we went down to the inlet beach early. The heat was only just starting to infuse the dry air, so that I still felt the edge of coldness. A group of three young people arrived and put down their towels just a short way along the sand from us. Celeste appeared to be engrossed in her book—an American book about government conspiracies—but I noticed that as she finished each page she looked up and let her eyes rest on them. I wondered what she was thinking, readying myself for whatever story she was going to tell me about their lives.

The group consisted of two guys and a girl. The girl was lying on her towel, reading a book, and one of the guys was sitting up, also reading—a political biography, I think—while the other jogged the length of the beach. Celeste and I put down our own books and went and splashed around in the water for a bit, and then returned and lay on the sand, and all the time Celeste kept turning her eyes towards them, not saying anything, until finally I said, 'Someone you know?'

'Someone I *might* know,' Celeste said. 'They seem cool.'

It annoyed me when she said that. *Someone I might know.* I think it got to me because I understood just what she meant. All three of them were beautiful to look at: tall and lean and strong. Without having any connection to them at all, Celeste had decided to make them hers. And it irritated me, because she didn't even know them and they obviously weren't hers at all, but I knew that it wouldn't take much for her to claim them, which was exactly what she did.

Celeste ended up inviting them back to our house. They came up onto the balcony and Celeste produced a slab of beers, which we drank together, and made a pot of mussels. We put on some music and the girl danced, her arms lifted into the air, eyes closed. She had long dark hair which fanned out around her body. I remember the way the runner smiled, the skin crinkling around his eyes making his face handsome. The quiet, almost smug expression on his friend with the shaved head, drinking a beer and leaning against the balcony, a little too cool to allow himself to join in. I felt torn. On the one hand, I was genuinely happy to be around the three of them. Celeste was right—they were cool. They were relaxed and fun, and perhaps a little pretentious, but being pretentious really wasn't the worst thing. On the other hand, despite the relaxed atmosphere that night, I was unable to connect with the three strangers in the way Celeste so easily did. I felt at a distance from them, like they were Celeste's friends, even though, like me, she'd only just met them. I felt like an interloper, an unwelcome guest, even though I was the host and they were visitors. So it was a relief when, in the early hours of the morning, they finally piled, drunk, into their car and drove away. They had to drive back to Melbourne that afternoon, and that was a relief too, though Celeste was bitterly disappointed.

'I miss them already,' she said, having a cigarette on the balcony in the pre-dawn light. And I pretended to miss them too, though I'm sure Celeste must have seen through my act because she said, 'You were pretty quiet tonight. Didn't you like them?'

And when I said I was just tired, she shook her head and said, 'If you're tired, don't stay up for me, just go to bed.'

'I'm worried about them,' I said, 'driving drunk like that.' Maybe I was put out because it had been my birthday, but Celeste had barely acknowledged it, and I felt dumb for being upset by that, because I knew I was old enough now that birthdays shouldn't really matter anymore.

'You're always worrying, Tilly,' she said. 'That's one of the problems with you.'

I had been sitting with her on the balcony, and now I stood up to go inside.

'Hey,' Celeste said, and I stopped and looked back at her. 'Happy birthday,' she said.

On cooler days, we walked along the ocean beach, the sea hurling salt spray into our faces. This was what we were doing one overcast day when Liam came to surf. Celeste and I were walking along the hard sand near the water's edge, wearing jumpers over our bathers against the cool wind blowing in from the sea. We were looking for shells. Celeste was a little ahead, filling the front pocket of her big yellow jumper with the most perfect specimens; we had an ongoing competition to find the most beautiful one. Behind her the grey-blue sea pounded the sand. We rarely swam here—the sea was too wild—but occasionally, as on this day, surfers would come, zipping themselves into wetsuits and strapping themselves to their boards, paddling out to catch the waves. Surfers often came on unsettled days like this, because the waves were bigger, but they rarely stayed long. The water was unpredictable, stirred up by the current flowing out from the inlet, and there was a long sand bank far out, just below the surface, that broke and sucked the ocean out like bathwater down a drain.

We'd been at the beach house about two weeks the day that Liam showed up. At first, I didn't recognise him. He pulled up with a mate and the two of them bounded across the sand, suits half-zipped, boards under their arms. Celeste and I were sitting on a dune by this time, our knees tucked up inside our jumpers, sifting through our shells.

'I think that's Liam,' I said, peering at the familiar figure. And we got up and ran down to meet him on the sand.

Liam's straight black shoulder-length hair was crusted with salt and sand. 'Hello, gorgeous,' he said, hugging me. 'Fancy finding you all the way down here.' He pulled Celeste to him next, kissing her ear.

Liam was working at a strawberry farm nearby, he told us, picking fruit. There was a whole group of them—travellers, mainly—and he said the couple who owned the place were kind. This was the same farm, of course, where Sem would later work.

At first, I felt excited to see Liam again—down on the beach, meeting his friend, all our hair blowing up in the wind and the taste of salt in our mouths. Unlike with the trio Celeste had adopted, I already had a connection with Liam through my mother and the Angel Street house, and so I didn't feel so much like an outsider or like Celeste was the one in charge. If anything, with Liam it was almost the other way around. I was the one who knew him, and Celeste was a little on the outer, especially because of her breakup with Liam's brother, Noah. I'd heard Liam mention it once at the Angel Street house, and he hadn't spoken favourably about Celeste. He seemed to think the breakup was entirely her fault. At the time, I'd thought it was pretty unfair of him. But when we saw him again on the beach, an ungenerous part of me was pleased to remember that Liam didn't really like Celeste, because it meant I wasn't at risk of being left on the outer. I was happy to see him. It was only later that I'd grow uncomfortable, thinking about Mum and the big fight she'd had with Liam before he left and what she might have said about me and everything that happened with Sem.

Sem's friend, Julien, was short and slender, on a working holiday from France. He was new to surfing, and excited to try something he saw as central to the Australian way of life.

'I'm not that good myself,' Liam said, laughing at Julien's excitement. They'd hired their gear from a surf shop in one of the nearby towns.

Celeste's mood had lifted now that Julien and Liam were there. Despite the cool day, and the tempestuous water, she stripped down to her bikini and ran into the ocean, shrieking at the cold. I guess she was showing off. I went back up to sit in the dunes while Liam and Julien paddled out into the ocean and sat up on their boards, appearing and then disappearing among the waves. The sky was grey with small patches of blue, and seagulls coasted around with their wings outstretched.

I can't say exactly when it became clear that while Julien was attempting to catch a wave, Liam was drifting further out. But suddenly Celeste was waving her hands and calling to them.

I'm sure Julien must have thought that Celeste was alerting them to a shark. He pulled his legs up onto his board and turned towards Liam, lifting his arms to wave, only to realise it was that other, more mysterious danger: a rip. Once Julien understood what was happening, he lay down on his board and began to paddle towards Liam, who was trying and failing to make his way out of the current by paddling at an angle into the shore.

It rapidly became clear that Julien wasn't going to be able to reach Liam, let alone help him. Julien was clumsy in the water, the board barely under his control. Celeste was already swimming out, her arms flashing against the water as she moved steadily through the waves. Seeing her, Julien turned on his board, and started coming in towards the safety of the shore.

It seemed like a long time that Celeste was swimming out to Liam, but in fact I don't think it could have been more than a minute or two. Once she reached him, she grabbed the front of his board and began tugging him across the current towards an outcrop of rocks that reached into the ocean at the far end of the beach. Grasping the plan, Liam started paddling in the same direction, and they moved together along the beach, not coming in towards the sand, but not moving any further out to sea either.

Meanwhile Julien had come up onto the sand, coughing and shivering, and started running around the curve of the beach to the rocks, and I got up and followed. We walked out between the rockpools, Julien searching out smooth places to stand barefoot among the sharp ridges, until he was right at the very edge, where the waves crashed. I came up behind him. Liam and Celeste were still in the water, moving towards us.

At last, they reached us. Celeste came up first, scrambling up onto the rocks with surprising agility. Liam had a harder time of it. Celeste and Julien were trying to grab his arms, but again and again he slid out of their grip. Celeste got down and knelt, reaching for him, and I could see that the sharp rocks were cutting up her knees. Finally, Celeste grabbed Liam's forearms and heaved and, with him bracing his feet against the rocks, he came up out of the water, breathless and bloody.

While this rescue was taking place, I felt as if I were watching it from afar. As if I wasn't really there. Of course, I was frightened for Liam and Celeste, but the emotion I felt most strongly was discomfort; I felt awkward, unsure what to do, and worried that I wasn't behaving appropriately. And so I stood back and hoped they wouldn't notice that I had done nothing to help.

Afterwards, we went up to the house. Julien was very quiet, his teeth chattering from the cold and the shock, even after a steaming mug of tea was put in his hands. He and Celeste went to the bathroom to dress the cuts on their legs and arms. Liam sat down at the kitchen table with me.

'How's your mum going?' he asked.

I can't remember what I replied, probably something flippant about her going off to the bush.

'I think she was taking it a lot harder than she let on,' Liam said. 'The situation with your foster brother. It was hard for her to see him again out of the blue. It reopened old wounds.'

I felt uncomfortable when Liam said that. I thought of Mum rambling about how Liam thought she was irresponsible, and how she'd included me in that description too. It was painful to realise that Liam might see me in that light and, embarrassingly, I found myself on the edge of tears. I think I was particularly upset because I knew Liam was right. I had been irresponsible when it came to Sem. And I looked up to Liam, so falling in his estimation stung particularly.

'I haven't spoken to Mum in a while,' I said. 'I think she's okay.' I could hear the quaver in my voice.

I think Liam must have understood that he'd touched a nerve, because he switched tack and started talking about Celeste instead.

'And how are *you*?' he asked. 'How's it been out here with Celeste?'

'Oh great,' I said. 'Really fun.'

'For sure,' Liam said. He looked down at the cuts on his palms, wincing a little. 'It's always a bit intense though, right, living with a friend. You can see a different side of people. I've got my fair share of horror stories, even from living with people who were really close friends.'

I could feel myself smiling at him. 'Thanks,' I said. 'It's good to hear that.'

'You take care of yourself, alright,' he said. 'Watch out for Celeste. Remember to stand up for yourself. And if you ever need me, well, you know where to find me.'

And then Celeste was back from the bathroom, Liam's friend in tow. 'What are you two talking about?' she asked, and the way she came and placed her hand on Liam's shoulder made me squirm.

'Oh, you know,' Liam said. 'Family stuff.'

Celeste laughed at that. 'What, like how you were fucking her mum?'

Liam shook off her hand and stood up. 'We should probably take off,' he said.

We walked them down to their van, and Liam and his friend drove off, leaving Celeste and me alone together again.

As dusk came on, I cooked: bacon and eggs. The oil spitted up hot from the pan, dotting my hands, while the bacon got fat-logged and soggy, not crisp the way Celeste made it. We ate and played a game of Scrabble, which we'd found in one of the cupboards. As we took it in turns to lay tiles on the board, the pregnant air outside finally broke into a storm, whipping the trees into a frenzy.

Over the next few days, Celeste's cuts dried into long dark scabs that she picked at idly, her grey eyes betraying nothing of what she felt about what had happened down by the ocean. Again and again I said to her, 'You saved him, you really are a hero,' and she just shook her head and smiled. 'No, seriously, you are,' I said, until finally she grew frustrated, and told me to drop it.

Celeste probably thought I was fawning and found it lame and annoying. But I couldn't stop. I really wanted her to agree that she'd been a hero. Because somehow in my mind that made my failure to help more forgivable. I was still thinking about Liam, and being irresponsible. If Celeste would just say she'd been a hero, then I'd only failed to reach heroic standards. But if she'd just done what anyone would have done, then what did that make me?

Chapter Eight

IT WAS JUST AFTER LIAM almost drowned that I decided to look for a job. I'm not sure what it was that drove me. Maybe it was something about my inertia that day on the rocks with Liam and Julien, my detachment, how I'd stood back and failed to help. Maybe it was Liam's gentle warning about Celeste. Or maybe it was just that I was running out of money—the little I'd saved from the Italian restaurant had long been spent on fuel and food and my half of the red car—less than half, in fact; Celeste paid more—and Peter's words still echoed in my mind: if I wanted to have any freedom, then I needed to have a job.

Celeste didn't think much of the idea.

'I just think there are better ways you could use your time,' she said, arranging shells in a square grid on the table by hue, dark grey in one corner, white in the corner opposing, pink in the third and yellow in the fourth. In between, the shells slowly changed colours, with a band of blue slicing through.

She swapped the positions of two purple-pink shells, examined the result, and then moved them back. 'I just think you have so much more potential than waiting tables. Don't you find it depressing?'

She was right to say that the job was depressing. Bijou—that was the name of the place—was a low building stranded halfway between our beach house and the small town with the camping ground. It was about a thirty-minute walk from us. In the weeks we'd been at the beach house, Celeste had been teaching me to drive on the quiet coastal roads, and while I wasn't confident enough to make it all the way to town—and I didn't have a licence—occasionally I drove the short distance to work.

Bijou marketed itself as a silent cinema-restaurant. The customers were mainly retirees—there were a lot of them in the area—who came to watch silent films projected onto a small pull-down screen while I served them various sliced meats in gravy with a side of steamed vegetables and, the chef-owner's special touch, mashed potatoes that had been shaped into a pear and crumbed, with a little stalk sticking out the top. The sign out the front of the place was illustrated with a big Charlie Chaplin cartoon. I was often asked when he would be on, though the whole time I worked there, they didn't show a Charlie Chaplin film once. But the patrons were nice and the job was easy enough, just a few nights a week, and so I felt good about it at first.

It was a little less than a week after I got the job that I came home to find that, for the first time, Celeste wasn't waiting for me, shuffling her shells about or painting on the balcony.

Usually, Celeste cooked us a late dinner, or I ate something at Bijou, but that night I was hungry, and when I opened the fridge there was just an eggplant and an old squeeze bottle of tomato sauce left by the owners of the house. I fried the eggplant in some oil and ate the greasy result at the table, and Celeste still wasn't home by the time I finished. It was almost one in the morning. I went to my room and read in bed, one eye on the time, and finally, at about 3 am, I heard a car in the driveway, footsteps clattering up the stairs.

'Hello,' I called, putting down my book and coming out into the hallway.

I could hear Celeste in the kitchen.

'Hello?' I called again, walking down the corridor.

Celeste was sitting at the kitchen table, wearing a shirt I'd never seen before. A bright yellow polo with a slice of pizza embroidered on the breast and, beneath it, *Rita's Pizza* in cursive font. In front of her, a pizza box lay open, with half of what looked like a supreme pizza inside.

'Want some?' she asked.

I started to walk over, drawn by the smell, oily and sweet.

'Well, you can't. It's all mine!' She laughed. She was drunk.

'That's okay,' I said. 'I ate earlier.'

She picked up a slice and took a bite. 'Looks like you're not the only one who can get a fucking job,' she said through a mouthful.

I felt my back stiffen. 'Didn't you say jobs were stupid?' I said before I could stop myself. I could feel my face getting hot.

'Obviously I don't think making money is stupid,' Celeste said, rolling her eyes. 'Can't you tell when I'm joking, Tilly?' She stood up, went to the sink and filled a glass of water from the tap. 'Besides, what else was I going to do with myself all day?' She smiled at me and sat back down. 'They've offered me a few shifts a week. Have a slice—go on. I was just teasing before.' She took a sip of water. 'Everyone there is awesome. They're so funny. We had after-work drinks with alcohol from the bar and heaps of pizza. Apparently, they do it all the time. This one guy, George, is cute. And Jess just cracks me up so bad. She does this funny thing with the pizza oven. So good.'

'I'm going to bed,' I said.

'Don't sulk just because I have new friends!' Celeste held her arms out towards me. 'I still love you too.'

'It's not that,' I said. But as I spoke, I could hear the emotion in my voice. Was that it? Was I just jealous? I shook my head. 'You're a hypocrite.' Now that I'd said it, I felt like there was no going back. I had to stand my ground. As much as I might want to sit down with her and have a slice of pizza and hear about the people she worked with and the funny thing with the oven, I felt committed to being angry, and my only option was to walk further in that lonely direction.

Celeste just cackled. 'So what? Go to bed, you old grouch. You'll feel better in the morning.'

⁓

The next morning, Celeste announced that we would go prawning down in the inlet that evening. I was embarrassed about my outburst the night before, but Celeste didn't even mention it. So I pushed the previous evening from my mind and focused on the prawning trip instead. Celeste had been saying for a while that she wanted to fish the inlet, but there were no rods or reels in the house, and we could never quite get our act together to drive into town to look for some. So, the fishing idea was always on hold, until the morning Celeste went exploring in the storage room under the house.

It was a dim little place, the storage room, narrow, built of thick concrete, with a single bare bulb in the middle of the ceiling. Cobwebs adorned everything, spun around an old canoe, life jackets rotted right through with mould, an axe, plastic tubs full of wires and corks, fish lures and plastic tape. And right at the back was an old prawning net, with a big hole in it.

Celeste brought the net up onto the balcony, where she bashed it against the rail to knock away the thickest spider webs. Then she set about mending the hole as best she could with a series of little knots.

We waited until dark and then set off for the inlet, twigs cracking under our feet. Celeste went ahead with the net and torch, and I walked behind with the second torch, my beam a little thinner, a little paler against the enormous shifting purple dark. In my other hand I carried a yellow plastic bucket that I had found under the sink. Above us all the stars were out.

After a time, the sticks beneath our feet gave way to sand— night sand that felt almost wet because it was so cool, now that the sun had gone down, and it made the hairs stand up on my arms. We became very quiet then, stealthy, with our silent beams of light darting erratically, picking up tufts of beach grass, and then the water, which glistened with the light from the moon. Celeste went in first and I followed. The water was shockingly cold around my ankles, so that I caught my breath, my gasp loud in the quiet night.

We probably spent about fifteen minutes casting our torches around, looking for prawns. The torchlight on the water looked beautiful, but there were no prawns in sight. Celeste had felt sure that the inlet was the place for them. She said their bodies would be buried in the sand beneath the shallow water, but we only saw pale stingrays, floating calmly past our feet.

'We'll catch a stingray instead,' Celeste said. I could hear excitement in her voice.

I wasn't into the idea. The stingrays were beautiful, and I wondered if they might also be endangered. Not to mention poisonous. But when I shared my reservations with Celeste, she was only annoyed.

'Don't be so uptight,' she said. 'Stingray is a delicacy. I'm not letting us leave empty-handed.'

It was easy to catch one. Celeste dipped the net and moved it slowly through the water and a stingray drifted right in.

She led the way back to the house, the bucket swinging against her leg as she walked. I was shivering in my jumper, my legs cold and wet. Inside, we huddled in front of the little portable radiator for a moment before changing into long pants and pulling on socks. As we turned our attention to our catch something unexpected happened. I'd been thinking that, just as it went without saying that Celeste would be the one to catch the stingray, it also went without saying that she would be the one to kill it. That was how most things went in our friendship: Celeste was the one who did things, and I was the one who stood by.

I told myself that my role wasn't entirely superfluous. It can be important sometimes to have an audience. Someone to do things with, or do things for. A witness. I still think that was true, for Celeste and me. If Celeste told me that she was practically living with Sem, then somehow my hearing those words made them true. If she said that I'd looked crazy that evening at Noah's party, calling to her across the lawn, then that was how it had been. Celeste showed me that simply by saying something with confidence, in a way that's persuasive to the listener, that alone can make a story real. Maybe if I had understood that back then, things might have turned out differently. I couldn't see that I had the power to change events, to affect them: the first step was to assert yourself with confidence. Instead, I spoke without thinking, careless about what consequences would flow. Or I looked to other people to do the telling, and let them decide for me how things should be.

I wonder, is that why I'm writing this for you now?

But I'm getting ahead of myself. I was telling you about the stingray.

When I lifted the bucket from the floor onto the formica table, Celeste drew a knife out of the block and then spun it in her hand, so that the hilt was extended towards me. I must have hesitated, and most likely my surprise showed in my face, because she said, 'Go on then,' and thrust the knife hilt forwards, as if to goad me into taking it from her hand. In the bucket, the stingray flapped sadly. It was not so beautiful now that it was unable to glide through the water. It looked strange and alien.

I just stood there without moving until finally Celeste took things into her own hands. Maybe this was the true dynamic between us: Celeste gave me the opportunity to act, and when I didn't take it, she did.

Celeste wrapped her hand in a tea towel then took the stingray from the bucket, setting it on the chopping board and holding it down while she stabbed it through with the knife, just to the side of its spine. It writhed and thrashed its barbed tail. Still holding it, Celeste withdrew the knife and brought it down again at the base of the tail, slicing the whole thing off. Then she looked up at me. 'I don't know how to kill it,' she said, and gave a short laugh. 'Where's the vital part?'

I didn't know either.

'Okay, okay,' she said, turning to the stove. 'I have an idea.'

Celeste set the kettle over the hob then, when it began to whistle, took it off the stove and poured boiling water over the wounded stingray on the chopping board. I watched as it thrashed, the skin on its back tightening, bright red blood coming out of its gills. That took me aback. I hadn't expected its blood to look so familiar. After a minute or so, it went still. Its skin had turned from sand to grey.

Celeste took the stingray and ran the knife down either side of the spine, taking off the wings, trickles of blood running over the chopping board and her hands. She rinsed the flesh in the sink and threw it into a pan.

There wasn't much meat, but what we had was sweet and succulent.

'Isn't it funny that when you eat stingray it's called skate,' I said. I'd been thinking about it as we prepared the meal. How we have to give some animals a new name before we can eat them.

Celeste smiled. 'I have a joke for you,' she said. 'What turns a stingray into skate?' She cackled and held up her knife. 'Me!'

———

Did Celeste know on the day we left—or earlier still: the day we went to see the car, or even the day she first suggested the trip—that Sem would come to join us at the house near Eden? She must have told him where to find us.

He arrived in the morning, early, while Celeste was still asleep. I was out on the balcony in my bathers, about to go down to the inlet to swim. The weather was warm, the water beyond the trees twinkling and bright, the ground dappled with sunlight that fell through the leaves above. When I saw Liam's yellow van parked behind the lemon tree, I was expecting to see Liam step out, but instead I saw Sem. He looked gaunt, the ropes and muscles of his arms standing out against his skin. It seemed like he had changed again in the time we had been away, his body more angular, joints looser.

'Hello,' I called out, waving from the balcony, trying not to look surprised. For some reason it seemed important not to betray anything of my real emotions at that moment. Not to show that I had actually believed it would just be Celeste and me alone at the beach house—or that she would at least ask me before inviting someone else. I wanted it to seem as if Celeste didn't keep anything from me, and to imply that it wouldn't bother me anyway. I didn't want Sem to realise that he was among the people I had been happy to escape.

'Hello, Matilda,' Sem called out, lifting his arm and waving back at me. He took the stairs two at a time and grabbed me around the waist, an awkward hug, his bones digging painfully into my side. 'Going to the beach?' he asked.

'Yes.' I went and pulled my towel off the railing where I had hung it to dry overnight.

'Well, see you later then,' he said. 'She's inside?'

'Yes,' I said again.

He was already opening the screen door, turning away from me. Just like that, I had been dismissed.

I went down to the beach, where everything was empty and bright, the sand and water white with glare, leaving Sem and Celeste to reunite in her dark room with the red-and-black woven blanket, the old posters of famous artworks I'd never seen in real life, the rustle of lemon leaves through the open window.

To distract myself, I decided I would swim right across the inlet. I waded through the shallows until the water reached my thighs, and then I began to swim. I made it to the sandbank, beyond which was the deep channel—far too deep for me to touch the bottom, the water dark and frightening-looking—that ran out to sea. I had never swum this stretch alone before. Usually I was with Celeste, letting the current whip us along for a moment before we scrambled back onto the sand. I had to close my eyes to throw myself in, swimming frantically until I got to the other side, much further down the sand than where I'd started, much closer to the rocks, my heart high up between my clavicles. As I was wading out to the far bank, I looked past the heads towards the ocean. Far out, among the waves, I saw the backs of dolphins, shining in the sunlight.

When I returned to the house it was early afternoon. Celeste and Sem were still in the back bedroom, their dim mutterings just audible from the corridor. I took some bread and butter back to my own room and read my encyclopedia until I fell asleep. When I woke, it was evening, and Celeste and Sem were out on the deck; I could hear their voices coming in through my window. I went out and they were standing side by side at the railing, watching the light change over the water. I fell into one of the deckchairs behind them, the wooden legs clacking under the stretch of the canvas.

'Hello, sleepyhead,' Celeste said, turning. 'How was the beach?'

'Great,' I said. 'I swam the channel.'

'Sem is making us dinner,' she said. 'I hope you're in the mood for fish.'

'I'm going to take you both fishing soon,' Sem said, grinning at me. 'Down at the jetty. You'll have to get up early, but it's worth it. You'll see.'

That evening, in celebration of Sem's arrival, Celeste cut our hair. We sat out on the balcony with old green towels around our shoulders, looking out at the inlet, while Celeste worked. I liked the feel of her fingers on my scalp. The sound of the scissors snipping, hair falling around my feet. It was getting dark by the time she did Sem, but her fingers still moved confidently around his head, the scissors catching the end of the light.

'You could get paid to do this,' Sem said.

'Yeah,' said Celeste. 'If I didn't have dreams for my life.'

Sem laughed.

'Hold still,' she said. 'If you laugh it will end up wonky.'

'I like it wonky,' Sem said. 'Don't be such a snob, anyway. I think you might enjoy being a hairdresser. Gossiping with all your clients. Making everyone beautiful. You'd be great at it.'

We drank after dinner that night, on the deck, until we were drunk. Sem danced wildly with Celeste, spinning her by her hands and then releasing her so she went spiralling into the plastic netting which creaked perilously and threatened to drop her into the trees below. Giddy, that night I slept with the windows and curtains open, looking down through the dark trees to where the moon hit the gentle waters of the inlet, listening to the surf pounding the ocean beach.

Chapter Nine

SEM CAME AND WENT FROM the beach house many times that summer. Sometimes he stayed away for just a night, and came back for long days that stretched out while we were in them only to fall away so abruptly that I lost track and could almost forget that there was a time when Sem wasn't around. I would sit instead squarely inside the moment: Sem striding down the beach with a cigarette hanging out of his mouth; swimming back to us through the inlet, arms flashing; or lying in one of the deckchairs, his limbs altogether too big for it, and so thin. And then Celeste and I would come back from a morning swim to find the house dim and cool and empty, or I would wake to the sound of car tyres crunching gravel, and he would be gone again.

When Sem was at the house, he and Celeste shared the room at the back, but when he was away Celeste would fall asleep on my bed, after hours of reading together, lying at angles across the covers, the smell of the sea in the sheets and our hair—even those fine golden hairs along our arms and legs and bellies; a smell like the inside of a cooked mussel, fishy and salty and warm.

I remember one afternoon, coming out to Celeste and Sem on the balcony. Celeste was taking a break from painting, resting with her elbows on the railing, looking out towards the inlet, and she turned at the sound of my feet on the squeaky deck. Sem was smoking a cigarette with his sunglasses on, sitting in a deck chair with one leg crossed over the other, a notebook on his knee, a pencil in his free hand. I must have been staring at Sem, because Celeste said, 'He's writing poetry.'

I shifted my gaze to her, and when I looked back at Sem, he'd rearranged himself, sitting with both feet on the deck, the notebook closed.

'Let's go down to the beach,' he said.

But later that evening, while Celeste was gathering flowers down below, Sem came and stood in the doorway of my room, where I was reading.

'You know, it's your mum who got me into poetry.'

I looked at him, his face illuminated by the light coming through the window. He looked handsome. There was an openness to his expression, like he was relaxed. Less guarded than usual.

'How?' I asked.

'When I lived with you guys, she gave me this book of poems.' He shrugged and laughed gently. 'Honestly, I didn't get most of them.'

'Right,' I said.

'Remember how you used to help me with English back then?' he said, leaning against the doorframe.

I did remember. The beautiful unusual ways he'd used words, and how I'd only been able to tell him he was wrong. I shifted uncomfortably. 'It was your favourite subject,' I said.

He kind of tilted his head to the side, smiling slightly. 'I guess,' he said. 'Actually, before I lived with you I went to this arts school for a few months, and they had photography classes, with a darkroom and everything. That was awesome.'

I thought about the photos in the back of his cupboard. How he'd hidden them there, almost as if he wanted to protect them from us.

'Can I ask you something?' I said.

'Sure.' He turned to look back down the hallway towards the kitchen. I could hear Celeste coming in through the flywire door.

'When we were kids, you had these photos in your cupboard. Why did you put them back there?'

He looked at me. 'It's funny you remember that. They were for an assignment I did. I got a good mark, and I wanted to put them up. I don't know why I chose the closet. I was a bit embarrassed about them, I guess.'

'So you took those photos?' I said.

'Yep.'

'They were beautiful,' I said. 'You didn't need to hide them away.'

And then Celeste was calling us from the kitchen, asking what we were doing back there and if it was time to eat.

Sem cooked us dinner that night. He chopped the vegetables expertly.

'You're good at that,' I said.

'It's in his blood,' said Celeste, from where she was leaning on the kitchen table. We watched as Sem swept the vegetables into a bowl. 'His dad was a chef.'

'A cook,' Sem said, putting oil into the pan and turning on the heat.

'He worked at this restaurant that was shaped like a train,' Celeste said. 'It was famous. Everyone knew the train restaurant.'

'It was my grandparents' restaurant,' Sem said. 'My dad worked there for a while.'

'Do you remember it?' I asked.

'Nah,' he said, sliding the vegetables into the pan. 'This was all before I was born.'

When Sem came to the beach house, Celeste put away her conspiracy books. There was no talk of aliens or government plots. It seemed that phase was over. Maybe it just proved that she was never truly that committed to it in the first place. Instead, she read thick paperbacks she found on the shelves in the living room.

It seemed like Sem picked up where Celeste had left off. He never talked directly about his time up north, but he said he liked being at the coast because we were untraceable; the area was known for being a black hole for mobile phone reception and there was no internet at the beach house. Or, coming back after days away at the farm, picking berries, he'd bring containers full of fruit and as we ate them he'd talk about chemical pesticides and the ways that the government and big corporations were keeping all sorts of data about the details of our lives.

At the time, I thought it was strange that Celeste gave up her theories right when Sem started to express them around me for the first time. I thought she would have wanted to bond with him over their shared interest. But now I wonder if perhaps it was easier for Celeste to enjoy those theories when Sem wasn't present. She could read her conspiracy books and imagine Sem reading the same thing. But when he was right there in the kitchen, pacing back and forth in front of the stove, thirty minutes into an angry diatribe about methods the government uses to control our minds, perhaps it was more difficult to feel a special bond. Better, then, to put the books away.

When Sem left the beach house, he said he was working at the berry farm, and that was true. But he always returned bleary and washed-out, tired and irritable and—despite his days of work—broke. I figured that Sem used drugs, but he probably wasn't the only person around me who did. The Angel Street house had been a pretty free place to grow up, in that respect. But I wondered whether there might be more to the story with Sem. Sometimes he stayed in bed for days. Or he'd fidget, jiggling his leg at dinner so I could feel the table shaking as we ate. I found myself looking at the insides of his arms, and then quickly pulling my eyes away, embarrassed that he might see me inspecting him. I didn't know much about intravenous drugs, but to me they were a different category. They scared me.

I'm ashamed now that I never asked Sem if he was okay. Maybe it was because of our history and my cowardice about the past. I didn't want to start a conversation that might lead back to why he'd had to leave our house all those years ago. Or maybe it was just because he was older than me. It didn't feel like my place to try to mother him. But mainly, I think, it's because I thought I would seem uncool. Like I didn't understand him or his world. If Celeste was fine with it, then I should be too.

I felt on unsteady ground those weeks after Sem came out to the coast. I think I was expecting him to be angry with me, because of what I'd said about him when we were younger. I imagined that, behind closed doors, he was talking to Celeste about me and what I'd done. But in fact, when we were together, Sem was often distant, or occupied with Celeste. They liked to cook together, while I sat at the kitchen table and watched. Or they'd sit on the balcony, while I went down to swim. And a lot of our conversations were really between the two of them—about their favourite music or people they knew—and I'd just sit quietly, listening in. On the rare occasion it was just the two of us, Sem would often fall into silence, and I got the impression he was lost in thought, hardly even aware I was there.

But then occasionally Sem was disconcertingly warm, almost intimate. In those moments, I'd again think of our time at

Carlisle Road, wondering if maybe the romance I'd imagined might not have had some reality to it after all. At those times it felt like he loved me, somehow—but was it was sibling love, friendship or, as in my adolescent fantasies, something more?

Like the day we went fishing. I woke to the sound of my bedroom door being flung open and felt Celeste poking me in the side. 'Get up, Tilly, we're going fishing.'

Mouths full of bacon and pockets full of bread, we climbed into the red car. Sem drove us past the white gums, their lean trunks standing smartly to attention along the side of the road, and through the little town, the camping ground soggy with morning dew, everything hazy with the salty spray that was blowing in off the sea. We reached the wharf early enough to beat the holiday-makers, joining fishermen with rods and baited lines sitting on upturned buckets and eskies.

Sem had organised everything: two hand reels, one red and one yellow, a proper fishing rod, bait and hooks. We sat on the damp wood among the old fish scales and muck, Celeste with the red wheel, me with the yellow and Sem with the rod. Sem showed us how to rig the lines with what he called jiffy hooks—ten little hooks running down the one line—and we dropped them into the flurry of silver darting around in the clear water below. Gradually the day opened, the sun turning its gaze onto us, onto our shoulders and the backs of our necks and the soft flesh behind our knees. Across the water, on the distant beach, a few holiday-makers appeared for a morning swim. Through the rotting wooden planks of the wharf we saw huge stingrays, the size of dinner tables, sliding beneath us.

The water was pristine, the sea so fertile, and sometimes a bare hook would slip through a fish's scales, or catch it by the eye. I caught the first fish. Long and silver with a sliver of yellow, twisting on the line. I swung it up over the jetty, and it flapped against the wood. Sem pressed it down against the deck and tore the hook free from its lip, and then, before I could ready myself or even anticipate what he was about to do, he thrust the fish into my hands and, surprised, I took it from him, and there I was, holding the strong slippery body, feeling the sharpness of the scales. The fish fought against me, twisting, and I was worried I would drop it, that it would escape, and so I had the urge to hold it tighter, but at the same time I also wanted to open my fingers and let it go, to free both the fish and myself. I stood with my hands outstretched, clutching the fish, not knowing what to do.

At last, Sem came to me, taking my hands in his, showing me how to press the fish hard against the wood of the wharf, how to pin it there with one hand. He gave me his knife, his hand warm on mine as he guided the blade into the neck of the fish, causing blood to run over my fingers. And I must have flinched, as the fish flapped wildly through its last moments of life, because Sem bumped me gently with his shoulder. I looked up at him, crouching over me, silhouetted against the morning sun. And when I gave the knife back to him, he winked at me, because to him I was just a kid. But later, when I was sitting a little apart, my line pressed against the pad of my finger and falling into the water below, Sem came over and sat beside me and reached around to press his own finger against the line, so he was embracing me, and he rested his chin on my shoulder, his face close to mine. 'Caught anything?' he whispered in my ear.

As our esky filled with fish, Sem said that he preferred to eat what he'd caught himself, because the meat at the supermarket was pumped full of hormones. I didn't think he was wrong—I'd also heard about the hormones in meat—but my general scepticism of Sem and Celeste's theories about the forces controlling us must have shown on my face.

'Don't look at me like I'm crazy,' Sem said. 'It's okay if you don't see things the way I do. It's just important to me that I make my own choices, that's all.'

Back at the house, we ate fried fish for lunch, crisp and silky, steam coming out when we cut through the batter. In the afternoon, Celeste and Sem went into the back bedroom—for a siesta, they said—and I went down to the ocean beach to collect abalone shells, little red ears with glowing mother of pearl interiors. When I returned to the house it was growing dark, and Celeste and Sem had filled a metal drum in the clearing by the house with kindling for a fire, beers already cracked open, the smell of smoke drifting through the air.

That night we drank. I danced with Sem on the balcony, the deck squeaking beneath our bare feet, and he held me tight, his cheek pressed against mine briefly, before he lurched away across the deck, looking for another drink. Later, in the darkness, I vomited into the bushes, my hands scraping against sticks and leaves, clawing the dry, dusty ground. And when I finally I stood up, I was alone.

I woke the next morning with Celeste lying beside me on the bed, both of us stinking and aching. Heavy-limbed, we took ourselves up and along the dusty corridor to the balcony, where we found Sem splayed out in one of the deckchairs.

'Morning,' he said, lifting his hand to shade his eyes. Together, the three of us went down to the inlet and threw ourselves into the icy water, splashing around then collapsing onto the sand, gritty and tired. My mind was empty, and I felt a dull pressure in my head. When we'd just about recovered, we went up to the house and fried what fish we had left, then Sem broke out a few more beers.

At sunset, we climbed into the car and Celeste drove us down to the pub by the wharf. We got beers, and then Sem went over to play pool, leaving Celeste and me sitting side by side at the bar.

Because of its significance, in terms of what happened later, I've spent a lot of time thinking about that pub. Beefy men with their scrawny wives, teens in bathers and shorts, locals in sandals with open pink-cheeked faces. Voices murmuring, country music on the radio, punctuated by the clack of pool balls. Outside, the sun sitting low and bright on the ocean, that end-of-day length in the shadows and in the rays of light. And then, settling over us gently, night.

Later, I went out to get some air and found Sem standing with his back to the wooden railing, smoking, a loose smile on his mouth. A woman was leaning towards him, deep in conversation, her thick brown hair pulled into a ponytail. Sem's eyes slid over to me as I came out but his expression didn't change and he didn't greet me. Instead he took the woman by the elbow and led her further along the deck, pointing at the ocean, showing her something out there, and I felt Celeste's hand on my arm.

'Fuck this.' She was slurring. 'Let's go.'

I followed her to the red car in the near-empty car park. I climbed into the back and she got in the front and we must have fallen asleep, because when I opened my eyes dawn was breaking over the flat ocean. My mouth was gluey with saliva and beer, my body restless and aching with cold. The lights in the pub were all off. No one was around.

Celeste and I got out of the car and stretched. Wordlessly, she got into the driver's seat, I got into the passenger side, and she drove us quietly through the town then along the dirt road to the beach house, the white trunks of the gum trees flashing by, my stomach sloshing with each bend.

We went straight down to the inlet, flopping onto the cool sand to wait for the sun to come up and warm us. I dozed for a bit, and woke to see Celeste in the water in her underwear. I joined her. It was cold, refreshing. Goosebumps on my arms. Celeste scooped up a great armful of water and chucked it at me. A smile broke below her tired eyes, and I felt a kind of relief, falling onto my back and kicking water at her in retaliation.

'Jesus, Tilly!' she yelled. 'It's in my eyes. Give it a rest.' But she was smiling. I dove under and grabbed her ankles, and she kicked herself free and struck off swimming, with me in pursuit, the two of us laughing and half-choking on seawater, letting the last night's tension float away.

⌒

During the next three or four days after the pub, when Sem didn't return to the beach house, Celeste swam laps across the inlet each morning while I sat on the sand. We worked the lunch shifts at our respective jobs. At night, Celeste's hair tied back, face beautiful in the dim light, we played Scrabble. Later, we lay together on my bed and read until we both fell asleep. We didn't talk about Sem's absence, the woman at the pub. I think I almost believed Celeste wasn't all that bothered by it. That she was somehow immune to doubt or sadness. Strong enough to swim through it, let it wash over her shoulders and leave it in her wake.

⌒

It was around this time that Celeste got me a job at Rita's Pizza. She came into my bedroom one evening and tossed a balled-up yellow polo shirt at me.

'What's this?' I asked.

'For your new job,' she said, walking over to the window.

'I already have a job,' I said.

'Just say thank you.' She was sliding the window open, letting in the air. 'You're going to love it.'

I looked at the yellow shirt, turning it over in my hands. I wanted to say, 'You can't just make decisions like this on my behalf without asking me,' but when I looked up, Celeste was already gone.

I quit my job at Bijou the next day and started at Rita's that evening; Celeste and I were rostered to work every night that week because a couple of the boys had gone surfing up the coast. The work itself was pretty easy, and most of the customers were friendly. Everywhere in town closed by 9 pm, and after that, it was just as Celeste had described. The chefs made up pizzas with extra toppings, whatever we wanted, and we helped ourselves to drinks from behind the bar. Then we'd take all the food and drinks down to the beach, where we ate and drank then drove home.

Alexis was our supervisor. She lived locally, and had been working at the pizza place longer than anyone else. The rest of us were mostly summer hires. She had a little kid, who stayed with her grandma when Alexis and her husband—who had a job at a cheese factory nearby—had to work at the same time. Alexis would always lock up at the end of each shift, and we'd report to her after we'd counted the till. She was the one who had the key to the cellar, too, where the alcohol was stored.

When Celeste and I arrived for our shift at the end of the week we found the atmosphere unusually sombre. I asked one of the other waiters about it and he pulled a face and said the owners were in and they were pissed.

Of course, Celeste found out the full story before I did. She told me in a whisper between serving customers.

'They went through the inventory. It's not really the missing food—they're chill about that—but apparently they've tallied up the value of the missing alcohol and they're talking about getting the police involved. So it's important that we don't mention the parties, okay? Otherwise they'll fire Alexis. We're all just going to say we don't know anything about it. They'll think it was stolen or something.'

'What?' I said. 'I thought we were allowed to help ourselves to food and drink?' My stomach turned icy at the mention of the police.

'Well, yeah, but it's meant to be a small single-topping pizza and a soft drink, not like bottles of vodka or whatever—obviously.'

'I didn't know,' I said.

'You seriously thought we were allowed to take all the store-room booze?' Celeste said, raising her eyebrows. She laughed. 'Don't look so scared. It's going to be fine. As if they'd fire all of us. And if they did, who even cares? We just have to look after Alexis, okay?'

After the dinner rush, we were called into the office one by one. Rita was sitting at the desk. This was the first time we'd met. She looked athletic, with sturdy, freckled shoulders and a clean pink-cheeked face. She gestured for me to sit in the plastic chair opposite and looked at me with stern, unreadable eyes.

'It'd be best if you were honest with me, Matilda,' she said. 'I know you're new, and going back through our inventory it looks like this has been going on for months. So, it's not on you. But I need to know the truth.'

I could feel myself blushing. 'I'm not really sure,' I said. I knew I must've looked guilty but I didn't know how to hide it.

'Come on,' Rita said. 'I'm not an unreasonable person. But I do need to know. Otherwise it's all on Alexis.'

———

At the time, it didn't seem like the wrong thing to do, to tell Rita about the staff parties. In a way, it seemed right. I was telling the truth, after all. And besides, I think my face basically gave it away. But when we turned up for our shifts the next day, Alexis had been fired, and everyone seemed to know it was my fault. None of the other staff would talk to me.

'Don't act so surprised,' Celeste said as she drove us home. 'You fucked up. I don't know what you were thinking.'

The next day, when it was time to leave for work, I said, 'I had a really bad night's sleep. Tell them I can't make it today.'

After Celeste left, I got up and went down to the inlet. It had been nearly two weeks but Sem still hadn't returned. I thought a swim might help clear my head. But as I paddled in the shallows, I knew I couldn't go back to the pizza place again. I'd shown them who I really was: a coward and a narc. I lay on my back and looked up at the pale blue sky. I had a little money saved, so I'd live on that for now. I didn't know what I would do when that ran out, as it inevitably would. Rely on Celeste, I supposed. And I already owed her for the car. I'd just have to be careful, I told myself. I'd deal with that when the time came.

Chapter Ten

SEM HAD BEEN GONE JUST long enough that I'd started to think
he might be gone for good when, unexpectedly, he returned.
It was evening and Celeste and I were lying together on my
bed reading when we heard the sound of a car on the gravel.
A door slammed, and I heard the car drive away. I glanced over
at Celeste, who still had her eyes fixed on her book. With what
I imagined was studied indifference, she turned the page. We
heard the clatter of feet coming up the stairs. The balcony door
slid open and shut. Feet came down the hallway then turned
into Celeste's room, the door bumping softly closed. Celeste
read for a few seconds more, then she closed her book and said,
'I think it's time I turned in.' She got up and left the room.

I expected to hear them talking—arguing about Sem being
away—but the house was quiet, and I fell asleep.

Next morning, I found them on the balcony. Sem was drinking a beer and gazing out over the trees to the inlet. Celeste was painting a big canvas, drops of paint falling from her brush onto the fibro deck. For all her talk about the limitations of Christina's art, Celeste wasn't necessarily a great artist herself. She did a lot of self-portraits, and I found them kind of ugly at first. Their great slabs of flesh and uneven eyes and ginormous teeth. They were almost frightening. It was only with time that they started to grow on me. I began to see how the portraits were full of varied emotions. Some were confident, others cowering, and some were amused, or unexpectedly defiant and proud. That morning I looked at Celeste's painting for a while, and then I went and sat in a deckchair by Sem. No one suggested we go down to the water, so after a while, I got up and went to the inlet by myself.

That was the day I found the dolphin. I walked further along the inlet than I had gone before, inland, to where the sand started to get reedy. The dolphin was half buried by the water's edge, rotting. It stank. I walked around it a couple of times, looking at the broken rubbery skin, the place where it had once had an eye. I thought it must have come in from the sea and become trapped in the inlet, mistakenly swimming towards the lake rather than away from it. Maybe it had been sick, or perhaps the tides had left it stranded. Or maybe it had been fleeing a shark which was still out there, circling.

I didn't go in for a swim. Instead, I walked back along the beach and climbed up the path to the house. As I was coming up the green steps, barefoot and sandy, I heard the sound of breaking glass. I stood there frozen. I heard Sem say something, and then Celeste, and then I heard Sem make a strange sound, a kind of yelp, like an animal.

Now, I wish I had sprung into action, rushed up the stairs and burst into the house to see what was happening and try to calm things down. That's what a better person would have done. But I don't like being around confrontation. And maybe I was worried that if I went in, some of their anger might turn on me. So, in the silence that followed Sem's sound, I climbed back down the stairs and walked across the grass to the narrow path to the surf beach, where I sat alone among the dunes.

I stayed there until dusk, and the cold began to settle in my arms and legs. Just when I was starting to think about going back to the house—my stomach was growling—I saw someone emerge from the trees a little way down the beach and stride towards the water. It was Sem. He took off his shirt and dropped it onto the sand, then ran and dived into the surf. It was a dangerous time to swim. Darkness and currents. And people said that dusk was when the sharks came out. But I didn't stay to watch him. I stood and went back to the beach house, where Celeste was sweeping up the shards of a blue vase that had sat on the table and which she'd occasionally filled with flowers she gathered.

'I'm sorry if we scared you off earlier,' she said, her face calm and expression neutral.

So she knew. She knew that I had been right there, on the stairs, and that I hadn't come in to help. That I had run away. I felt myself blushing, caught out. I wanted to ask what the fight had been about, but that would mean agreeing I'd been listening outside, and hadn't come in to help. And, as with my history with Sem, or the day that Liam almost drowned, it made me uncomfortable to confront that side of myself, the side that failed to act.

'Oh,' I said. 'So you're okay?'

'Of course I am,' she said.

And I left it at that.

———

After their fight, the atmosphere between Celeste and Sem was tense. Celeste spent her days out on the balcony, painting. I stuck to reading, sitting in the deckchair with my encyclopedia, or one of the thick paperbacks Celeste had finished with. Sem rarely joined us; he slept late, then went alone down to the surf beach, returning brilliant with sunburn to sit out on the deck and smoke cigarettes. Sometimes, if Celeste was still painting when he returned, he'd say something about her work. One afternoon, he remarked, casually, that if you looked at it a certain way, Celeste's leg in her painting looked like a little dog, jumping up. When I looked, I could see what he meant. There did seem to be a dog, standing on its hind legs, looking up at her. But Celeste's back immediately stiffened.

'It doesn't help to have you commenting on the work before it's even done,' she said, stabbing her brush into her palette. 'What am I meant to take away from that? It looks like a dog? What kind of feedback is that?'

Other times, Sem looked at Celeste's paintings as if he were appraising them, but said nothing, but that was almost worse. It's funny, thinking back, because I never said anything either. But I guess they were used to that from me.

'What is it that interests you?' Celeste asked me abruptly one night, as if we were already in the middle of a conversation. We were reading on my bed while Sem smoked on the balcony.

'Huh?' I said, confused. 'What do you mean?'

'I mean, what are you interested in, Tilly? *Are* you even interested in anything?'

I paused for a moment, trying to think of how to respond. 'I'm interested in just being here and having a good time with you guys,' I said. I hoped this would serve as a distraction from the real question, which I was struggling to answer. About a month earlier I'd quietly received and deferred a university placement. I didn't have any plans for what I'd do next. When I looked inside myself for passion—which I did increasingly as the days slipped along, carrying me with them, rudderless—I found instead an emptiness that was almost peaceful in its spaciousness.

'Are you, though?' Celeste asked. 'You don't show it. If anything, you seem *un*interested in hanging out with us. Especially when Sem's around. It's like you're nervous all the time. It's tiring, you know.'

So, she was angry.

She's angry with Sem, I thought. *She's just taking it out on me.*

I looked up and met Celeste's eyes, and they were dark, like pebbles.

She sighed and looked back at her book, and I thought maybe the conversation was over. But she looked up again. 'You should think about it, you know. What you're interested in. You can't just let life slide past you. You have to claim something for yourself before it's too late.'

'Okay,' I said. 'Yeah, thanks. That's a good idea.'

Now, in retrospect, I wonder if Celeste really was frustrated with me, or if I was right and her frustration had more to do with her own situation. She would have already known that night that she was pregnant. It must have been on her mind. Maybe that was what she meant about claiming something for yourself. Like my own mum, on the couch, just a few months before. *You have to keep something for yourself,* she'd said. *Always keep something back just for you.* She'd been talking about marriage, but she could just as easily have been talking about motherhood.

But, at the time, I didn't yet know that Celeste was pregnant, and even if I had, I don't think I would have really been capable of understanding how that might make her feel. In my mind, things were more black and white: either she was angry with Sem, or she was angry with me. The baby would have been a complicating element that I wouldn't have known how to parse. So, I decided Celeste was angry with Sem—they'd been fighting, after all—and tried to put it out of my mind.

Still, the next day, I avoided Celeste. I left her to paint on the balcony and went for a walk through the bush, and when I came back, Sem was sitting in one of the deckchairs with a beer in his hand and a small smile on his lips.

'I'm taking you both to Eden,' he informed me as I walked across the deck. 'I think we could do with an outing.'

Looking back, Celeste must have told him about the baby that morning, while I was down walking among the trees.

Maybe it was because of the conversation I'd had with Celeste the night before, and her intimation that I was self-absorbed, but as we got into the car I felt determined to prove to both Celeste and Sem that I was really present. I challenged myself on the car ride to say as many things as I could, but being in the back seat while they were in the front made it difficult, and I found myself awkwardly leaning forwards, making boring observations that received only obligatory responses, if any at all.

Down at the port we visited the whaling museum, then ate fish and chips—paid for by Sem—at a wooden picnic table on a patch of grass down by the water. Afterwards, Sem lit a cigarette and put his arm around Celeste, and she dropped her head onto his chest.

'Family,' Sem said. And Celeste nodded.

'Worth celebrating,' he said.

The sun was going down and Sem's face looked gaunt, his eyes resting lightly on everything, glancing into mine and then immediately flashing away.

'Did you know that my dad named me?' he asked.

Celeste lifted her head from his chest. 'Sem,' she said, smiling.

'Semyon,' Sem said. 'It's Russian for Simon.'

They were sitting together at the picnic table, and I was nearby on the grass.

'My dad's best friend was Russian. His name was Semyon. He introduced my parents, so maybe they felt they owed him. Or maybe mum just really loved the name.'

'I like Tamara,' Celeste said quietly.

'Tamara,' Sem said. He pulled a kind of face. 'Well, I like Judy. It was my granny's name.'

They kept talking quietly while I sat on the lawn, watching, plucking idly at the grass. It felt comfortable, the three of us, down by the water, that evening.

I didn't understand at the time what they were celebrating. But I was happy because all the tension of the previous week seemed to have mysteriously slipped away. When Celeste didn't reach for a beer, I didn't reach for one either, thinking that she was being sensible and that I should follow her lead, that I might always be able to learn from her how to behave. I must have known that something was up, but I didn't ask Sem what he meant about celebrating. Nor did I find a moment to ask Celeste what had changed between them. I was afraid that it should have been clear already. That I should have understood on my own, and to ask would reveal that I was just a kid, and they would laugh at me. It was the most unbearable thing, being seen as naive.

But still, that evening in Eden, on that patch of grass by the sea, greasy-fingered, with Celeste's head resting against Sem's chest—I want you to know about that night. The two of them together, whispering names. That moment is yours. And in fact you were there, in a way. Hidden inside Celeste, in some early form.

That day down at Eden was so lovely that I was surprised to wake the next morning to the sound of tyres on the gravel and come out of my bedroom to find that Sem had left again. But Celeste was in the kitchen making breakfast and acting as if nothing was wrong, so once again I hid my confusion and carried on as if everything were fine.

It was a few days after the trip to Eden—Sem still had not returned—when Celeste told me she was pregnant. We were sitting out on the balcony, waiting for the kookaburras to come and eat the raw mince we'd laid out for them. She looked a little smug when she told me, and I thought to myself that it was probably because she was revealing another bond that she and Sem shared, and from which I had been excluded.

Celeste's pregnancy only deepened my confusion about Sem's abrupt disappearance. I felt angry at him on Celeste's behalf, and angry at her too, because she wasn't sticking up for herself. At least, that's what I told myself. But perhaps some of the anger was about feeling left out, too.

'It's rubbish that he's taken off,' I said. 'This is a time when he should stick around.'

Celeste said, 'He's working at the berry farm. He needs the money, you know. Besides, it's the atmosphere around here that he can't take. And—please don't take this the wrong way—but it's also being around you. It brings up all that stuff from when you were younger.'

Part of me wishes that Sem had been there when Celeste blamed me for his absence, because I believe in that moment I was ready to ask him straight out: *What actually happened between us when we were young?* He might have looked at me and said, 'Remember how they fought, your mum and dad? Do you think they would have hesitated to use you against each other?' And he would have explained to me about leading questions, and custody battles, and divorce. And then maybe I would have understood something that I now think must be closer to the truth—or, if not truth, something that at least would have allowed us all to go on living peacefully.

Or maybe he would have been angry. Maybe he would have finally told me how much I'd hurt him. And perhaps I would have been able to confess that I hadn't known how serious the impact of my words would be. How I had felt about him, back then, maybe even still, and how I'd been an idiot to try to speak that romance into reality.

If I had only spoken to Sem, I might have begun to understand how it was for him. Living with me out at the coast after everything that had happened. But he wasn't there, and perhaps that's just as well. I probably would have only hurt him again.

Chapter Eleven

IT WAS TOWARDS THE END of summer, just before Celeste's birthday, when the rainstorm struck. For three days it rained continuously, fat droplets that drummed the corrugated roof and made the water of the inlet dark and shimmering. It was this rain that turned our water bad.

There had been some instructions, when we first moved into the house, about general upkeep. Closing the front gate, checking the fruit trees, how to clean the shower drain, things like that. We barely read it and immediately put it out of our minds. But there was, I think, a note about the gutters, which needed to be regularly cleaned. So when it rained at the end of that summer, all the debris that had been accumulating in them was washed into the tank, turning our water brown and cloudy with muck.

We found out one morning when I went to get a glass of water from the kitchen. Celeste had just got back from a doctor's appointment. I took the cup over to show her.

'Gross,' she said, pulling a face.

The water didn't seem safe to keep drinking. So Celeste went to the fridge and prised a can of beer from its plastic ring.

'Catch,' she said, tossing it to me, and I fumbled it and it glanced off a chair leg to roll across the floor, leaving a dent in the corner of the can. When I popped it open the beer fizzed over, cold and sticky on my hands, on my shins, on the floor. The floor was still sticky when I left that house. We were not ones to clean. We just let the heat carry us along. Which is why, when the tank got contaminated, we didn't immediately rush down to the car and drive to town to buy fresh water. We didn't get on the phone to find someone to come and take a look at it. Celeste just went in to Rita's to work the lunchtime shift. And I lay on the sandy couch and drank beer. But when Celeste came home that evening and went to lie down for a nap, I found myself thinking that she should go out and fix the situation. Bring home a proper supply of water. She was pregnant, and that was what a mother should do. I guess, really, I wanted her to take care of me too.

The next morning, I finally suggested that we go into town to find someone to clean the tank. Celeste was in her room, lying across her bed, reading. I asked if she would drive us. But she was too tired.

'Here.' She threw me a bottle of water from beside her bed. She'd brought it back from work, I assumed. 'I'll take you tomorrow,' she said. But the way she said it, tomorrow meant sometime in the distant future, nothing so specific as the very next day. She had been this way since Sem had last left, and since she'd told me about the baby. She seemed tired. Not her usual energetic self.

So, I spent the rest of that day and the next lying around in the front room drinking beer after beer, my head thickening, until I stumbled down the corridor and collapsed into bed. Celeste went out to work and came home, but she didn't bring any water for me. In the middle of the night, I woke with a throbbing headache to hear shuffling and clanking. I came out and found Celeste in the kitchen, boiling a saucepan of water on the stove.

'What are you doing?' I asked.

She carefully poured the boiling water into two mugs and handed one to me.

I must have hesitated because she said, 'It will be hot, but safe, I think. If you boil water properly, you're good.'

And so I brought the cup to my lips and drank. The water was hot and tasted like metal. We stayed like that together for a few minutes, drinking.

That night we agreed that the next day we would drive to the closest town to buy a good supply of water. And while we were there, we would find someone who could come to clean the tank. Celeste said she'd pay for it.

'Don't worry,' she said. 'I'm sure the owners will reimburse me when I explain.' But our words rang empty as we spoke them, like acquaintances promising to have coffee sometime, or teenagers earnestly declaring their plans to change the world. By morning our words would vanish, leaving only a stain of embarrassment that we'd been so optimistic about ourselves.

Next morning, I woke to the sound of tyres on the gravel outside. It was early, pale light leaching in between the heavy curtains. My head was aching and my body was heavy, from too many beers. I was feeling so unwell that I forgot about the situation with the tank. I got up and went into the bathroom and turned on the tap. I bent my head and put my hands into the flow and started scooping water into my mouth, only to remember the brown muck, and start spitting it back out. And I hardly had time to register the error because already Sem's boots were coming down the corridor, Celeste's bedroom door creaking open on its hinges, and I heard him say, 'Happy Birthday, C.'

I came out into the hallway to see Celeste pulling away from Sem almost angrily.

'I didn't think you'd remember,' she said, walking down the corridor, not looking back at him. 'It's been long enough.'

It was her birthday. He'd remembered—and I had somehow managed to forget.

Things were off-kilter all that day. We spent the morning separately, each doing our own thing. Celeste painted on the balcony. Around lunchtime she drove into town and came back with a slab of water.

'Take it slow,' she said, as I eagerly twisted off a cap. 'We want these to last a while.'

Sem slept in Celeste's room until late afternoon, when we started drinking—at least, Sem and I did. I felt myself getting woozy with alcohol and let the hours slip away until night started to fall, and that was when Sem gave Celeste her gift.

Sem had had the gift made specially for Celeste, by an artist who lived a bit further along the coast. A ceramics artist, Sem explained, who had moved down from the city and built two huge kilns, for firing pottery. Sem had asked the artist to make a bowl, with a mottled green and blue glaze. It really was very beautiful, and I could tell that Celeste was thrilled. She held it in her hands and carefully turned it, admiring it from different angles, and then she went and put it in her bedroom, her face lit up by a huge smile.

It was the present that set the evening back on a good track. Celeste decided that she wanted to go to the pub. She wasn't drinking, but she wanted to go anyway. Sem drove us in the red car, already drunk, soaring through the trees. He and Celeste seemed so fearless, laughing and chatting, while I sat quietly in the back, still not quite over my embarrassment at having forgotten Celeste's birthday. She was turning twenty-one.

At the pub, Celeste drank lemonade while Sem and I had beers, and we played pool. I was terrible, my balls rolling sadly across the felt, no satisfying clacks. I drank a lot. I think Sem did too. The pub was a blur of faces, Sem and Celeste coming and going, another beer pressed into my eager hand. Celeste took off her shoes at one point, and danced in bare feet, but Sem wasn't around. I was worried that he'd gone off with another woman again, and at one point I saw him leaning against the verandah railing, cigarette in hand, talking with the woman with the thick brown hair. I was struck by the coldness of his expression, despite his smile. When I think of Sem now I try to remember him as he was when we lived at Carlisle Road, but often my thoughts return to the night of Celeste's birthday, Sem strung out, his joints held at angry angles, something bitter, almost spiteful, in the turn of his mouth, standing in the darkness, smoking a cigarette with a stranger. Well, a stranger to me and Celeste.

I'm trying very hard to think clearly, to remember exactly how it happened. But it is difficult, because I was very drunk, and because of the time that's now passed. It's difficult also because I have tried so often to remember, so now I can't be sure if I'm really remembering that night, or if I'm remembering an earlier remembering. But here is what I think is the truth, or something close to it.

I didn't see the start of the fight. I was inside, at the bar, getting beers. When I came outside, a pint in each hand—one for me and one for Sem—Celeste was already storming away from him and she bumped into me, sloshing beer all over us and on the ground.

'Of course,' she said, gesturing furiously at the drinks and her wet bare feet.

'Calm down, Celeste,' Sem called, and Celeste turned back to look at him. He was still over with the brunette, and I remember thinking, *Just come away from there, just come over here to Celeste*, and maybe I even said it aloud because he looked at me in surprise and did step away from the railing and come over to us. But this only seemed to make Celeste more furious, and when he put his hand on her arm she twisted away from him and I dropped one of the beers and the glass shattered all over the ground, and she was walking through the glass, no shoes on, and Sem was trying to pull her back, shouting, 'Your feet, your feet,' and she was yelling back, 'Fuck my feet,' and she left a trail of bloody smears as she stalked back through the pub and out the front door.

Suddenly Sem's face was close to mine, transformed into something inaccessible and ugly. 'Would it kill you to be a bit less clumsy? She's fucking pregnant,' he said. His breath smelled sour. And then he was following Celeste through the bar, and there was nothing left for me to do but follow them out to the car, where I found Celeste in the passenger seat and Sem climbing into the driver's side.

Sem drove us back through the town, and then through the blur of trees, the headlights lighting up the road as it swiftly disappeared beneath our wheels. Bottles and cans of beer were rolling around the floor at my feet. Sem and Celeste were really arguing now. They were shouting over each other, yelling about the woman in the pub, about the baby and the future, and then Celeste turned and opened the car door, as if she were going to throw herself out onto the road, and Sem leaned across and grabbed her by the hair, pulling her back roughly towards him. For a moment he lost control and the car veered wildly, and I screamed, seeing those tall trees, the dizzying drop to our left suddenly seeming very real. Sem pulled the car back sharply, my head hitting the window, a moment of disorientation in which I could hear myself screaming again, my voice sounding thin and high and airless.

The violent motion of the car and my screams seemed to have interrupted the fight, and we were all quiet now, as Sem drove. Celeste turned in her seat and looked back at me, eyebrows raised, and suddenly we were both laughing. Not Sem, though. His eyes were on the road ahead, his face stony with anger, driving into the dark.

'You'll get us all killed,' he said. 'You'd like that, wouldn't you? What a great mum.'

That set them off again, arguing just as intensely as before, as we hurtled up to the house. Sem parked by the water tank and opened his door to get out of the car.

'Keep driving,' Celeste said, not moving from her seat. 'I want to go down to the ocean and look at the stars.'

'I think it's time we called it a night,' Sem said. His voice was cold with anger.

'It's my birthday,' Celeste said. 'You can't stop me.'

Sem swore and closed his door. He started driving again, taking us along a track that led to a clearing down near the rocks between the inlet and the beach, where surfers sometimes camped. 'You're unbelievable,' he said.

Celeste had started to cry, and now she turned and tried to smile at me through her tears. 'Tilly gets me, don't you?' she said, reaching back between the seats to hold my hand, our arms stretching across the car, lurching in an uncomfortable dance as the car bumped along the uneven track.

Sem parked in the clearing. I remember the car's headlights shifting across rocks and trees, everything coming into the light and then falling out of it.

I had taken my shoes off and could feel sticks and leaves in the sand with my feet. The stars were out in crowds. And the air around us was thick. Full of dust the car had thrown up. I can remember the warm beer can in my hand. I remember looking out at the ocean. The sound of the waves crashing against the rocks. It sounded like a powerful animal roaring at us.

I remember Celeste and Sem arguing again, and then the argument dying down. Celeste angrily picking glass out of her feet, sitting on a log by the edge of the clearing, alone, lit up by the car's headlights.

I remember my hands in the ocean. Salty spray hitting my cheeks. Moonlight on the waves.

I must have blacked out. I couldn't tell you what my last memory was. It's more like a slow fade-out. Things becoming less distinct. More fractured. And, eventually, nothing at all.

Part III

Part III

Chapter Twelve

I HAVE BEEN HOLDING OFF talking about Peter's documentary. It's been seven or eight months now since it came out, and I think perhaps I haven't spoken about it yet because I'm not sure if you will ever watch it, and how important it will seem to you. I think part of me hopes that by the time you're old enough to read this, Peter's documentary will have been forgotten, and time will show that this story wasn't the beginning of his illustrious career but just a flash in the pan, disappearing back into the rest of the mud.

When it first came out, the documentary didn't get very much attention. Peter had produced it with a friend who was starting up a small production company, and they put it together pretty quickly on a tiny budget. It was screened as part of an indie film festival on the South Coast, and I thought that would be the end of it. I had decided I wasn't going to see it. But when Peter won an award—a prize for emerging filmmakers—there was a special screening in Sydney, Peter invited me and I went along. Still, I thought that would be as far as things went. And, by a few weeks later, the documentary did seem almost forgotten.

But then I was committed to stand trial, and right around the same time Peter managed to get the documentary signed up to a streaming service, and suddenly the Office of the Director of Public Prosecutions was involved, moving to suppress the release on the grounds that it might prejudice the jury at my trial. The media picked it up as part of a bigger story about freedom of speech and the tension between justice in the courts and justice in the hands of the community—young people, they argued, were finding new avenues of justice in documentary-making and social media. Suddenly everyone wanted to see it, and even though it was *technically* banned, of course anyone who was really interested could find it easily enough online.

It got so that every time I left the house, I felt like everyone's eyes were on me. That's part of the reason I came out to live at the lakes for a bit. To get away from it all. And even out here I prefer to keep to myself.

It was about six months ago that the injunction was passed. My lawyer, Alison, says that before my trial they will ask each juror if they have seen the documentary and, if they have, they'll be forbidden to participate. We'll just have to take their word for it, but Alison says I shouldn't worry about that because, really, the documentary is more likely to help my case than harm it. You see, in the end, Peter found a way to tell a story that exonerated me. I wonder, sometimes, how he was able to piece it all together in that way. Was it like discovering something, or more like creating it? Was it about finding the truth, or protecting me, or just telling a good story that would kickstart his career?

I often find myself thinking about the documentary and you. When I imagine you, I tend to think of you with Christina. It's easier that way, because of the uncertainty about what will happen to Celeste. I know you'll always have Christina. Sometimes I think that she will try to keep the documentary from you. But then I can also imagine that she might want to sit down with you and watch it together. Maybe you won't be interested. Perhaps it will seem old-fashioned or boring to you. Maybe documentaries will be a thing of the past by then. Maybe this whole story will be all but forgotten, and the documentary quite difficult to find. Or maybe Peter will be famous. Everyone is saying that this documentary is the launching pad for his career. All the controversy has served him very well.

If you don't ever watch the documentary, or if you read this while you are still making up your mind whether to see it or not, I will tell you the parts of it that you should really know, because it's important, I think, in terms of understanding how everything went. Essentially, in the documentary, Peter tells three stories of your father, Sem. The first is the story of a lost boy. The second is a story of revenge. And the third, the story that Peter has made prevail in the end, is a story of manipulation.

It must be at least six months now since I saw the documentary myself, but I remember it starts on the ocean beach, at the house near Eden, with surfers on the waves. Music first, and then my voice. When I watched the documentary, I thought that my voice sounded quite hesitant; there were lots of pauses, and sometimes I stopped mid-sentence before going on. I was recalling the day that Liam came and almost drowned in the rip, and how Celeste saved him. I don't really remember telling Peter about that for the documentary. From the way my voice sounds—so hesitant—I guess the story had some significance, at least in my mind. It wasn't just something that came up, but something that I thought might be important. I'm clearly taking care to get it right. Perhaps I told Peter about it when he was recording me on the drive up north from Eden into the desert, after we had left the beach house. To my mind, that makes the most sense. Probably, as I told the story, I was thinking of how they'd searched the ocean for Sem's body. That one possible explanation for his disappearance was that he had gone swimming and been caught in a rip. I think that's why I'm speaking with such care.

The documentary starts with the ocean beach, and my voice telling the story of Liam and the rip, and then Peter shifts to a photo of the Carlisle Road house, as it was back when we all lived there, Celeste and Sem and me, the place half-demolished by the storm. There was a tear in the corner of the photo, and when I watched the documentary I thought that Peter had probably been glad of that tear, because it attested to the photo's realness and, also, its fragility. The photo would gradually fade and eventually disappear, and the moment it captured had already been lost to time: the happiness we felt at that house, our childhood innocence, all of it vanishing.

In the photo, Celeste and Sem and I are posing in the front garden in our swimsuits and, behind us, a sprinkler is spraying a thin fountain over the grass. It can't have been too late in the summer, because Sem doesn't yet have his cast on, but we're all sunburned and brown. By this point in the documentary, I've finished telling the story about Liam and the rip, and the audio goes quiet. And then Peter brings in my mother's voice, talking about Sem as a child, and the things that happened to him before we ever met him, things I never even knew about until I saw Peter's documentary for the first time. As my mother talks, Peter zooms in on Sem in the photograph, cutting first me and then Celeste out of the frame, until it is just Sem standing there, a little out of focus, tall and skinny, his eyes hidden beneath the fringe of his dark hair.

When I watched the documentary, I think I was hoping I'd find answers. I guess I thought the documentary was art—Peter always spoke about it that way—and I thought in art there might be truth. But, to be honest, the documentary wasn't really art in the way I was expecting. Not like Celeste's paintings at the beach house. For all that I found Celeste difficult, her art was straightforward. Sometimes I felt almost embarrassed when I looked at her portraits, because they seemed so personal and private. I remember one painting in particular, where she'd made herself small and hunched, her back curved and her face turned away. This was when she and Sem were fighting.

When I looked at that painting, I think I saw something of how she felt inside.

Peter's film didn't have any of that unguardedness. When I watched it, I learned nothing about him, not even what motivated him to make the film in the first place. Perhaps the only thing it showed me was that Peter had what it took to forge a career as a filmmaker. When I watched the documentary, I could always sense him behind each frame, orchestrating things. Even though when I saw it, the documentary had only won a single, rather modest, award and hadn't yet become the sensation it is now, the elements of success were there. It was so clear that Peter had decided, above all, to make a seamless narrative out of the fragments of our lives. At times, he even stepped in and narrated. It was all so controlled. I couldn't trust it.

The morning after Celeste's birthday I woke to the sound of rain. I was in my bed and expected to find Celeste sprawled beside me, but when I rolled over, she wasn't there. I sat up and looked out the window. The sky was grey, the balcony slick and wet, reflecting mottled clouds.

My body ached. From my belly, through my ribs, up my neck, between my teeth and behind my eyes. The muscles in my shoulders and arms were stiff and weak. When I stood, my legs hurt too, a deep ache in the muscles. And my head, where it had smacked against the car window, had a tender egg on it. I was dirty, with twigs and sand all through my clothes and hair. My feet and hands stung, and later, when I rinsed them in the ocean, I would discover they were cut and beginning to scab in long brown lines. I was salty and stiff-haired, as if I'd been swimming in the ocean.

I climbed out of bed and went to Celeste's room, peered in through her door. She was lying on her bed, alone. Sem wasn't there. Celeste was still sleeping, and I could see that, like me, she was a salty, sandy mess. And she was cut all up the front of her legs and knees. Her palms, resting on the sheets, were bloody.

I headed to the kitchen, my throat dry. But, of course, the water wasn't good to drink, and I couldn't be bothered boiling up a pan on the stove. Miserable and aching, I put on my bathers. It was still raining, and my towel on the balcony was soaked, so I left it there. I went down and followed the path to the inlet.

The sand was pockmarked and cool and the water's surface was broken and trembling as I bathed. I plunged my head beneath the water and opened my mouth. It tasted salty. I opened my eyes, stinging with salt, and looked into the brackish haze. Tilting my head, I turned my mouth to the sky and drank the raindrops that fell in. I cleaned my hands and my feet, discovering long scratches, running my fingers along their raw lengths. After half an hour or so in the water, I went back up to the house to find Celeste outside on the balcony in the rain, pulling our beach towels, now sodden and heavy, from the railings.

I was too exhausted to bother talking. I assumed she felt the same. I passed her without speaking and went inside where it was warm, the place alive with the sound of the rain striking the corrugated-tin roof. Aside from the rain, everything was still; there was no sign of Sem. I took a jumper from my room and came back out to the kitchen.

Celeste was still on the balcony, standing under the narrow overhang of roof, twisting the towels to wring out as much water as she could and then tossing them inside in a heap on the floor. She came in, dripping rain from her hair and elbows, and hung the towels over the backs of our kitchen chairs. Then she went down the hall and I heard the sound of her bedroom door closing.

I lay on the couch and let the sound of the rain soothe me back to sleep. As I was drifting off, I thought about what would happen when Sem came back. He and Celeste would have another fight, probably. Maybe break another vase. I imagined that this time I wouldn't hesitate on the stairs, or turn and head back to the beach. I'd come into the room and witness the broken vase on the floor and I'd . . . do *something*. Somehow I'd become the person who knew how to act.

⌒

When I woke, Celeste was in the kitchen behind me, making dinner. She had cleaned herself up since the morning. No more sand or blood. Her hair was dry and salt-stiff, so I realised she must have gone swimming too.

'How do you feel?' she asked. She was flipping sausages, the meat sizzling in the pan, and I got up, groggy, went over and stood behind her, picking up one of the empty plates she had resting on the chopping board.

'Okay,' I said.

With a knife, she skewered a sausage and transferred it from the pan to the plate I was holding. She turned back to the stove, and did the same for herself. I was expecting her to say something. Maybe something about the previous night, the fighting, the intense drive back from the pub. But she was quiet. As she picked up her plate, I noticed that her hands were shaking. I could smell the sea on her skin. Her silence unsettled me.

I took my plate to the table, sat, and started to eat. After a moment, Celeste came and sat opposite me. We sat like that for a while, without speaking, as I ate. When I looked up, her face was pale.

'Hung over?' I asked.

'I wasn't drinking,' she said. She looked confused for a moment, and then her face hardened and became cold. 'You have nothing at all to say about last night?' she asked.

'I guess I blacked out,' I said, shrugging. I had another bite of sausage.

'You blacked out,' she said. 'Okay.'

'It was a crazy night,' I said. I think I was hoping to spur her into conversation, but instead she continued to sit and regard me with an accusatory expression on her face.

'You wanted to light up the water,' she said. 'Do you remember that?'

'Not really.'

'You wanted to shine the headlights on the ocean. You thought it would be beautiful.'

I laughed. 'That sounds like a stupid drunk idea.'

These days, I spend so much of my time going back over the events of that summer. And then I go back further, to when we were younger and to the places we lived. It's a bad habit. Because each time I send my mind back, I'm liable to change things. I can't help but imagine other ways that things might have gone. And once I've imagined something, it's surprisingly easy to remember that imagined version of events, instead of what really happened. The more I return to the fantasy, the more real it seems. So, in the end, I wonder if all I'm remembering are the stories that I've told myself, and I've only succeeded in pushing the truth I'm seeking even further away. Sometimes, for days or even weeks, I will try to stop, to keep my mind only in the present. But I always give in and return to the past again, hoping that this time everything will be clear to me, that I will know what was true.

Sitting at the table that evening, Celeste told me a story of what happened the night of her birthday. My own memories were patchy, and there were blanks from when I blacked out, so she filled them in for me. She told me this story quietly, with her untouched food in front of her, and there was something almost matter of fact about her demeanour that was so at odds with the story she told.

I've returned to Celeste's story so many times, comparing her version to the few impressions I retained. Assessing her words in the light of everything I know about her. Reviewing again everything that happened between us. About halfway through Peter's documentary, when he is starting to tell Sem's story from the beginning a second time, he recreates scenes from Celeste's birthday, and now that is the version that plays in my own mind when I try to remember that night. Like a videocassette that's been taped over. It's impossible to see clearly anymore.

Peter used actors to play us. When I first saw them, I was unexpectedly relieved. Until that moment, I guess I'd thought it might be like seeing a ghost, or my own reflection in a funhouse mirror. A distorted kind of nightmare. But the three actors looked nothing like us. The actor playing Celeste had none of her magnetism. The film version of Sem had none of his warmth. And there was a certain confidence to the way I stepped out of the car and looked around, at ease, lifting my hands to smooth my hair out of my face, talking casually to the other two, that was flattering but unfamiliar.

In the documentary, before we go to the pub for Celeste's birthday, we swim. Shivering in our bathers, goosebumps on our arms and legs and the skin across the bases of our necks. Only then do we go to the pub. We drink beers. Celeste and Sem dance and then they fight. Celeste goes outside and throws her glass over the railing and it smashes on the rocks below. When I saw the documentary, it struck me that I didn't remember telling Peter that Celeste had thrown her glass like that. Was that really how it happened? Or was there creative licence when it came to re-enactment? It didn't seem like there should be, in a documentary. But maybe I'm holding Peter to too high a standard. Maybe we all embroider the truth sometimes.

On the way home, the audience watches the car drive past flashing white trees and then, seen from above, the car door swings open and closed and I know that is Celeste, threatening to hurl herself out onto the road. Down in the clearing by the ocean, the actors pretend to drink and argue. Peter shows the rocks and the ocean and the trees trembling in the breeze. And then: fade to black.

When I watched that scene in the documentary I felt let down. As if I had been listening to a story that stopped abruptly partway through. I wanted to find out what happened in the end. Did Sem go down to the water for a late-night swim only to be swept away by the currents? Or did he walk back to the road and hitch a ride into town, to get away from Celeste and the arguing and the baby that was on the way? Did Celeste smash a bottle over his head or strike him with a stick and drag his body out into the sea?

Or did he just get tired? Did he unfurl his swag from the boot of the car and take it around the front, out of the way, near the tea-trees to get some sleep? And did I, hideously drunk, get behind the wheel of the car and attempt a five- or six- or seven-point turn, clumsily trying to turn the car towards the ocean? And did the wheels, on the third or the fourth or the fifth angle of the turn, catch and stick and then finally drive over something on the ground? Canvas and a soft, sleeping, beloved body resting innocently inside. Was that what happened? Or is that just my imagination, fed by Celeste? Is that just a story she told me one night, her food lying uneaten in front of her? Yet another way for her to control me, to make me doubt and fear myself? Was that awful version of events perhaps less shameful than telling me that he had taken off and left her, pregnant, to fend for herself? Or an alibi for something horrific that she herself might have done to Sem, in the heat of the moment?

Or was it true?

I can hardly remember the hours after Celeste told me what had happened that night. I know I went to my room. Climbed into bed, curled up, closed my eyes. The red car. Headlights catching the outline of tea-trees and underbrush. The sickening pull of the wheels.

There was a terrible rushing of the world towards me, horror coming at me from all directions, and all I could do was try to escape, try to make myself so small, in a place so dark, that the terror would not be able to reach me.

I stayed in bed, curled into a ball. Celeste moved around the house, and then it grew quiet. She must have gone to sleep. Still, I stayed beneath the blankets. My limbs felt stiff and sore. Maybe I slept for a few hours. Then I woke, still unable to move. Through it all, there was just one distant gleam of light: the possibility that Celeste was lying, that I might be innocent after all. I made pacts with fate. If I could be innocent, then

I would finally talk to Sem about what had happened in the past. I would leave the beach house and Celeste and begin my real life, with purpose. I'd reform my personality. Find a way to do something good in the world. If only what Celeste said wasn't true.

I think it was that distant hope that eventually got me out of bed.

I went to the kitchen and took one of the torches to go down to the clearing by the rocks, where the red car was still parked. It was almost morning, and so, as my eyes adjusted to the pale light, I didn't really need the torch, but I cast it around the corners of the clearing anyway, looking for some sort of clue as to what had happened. What I might have done.

Celeste's words from earlier, as we sat opposite each other at the table, haunted me. 'You wanted to shine the headlights on the ocean. You thought it would be beautiful.'

I cast my torch around the clearing, and I could remember it—or I thought I could; perhaps Celeste's words had just conjured the image in my mind: headlights falling across the underbrush, the thin trunks of the spindly tea-trees, as I turned towards the sea.

'You must have got the keys from Sem before he went to sleep.'

I shone the torch on the back of the red car and then the front. But there was nothing to see. Maybe the rain had washed it clean. Maybe the canvas of the swag had protected it. Or maybe there was nothing to find. Maybe I was somehow innocent after all?

'He was sleeping in the swag, I'd started to clean up the clearing, and then you got in the car.'

I lowered myself onto the damp ground and turned off the torch. I stayed there for a long time. The clearing felt calm and quiet, colours muted in the half-dark.

'He'd set up his swag in front of the car. I wasn't sure if he was dead. I had to check.'

I sat in the clearing, alone, waiting for the sun to come up.

'Once I looked I was certain. There would have been no use calling an ambulance.'

In my mind, I could see the lights from the car swinging around, over the tea-trees and then the water, as I moved the car. In reality, before me, the pre-dawn sea was dark.

'I had to make a decision for us both. I dragged the swag, with him in it, out between the tea-trees and over the rocks. It took forever. You tried to help but you were useless. Then I rolled him into the sea.'

The first light was starting to break over the ocean and, sitting in the clearing, I felt that if I looked down at myself, I might discover my body had disappeared, left behind in the darkness. I hoped that might be the case. I felt like I had been plucked out of the world and placed somewhere else, alone. It's a feeling that has stayed with me ever since. I'm in the place where things end. No friends. No future. No light or sound or hope. Only, behind me, the past, the path that led me here.

Chapter Thirteen

THE FIRST STORY THAT PETER chose to tell in his documentary about your father was not the story that Celeste told me the day after her birthday. He does not start with the body in the swag, the drunk girl behind the wheel. Peter starts with the story of a lost boy. He begins the story even earlier than I did here, in this retelling for you. He starts right back before I ever knew Sem, on the day that he was born.

My mum begins the narration, her voice first played over the photo of Celeste and Sem and me at Carlisle Road. She's describing Sem's parents, how they met when they were young and then Sem's mother got pregnant. 'Sem was her first child,' Mum says. As she continues to speak, the documentary shifts to a re-enactment. In Peter's documentary, Sem's mum is a young woman with slender freckled arms, holding a baby wrapped in a hospital blanket. Sem's dad is a pair of calloused hands, taking the bundle from her arms. 'Sem would have been less than two,' Mum's voice says, 'when his father died.' Peter shows us a wrecked car, police lights flashing on the road, a cemetery.

'Three years later, Sem's mum married her new partner, and over the next five years she had four more little kids. But her new partner left her soon after the last one was born,' my mum narrates. Peter shows us dirty white sneakers, walking out a door. I thought, when I watched it, that this part felt a little cheap in Peter's documentary. He dressed the actor who played Sem's mum in tight denim shorts, with thick black eyeliner and badly dyed red hair. I really wanted to know, when I watched the documentary, if it was the actor who had coloured her hair—if that was how she wore it in her day-to-day life—or if they'd dyed it for the role. I thought details like that might reveal something about the relationship between the documentary and the truth.

Peter shows a house overrun by kids, and a mother struggling to cope. A messy room cluttered with toys. A baby crying while a toddler throws a tantrum, rolling on the floor. An image of a telephone—one of those old-fashioned ones, with a curly white cord—and a voice reporting Sem getting into trouble at school. A group of boys in a circle, chanting for a fight.

'Sem went to live with his grandmother for a while,' Mum says. The camera goes up a front path, with roses either side. The front door opens, and a boy's legs run inside.

At this point, the re-enactment cuts away to the video of the interview with my mother. She is sitting at the kitchen table in the Angel Street house, and it must be late afternoon, because the orange light coming through the windows hits the table at long angles, making my mother's features look more pronounced and softening her skin. As she talks, Mum rests her hands on the wooden tabletop. She is talking about Sem, and things that happened to him before he came to live with us. I don't know if my mother or Peter felt any qualms about sharing the details of Sem's childhood so publicly in the documentary, when Sem wasn't around to give his consent. Perhaps they held certain things back, and only shared the most relevant bits. Nothing my mum said seemed gratuitous. I preferred it to the re-enactment. But, still, I wonder if Sem would have told it the same way. Or at all.

'Sem first went into foster care when he was ten years old,' my mother says, very clearly and evenly, as if this is something that she has rehearsed. 'He'd been living with his grandmother. They'd been very close. When she got lung cancer, I gather it was too difficult for her to keep looking after Sem. He went back to his mother at first, but she'd found him too much of a handful even before everything with his grandmother. She was juggling work and childcare as a single mum and I think it all just got too much. There was an incident where she left the children unattended for a whole day, even the toddler. And the house wasn't clean. It wasn't a safe environment. The children were put into care. They tried to keep the little ones together, but Sem had already been living separately, so he went on his own. Initially, it was only meant to be short-term.

'When his grandmother died, Sem started having more severe behavioural problems. He moved through a few homes during that period, before he came to us.'

My mother's voice became emotional at this point in the interview. 'They dropped him off at our house at about six o'clock in the evening, this awkward teenage boy, scowling in the living room. The social workers said he had a sports trophy to show us. Best and Fairest. But when he went through his bag, he couldn't find it. He must have left it behind. You'd expect a child to be sad or angry in a moment like that. But Sem was stressed. Almost afraid. He kept anxiously going back through his bag. As if that trophy would have proved something to us. That's what broke my heart.'

Telling you this story makes me think, again, about how disingenuous Peter could be. Because it's clear to me now that the re-enactment of Sem's birth and childhood, the first interview with my mother, all of that was to set the stage for a story that Peter didn't believe was true, or at least wasn't the whole truth. It was just a convenient place to start a documentary, to *set the scene*. That's not to say that my mother was lying in her interview. The things she said about Sem's childhood were all correct, as far as I know. And all the other things Peter depicted in the documentary, right up to the disappearance, they were all more or less fact. Even the possibilities Peter presents for what happened to Sem, the ways in which he might have been swallowed up by the world, or erased himself—as far as I know, Peter thought they could be true. But there was an untruth in what was left out of this story. Peter presented Sem's life this first time in a neat order, each thing seeming to lead almost inevitably to the next, so that Peter could eventually arrive at a certain conclusion: that Sem was lost and seeking meaning. That his childhood had forced him into a place where he had no options and nowhere to go. A young man who was looking for connection everywhere: in drugs, in women, even in conspiracies. A Sem who might have taken his own life. A Sem who might have run away and left us all. Who could have taken a night swim in dangerous waters and been sucked out to sea. Someone who was broken, who was always going to disappear.

There was no mention in this version of the story of Sem's jobs, or that he loved to cook, and wrote poetry. Peter didn't account for the fact that lots of people get a bit lost, but still pull through. Or how people who seem fine can be the ones in trouble. And, most of all, Peter didn't account for other people. For my parents, and Celeste, and me. How our actions affected Sem. He didn't account for our problems, or our accidents or mistakes. In Peter's first version, Sem's life was set on a certain pre-ordained path that was always headed for ruin.

I remember I asked Peter about it. He came around to see me a few days after the documentary screened in Sydney, bringing with him a bunch of flowers, as if I was his movie star and not his subject, and my mum let him in, fussing about putting the flowers into water, as if he was spoiling me.

'Why did you start by telling that story about Sem and his childhood and that dumb stuff about the aliens? Nothing about my family, or Celeste and me? You made it sound like it had nothing to do with us. Like he was just always going to vanish, and there was nothing to be done.'

When I said this, Peter smiled. It reminded me of how he used to smile when I talked about Celeste, right back at the beginning of our relationship, before I went with her to the coast. A superior, knowing smile.

He said, 'I told it for completeness. I wouldn't have been telling the whole story if I didn't start there. It's not like I don't get to everything else later on. But it wouldn't be much of a documentary if I started at the very end. And besides, people wouldn't believe it, if I just started with the conclusion. Part of the persuasiveness is the process of leading them there.'

I've thought a lot about that conversation with Peter. I've come to realise that persuasive storytelling was what Peter was really all about. He claimed he was interested in the truth, but I want you to understand that Peter and his documentaries aren't really things that you can trust.

———

After Celeste's birthday, after she told me what I had done to Sem, I had trouble getting out of bed. Most days I lay on the mattress, waiting for Celeste to bring me bottles of water, because the tank was still contaminated. Sometimes, if I'd opened the curtains, I would see Celeste out on the deck, painting or reading, but other days I kept the curtains closed and would only hear her when she came inside to fix some food or, at night, when she padded down the hallway to her own room to sleep.

She came into my room once, very early on, and sat on the end of my bed.

'We have to talk about what's going to happen next,' she said. 'I know you're not well, but we need to talk about this now.' She put her hand on my foot, through the covers. 'We're going to wait, okay? We'll wait, like we think he's coming back, and then, when enough time has passed, we'll report him missing. They'll just think he took off. Or drowned. We can do this, Tilly. It's going to be alright.'

I can't remember if I said anything in reply. Those days are hard to recall. From time to time, I must have got up to use the toilet. Celeste brought me meals and, when hunger got the better of my grief, I ate greedily and then left the plates, which she cleared away. I tried to silence my wants. My hunger, and my desire to be comforted, and a longing for the sun on my face. Those things were for people who were part of the world. I stayed in my room, where I was safe from what I had done and the world was safe from me.

I felt like I would stay in bed forever. And there was no obvious moment when things got better. It didn't happen like that. But gradually, I started leaving the bed, walking around the room. I remember looking out the window, across the balcony and over the tops of the trees to the inlet, where the water still flowed as it always had, the gum trees on the far bank as tall and pale as they had always been, the light changing each day, morning, midday, evening, night.

One afternoon, I went out onto the balcony and looked at the water. Celeste brought out a chair and I sat in it and she cut my hair. Just like that day with Sem. Her hands on my scalp. Afterwards, I went inside with her, and together we chopped vegetables for dinner. Somehow, life was going on. But Sem did not return.

It was two or three days after I left my room that I went down to the inlet and swam. I passed the red car, back in the driveway. Celeste must have moved it. When I got to the inlet I struck out into the deep channel towards the far bank and I felt certain that I would die out there. I deserved it, for what I had done. I would be swept out to sea, or taken by a shark, and my body would rest with Sem's. I would suffer the same fate that I had bestowed upon him. Instead, I made it across and back unscathed.

I returned to the house, still dripping wet, and found Celeste reading on the deck. The swim had helped to clear my mind. If I couldn't remember what happened, surely the best thing was to confess and let the police investigate. Then it wouldn't be my burden anymore. 'I want to go to the police,' I said to Celeste.

She put down her book. 'You're not thinking straight. I've put everything on the line for you, Tilly. If you go to the police, what do you think they'll do to me? I threw his body in the sea. Anyone knows that's a crime.'

'I didn't ask you to do that,' I said.

'Well, I did it anyway,' she said. 'For you. So just be grateful. Don't go making things hard.'

'I hate this,' I said. 'It feels wrong.'

'It's not all about you.' Celeste glared at me. 'It's about the three of us.'

I felt tears coming to my eyes. Everything felt out of my control.

'We're going to wait,' she said. 'We'll wait and then we'll go to the police and we'll say he's missing, like he always goes missing.' She stood and took my hands in hers. 'It will be okay,' she said. 'You have to think clearly. You could go to prison.'

'Maybe that's what I deserve.' I meant it to sound serious, but it came out plaintive and whiny.

Celeste squeezed my hands. 'It was an accident.'

———

Peter recreated this scene in his documentary, towards the end of the film, when he is building towards the denouement. It's Peter's version of events that I now have in my mind when I try to remember that day. I see myself being pulled into Celeste's arms—the mousy brown hair of the actor who played me, and the strong arms of the girl who played Celeste. When I watched that scene in the documentary, I thought I understood the actor playing my role. We were the same. Celeste had spoken so firmly, and I had followed along, reciting lines from her script, doing what I was told to do and saying what I was told to say.

———

A few days later, Celeste drove us to the police station near the pub. We had agreed that she would do all the talking. She'd say that Sem had disappeared, and we were worried because he'd never stayed away so long before. It was more than two weeks since we'd seen him and we didn't know where he might be.

The building didn't look like a police station. It looked like a house. Other than the blue police sign out front, it looked like any of the other single-storey fibro houses in town. Celeste parked out front and we walked up the brick path to the front door, where Celeste knocked. It was chilly, and we pulled our jackets firmly around our bodies, a salty breeze blowing up from the ocean, seagulls whirling overhead.

After a minute or so Celeste knocked again, more urgently this time. Again, we waited.

When there was still no response, I went and pressed my face up to the window and called, 'Hello?' But no one came. I looked over at Celeste, who shrugged.

The pub was just down the road, so we walked there and sat at the deserted bar. I wasn't sure if I imagined the publican's eyes resting for just a moment on Celeste's middle—her pregnancy was just starting to show—before Celeste asked for two orange juices. The publican poured them and returned to wiping down the tables, everything dim and reeking of beer.

'When does the police station open?' I asked the publican, when she resumed her post behind the bar.

'Whenever Rob wakes up,' she said. 'Which won't be too early today,' she added with a grimace. 'He was here pretty late last night.'

I nodded and looked down into my juice, and she must have taken pity on us because she wrote his phone number on a napkin and told us that if we really had to, we could call.

Celeste phoned from out the front of the pub, her face serious, hair tucked behind her ears. When she spoke, she turned her body away from me, cupping the phone against the wind.

'Just a little concerned,' I heard her say. 'It's been a few weeks.'

She hung up and we walked slowly back to the station. This time when Celeste knocked I could hear movement behind the door and, after a short wait, it opened to reveal a stocky man, maybe forty years old, balding, wearing shorts and a polo shirt. His face was covered with coarse stubble, pale blue eyes looking out, and his feet were wedged into a pair of leather sandals.

'Come in,' he said. 'Tell me more about this business that just couldn't wait.'

We followed him down a short corridor and into an office.

'Take a seat,' he said, gesturing to a brown floral sofa. 'Unless you'd rather we go to the main station? It's a bit of a drive.'

I took a seat next to Celeste. The policeman sat opposite us on a swivel chair, kicking one leg up to rest on the other, his heel on a coffee table on which two plastic binders languished with a birdwatching book.

Celeste was calm and matter of fact. She ran through the details: Sem's name, age, the date we saw him last, that it had been her birthday. 'It's not unusual for him to come and go,' she said, 'which is why we didn't come in earlier. But now it's been more than two weeks, we're starting to get a little concerned.'

'Tall skinny guy?' the policeman asked. 'Dark hair?'

Celeste nodded.

'Seen him round the place,' he said. 'Usually notice when someone new blows in, with a small town like this. Living with you then, was he?'

'Most of the time,' Celeste said.

'But not all the time?'

'No.'

The policeman's eyes drifted down from Celeste's face to her belly. She had unzipped her jacket and the small bump of her pregnancy was pushing against her t-shirt. I wasn't sure if he could tell.

'And when he wasn't with you?' he asked.

'He had a job picking berries,' Celeste said. She named the farm.

'Well,' the police officer said, 'I know a few people I can talk to. Most likely he's up there with the other local fruit pickers. I'm sorry, love.' He swung his feet off the table and sat forwards, resting his elbows on his spread knees and clasping his hands between them, as if in prayer, a small frown turning down the corners of his mouth. 'Men, right? Real bastards, the lot of us.' He sat up straight and put his hands on his knees. 'I'll see if I can talk some sense into him. Remind him that a man has responsibilities back home.'

We gave him our address and Celeste shook his hand as we left. 'Lovely to meet you, Sergeant McIntyre,' she said.

⌐

Celeste drove us back to the house and made burgers that we ate quietly at the kitchen table. My mouth coated with grease, head heavy, I went and lay on my bed and for the first time thought fondly of the big house on Angel Street, where Mum was waiting for me, and where Peter was just around the corner, always happy to come and take me out for a meal. A different world, now in the past, but, I thought, it might still be waiting there for me. If I returned, perhaps I would find everything as it had been, and I could be innocent again. Or, if not innocent, at least more human. Part of the world once more.

Next morning, I broached the idea with Celeste.

'What would you even do back there?' she asked. She was reading on the balcony. 'And what about your mum? How could you stand to live with her? I thought you hated it there.'

'Well,' I said, aware that I was measuring my words carefully, 'I was thinking we could get our own place.'

Celeste looked up from her book. 'With what money?' she asked, eyebrows raised.

'I could get another job,' I said.

'Don't make me sad.'

'It's just—I don't know—what are we even doing here?' I asked.

'What do you mean?'

'Summer's over.'

'And?'

'I don't know,' I said. 'Just forget it.'

After that, we sat together and read in silence. It was a relief, to escape into my book. The story of a family in Ireland, the children growing up through the chapters. It was liberating to step into their lives. When I was reading, I didn't have to be me.

Finally, Celeste looked over at me. 'It won't make any difference.'

I could feel my face burning with a mix of shame and fear. The awfulness of talking about what had happened, and making it real.

'You can't escape it just by going back to the city,' she said.

'Well, I don't know what to do,' I said. We'd lied to the police. We'd covered it up. If I really had killed Sem, and we were going to try to go on living this way, the only option was to try to forget and escape.

'Trust me,' Celeste said. 'We're going to get through this, okay?'

I looked back at my book.

'We still have the house for another few months if we want,' she added. 'Mum's friends will be away for six months at least.'

I nodded, not looking at her.

'You have to trust me,' she said.

I thought about that shattered blue vase. I imagined that one of them had thrown it at the other. I thought of Sem's thin arms, his fall from the bridge all those years ago. And I thought of Celeste's strong arms, her unreadable eyes, her angry voice coming down the stairs while I stood below, uncertain how to act, and how furious she had been on her birthday, threatening to throw herself out onto the road, her voice so loud inside the car. I thought of the tension between us. I imagined Celeste hurling that vase at Sem, while I stood on the stairs outside, too frightened to act.

And I thought too about the lies we'd told the police. Celeste had made me complicit. The moment when I could have told the truth, could have confessed or said that I didn't remember, had passed. I didn't like it, but what could I do? As Celeste said, if I went back on our story now, I'd be putting her in just as much trouble as me.

In retrospect, I can see that in fact I did have some power, more than I knew. Celeste needed me as much as I needed her. We had to keep up the story together. But at the time, I didn't feel at all powerful. I felt that I had to do what Celeste told me. And it was scary, because I wasn't entirely sure if I could trust her. In the back of my mind I kept wondering if, as well as lying to the police, she might also be lying to me. I was trapped. How could I leave when I couldn't even drive myself away?

I looked up at Celeste, reading so calmly, and I felt afraid. It seemed like everything I knew of the outside world was now coming to me through Celeste. Even the water I drank depended on her trips into town. There was no possibility of me striking out on my own.

⸺

I always saw Sem as grown up. When we were teenagers at Carlisle Road, and later at Angel Street and down at Eden. There were less than two years between us, but Sem always seemed much older than me. Like he knew so much more about the world. When I was with him, I wanted him to see me as grown up too. I hated that, to him, I was just a child.

Maybe, in a way, Sem did teach me to grow up. What happened to Sem at Eden, and everything that followed, showed me that actions have real consequences. Perhaps that's what it is to be an adult: to have to live with what you have done. Maybe Sem showed me even earlier what adulthood was like. To be taken into a room and asked to speak. An adult knows that real people and their fates depend upon their words. Adults are responsible for themselves in the world, and responsible for those that they love. It's taken me a long time to understand that. And on the balcony that day with Celeste, I was still very much a child.

Later that week, we ran out of drinking water again. Celeste went to the fridge and pulled out a beer, popping the can with a satisfying hiss. I thought about the beer and the baby. But those kinds of thoughts were hard to hold in my mind. Since Sem had gone I found it hard to concentrate on much, and besides, Celeste didn't drink the beer, but pressed it into my hands, and I took a sip.

By the afternoon, my mouth was furry and my head felt full of fog. I told myself I wouldn't have another, I'd had too many already, but then I felt so thirsty that I found myself back at the fridge, a cold can in my hand, the liquid moistening my mouth only briefly before it felt dry again, and I would need yet another drink.

The hours disappeared. Celeste went out in the middle of the day, but when she came back, she didn't give me any water, and I was too woozy to think to ask for it—or maybe part of me preferred the beer, the way it muted the world around me, put some distance between my mind and my body and what I had done. Late in the afternoon, as I lay on the couch, I heard the sound of tyres approaching down the track and for a moment my heart lifted: Sem was back.

Except, it wasn't Sem. It was Sergeant Robert McIntyre—come to check in on us, he said, his eyes lingering on the beer cans around the living room, our stuff haphazardly strewn about, Sem's jacket draped over one of the chairs.

Celeste immediately sprang into action, her hand on his arm, offering him something to drink. And when he asked for a glass of water, Celeste poured it from a bottle, explaining about the situation with the tank as if it had just happened, leading him out and down to look at the guttering, explaining about the contamination, while I stood at the top of the stairs, noticing that Celeste wasn't even wearing a jacket, despite the cold, hearing the hollow ring of her laugh echoing from below. She turned and caught my eye, her cheeks pink, standing beside the red car.

Back inside, Sergeant McIntyre sat on the couch. His gaze lingered on Celeste, sitting opposite him, and my eyes followed his, taking in her tanned arms, the expanse of leg below her shorts, her pink face, her grey eyes and wide smile. She leaned towards him, her breasts pressing against her top.

'Thanks for coming to see us,' she said, smiling. 'I'm glad you're taking this seriously.'

Sergeant McIntyre said he'd been to visit the berry farm and asked around, but Sem hadn't turned up. Now, he wanted to know again about the last time we'd seen him. Did he seem okay? Was there anything unusual about his behaviour? 'Routine questions,' he assured us. 'Chances are he's just taken off and he'll show up in a week or two. You said he was often coming and going?'

'Well,' Celeste said, 'like we said the other day, the last time we saw Sem was the night of my birthday. We went down to the pub. Sem had a few, but he said he'd be fine to drive home, so we agreed. Foolish, really. Though maybe he was under the limit. He can really hold his drink.'

'It's okay,' Sergeant McIntyre said. 'I'm not going after him for drunk driving.'

'Phew,' Celeste said, manufacturing a relieved smile. 'I was worried for a moment.' She pressed her hand against her chest theatrically before carrying on. 'Well, we drove home and had a few more beers down by the beach. Then us girls got tired, so we came back up to the house, but Sem said he wanted to stay down there for a while, watching the moon.'

I felt myself nodding dumbly and smiling. Was that what happened? It seemed right. It seemed close enough. I was very drunk, I realised. It was difficult to hold on to the moment. Everything was slipping.

'He slept down there?' Sergeant McIntyre asked.

'I don't know,' Celeste said. 'That's the last we saw of him. We presumed he'd found a lift back into town.'

'Okay,' the policeman said. 'Was there any chance he could have gone for a late-night swim?'

Celeste turned now to look at me, her eyes locking onto mine. 'I'm not really sure,' she said.

I felt Celeste's eyes like a weight, an obligation, and so I said, 'It's possible. I've seen him swimming at night before. He wasn't afraid.' I thought, as I said this, that it wasn't a lie. I remembered the day the blue vase was smashed, watching Sem stride down to the sea and swim, seeming unconcerned for his own safety.

'Right,' the police officer said. 'That's something to consider then. There's a powerful current out there.'

'Yes,' I said. I was warming up a little. 'I always worried about him, but there's no stopping Sem once he's made up his mind.'

'I see,' Sergeant McIntyre said. 'I'll talk to the boys at the station. Wouldn't be the first time someone's got into trouble in the surf around here. Not that you should worry. Like I said, he'll probably turn up. And ladies, easy on the beers.'

'Yes, Sergeant,' Celeste said, leaning back and placing her hand on her belly. 'I'm pregnant, you might have noticed, so I've been sticking to orange juice.' She laughed. 'I've had so much of it, when this baby's born, I'll have to plant him or her an orange tree!'

Now, I often think back to that afternoon with Sergeant McIntyre at the beach house. I remember how out of it I was from all the beers. And it strikes me how little I really recall of that scene. Whether Celeste truly had been drinking orange juice, and I hadn't noticed, or if that was just another story she made up for the police. Whether she'd encouraged me to drink beer, or if that had been my choice. After all, it wasn't her job to look after me. I could have gone and fetched some water myself, couldn't I?

And then there's what happened later that evening. I was still lying on the couch, half drunk, when Celeste said she was turning in. And before walking down the corridor that led to our rooms, she stopped and said, 'Don't think I don't know about you. The way you looked at Sem. Always so hungry for his attention. You wished he wanted you. You're fucked up, Tilly.'

I just gaped at her.

'Is that why you killed him?' she asked. 'Because he wouldn't love you?' She stood there in the doorway, staring at me, and then it was as if something inside her broke, and she came over and pulled me into a hug.

'It's okay, Tilly,' she said. 'It's okay. I'm sorry. I'm so sorry. I'm going to look after you. I promise I will.' She was sobbing, and so, after a moment, I put my arms around her and held her. We stayed that way for a few minutes. When Celeste pulled away she wiped her eyes and kind of laughed.

'Sorry,' she said, and pulled a face, as if that would lighten the mood.

'It's okay,' I said.

I stayed up for a while, on the couch, after she went to bed. I didn't know quite what to make of Celeste's outburst. I guess I wasn't sure if what I'd witnessed had been—as it appeared—an emotional outburst, genuinely out of Celeste's control, or if it was perhaps something more calculated, to upset me, or throw me off balance, or somehow keep me under her control. Even looking back now, it's difficult to really know.

The police came to the house and took Sem's things—his toothbrush and notebook. They searched the ocean with helicopters and boats. I heard them, early one morning, thudding through my dreams. There was a story in the local paper about Sem's disappearance. And then a week or so later it appeared in the national press. I remember waiting for the next logical development: the news story about his childhood. For my name to flash across the screen. A description of how my family had thrown him out when he was little more than a kid. I thought that maybe, when I read that piece, I would understand at last what had really happened all those years ago. But the article I was anticipating never appeared. To the media, Sem was still a person without a past. And, besides, his time with us was just a fragment of his history, anyway. At that stage, the media wouldn't have been too interested in me.

I cut the stories out of the paper and kept them in a drawer in my room. And then, thinking one afternoon that this was the behaviour of a guilty person, a killer, I took them out and tore them into strips and stuffed them into the rubbish bin. Went back to my room and lay down. Wondered if destroying them made me look guiltier still.

I was waiting for my mum to call. Or for her to get in her car and drive down to the beach to find us. I thought she would come. To look for Sem or to look after me. So when I heard tyres on gravel early one afternoon while Celeste and I were out on the deck, sitting quietly, I assumed it was Mum, and I was surprised when, after the creaking of footsteps on the

stairs, I turned in my chair to see Peter standing at the edge
of the balcony, a big black duffel bag hanging from each hand.

'Oh, Matilda,' he said, and to my slight surprise, I found that
I was happy to see him. I went over and put my arms around
his neck and he dropped his bags and put his arms around me,
laughing a little awkwardly. It had been a long time since I'd
held anyone like that, or been held. The feeling of his body
against mine, that soft warmth, washed over me like relief.

Chapter Fourteen

PETER USED MANY ACTORS TO play Sem. Different actors for different ages. And he used various tricks when deploying them. For example, Peter rarely showed the actors' faces. We never saw the expression of the dark-haired boy who played Sem as a teen, or of the skinny actor who played him as a young man. We were always just catching the backs of their heads, or their torsos and arms, hands, ankles, shoes. Peter liked to apply a milky filter to these recreated scenes. A weakening of the colours, as if to gently excuse himself from the absolute truth. And, I think, there was meant to be something tantalising about all these half-glimpses and misty moments. It was meant to make us forget to care about what was real and just want more.

So, it was with actors and old photographs and interviews—mainly with my mother—that Peter recreated Sem's time living with my family. We saw Sem's purpled knees—or, rather, the purpled knees of the actor who played him—drawn up to his chest as he hid beneath a picnic table in the park. Now, it is those purpled knees I think of when I think of Sem. And when I remember Sem running away from home, I see the flash of an actor's ankles running out a door, even though Sem never ran out of our house like that, he usually disappeared from school, or vanished in the night. I hear voices belonging to people who are strangers, performers, people who hadn't been there and didn't understand anything about what had gone on.

Peter went to Canberra when he was recording the documentary, to get some footage of the bridge. It looked the same as it had when I was younger. Peter got one dizzying shot of the drop over the edge, and seeing it on screen I was surprised that Sem had managed to survive his fall with so little injury. It was a long drop. In Peter's recreation, Sem didn't slip and fall, though I'm sure I must have told him that's how it really happened. Instead, he used my mother's version of events. In Peter's retelling, Sem jumped.

After showing us the bridge and telling the story—as recounted by my mother—of Sem's suicidal jump and near death, Peter went on to tell a story about Sem's life as a young man after he left our family. Peter narrates this section himself, describing how Sem lived with another family for several years before reconnecting with his mother, Janine, after he turned eighteen. Janine died of lung cancer, just like her own mother, around the time that Sem went up north. When I saw the documentary, and learned for the first time that Janine had died, I felt disappointed that Sem had never talked about it with me. And then, almost immediately, the disappointment was washed through with guilt. Because I wished that he had talked about it with me not because I thought it might have helped him, or because I worried that he needed support, but because it would have meant that he trusted me and we were close, and I wished our relationship had been like that.

Peter went on. Sem had casual labouring jobs, mainly working in people's gardens or repairing houses. Interspersed with Peter's narration were fragments of interviews he'd recorded with people I'd either never met, or met only briefly, but who seemed to know Sem well. His housemate. A few girls. Some friends. They told stories of how erratic Sem was. Drugs. Parties. Trips into the bush or to the desert. His theories of government oversight and control. Occasionally, Peter spliced in photographs of Sem throughout the years, his face changing in line with the story that was being told, of a boy who was destined for trouble from the moment he was born, who was constantly rejected and hurt, who ran away and jumped off bridges trying to erase himself, searching in increasingly unlikely places for a home, somewhere he could belong.

Of course, I didn't know when I first started watching the documentary that Peter would go on to tell three versions of Sem's life. So, I remember feeling almost sick during the interview with my mother, waiting for them to get to Mrs Rose and the question of what had happened between Sem and me when we were younger, and feeling almost giddy when I realised that the documentary had moved on, that Sem was a young adult already and the question of Sem and me hadn't come up, and wouldn't be mentioned in this first retelling of the story at all.

That's not to say that Peter didn't use my interviews in this first version of Sem's life. On the contrary, large parts are told through my voice, as I recount the time that Sem went up north, and how he came and went from the house by the beach. Peter never really concludes this version. He takes us to the point where this troubled young man, struggling with drugs, learns that he's soon to be a father. And then he leaves it up to us, the audience. Did Sem—as he often liked to do, Peter suggests—go swimming in the ocean beach alone late at night and get swept out to sea? Here, Peter returns to the audio of me talking about the day Liam was caught in the rip. Did he take his own life—out in the ocean, or somewhere in the bush? Here, Peter returns to the interview with my mother, describing how Sem went over the bridge. Perhaps he overdosed? A housemate in the city describes Sem's drug use. Could Sem still be alive, taking up with a new group of people who know nothing of his past and trying to find some connection there? An interview with some of the hippies up north, talking about Sem's search for community. And finally—and there is a smug little smile in Peter's voice as he suggests it— maybe Sem had some sort of extra-terrestrial encounter in the desert, like something from a science fiction movie—and ended up in the sky after all. There is a brief snippet of an interview recorded up north with a young couple talking about their friend who got abducted. Peter wanted his documentary to be taken seriously, so this last idea is presented almost as a joke, or as a metaphor. A romantic gesture towards the mysterious circumstances in which Sem disappeared. Peter ends this first telling of Sem's story with a shot of the night sky, taken from out in the desert. So many stars.

Peter arrived at the beach house just at the moment I needed him, before I even knew that he was what I needed. He immediately set to work. Tidying the house. Paying for a guy to come and clean the tank. Making sure Celeste was going to her medical appointments.

Peter made no secret of the fact that he'd come to make a documentary about Sem, and his disappearance. 'I thought I'd give it a go,' he said. 'If he shows up and it's all for nothing, it will have been some good practice anyway.'

I think it was because of the documentary and how I'd treated him before I left that, initially, Peter was a little hesitant to fall back into a relationship with me. That first night, he said he'd sleep on the couch, and it took quite some persuading for him to agree to sleep in my room instead. And even then, he stayed strictly on his side of the mattress, and in the following days, as he cleaned and organised, I had the sense that he wanted to keep a little distance from me.

But on my side, I wanted to be close to Peter again. When I think of that time I particularly remember one afternoon at the beach a few days after he arrived, the three of us sitting on the sand: Celeste, Peter and me. Summer had ended, and this was one of the last warm days, warm enough to sit out for a while after swimming before wrapping ourselves in towels.

That day at the beach, the three of us sitting on the sand, was so similar to the day we'd gone to the pool together, months earlier, before we'd even decided to go down the coast. But whereas Peter's presence had been uncomfortable that day at the pool, now I was glad to have him around. There was something reassuring about him. He was so solid and cheerful. I could almost forget what had happened and what Celeste said I had done. Peter was an anchor to the world before.

Of course, there was a flip side. I remember watching him bounding across the sand to the water, his sunglasses flying off his head, and in that moment he seemed to belong to a world far apart from the one I was in: a world that I would never have access to again. In Peter's world, there was potential. Futures stretched in front for him to choose between, and because of all this future awaiting, he could be content in the present moment, plunging into the water or lying in the sun. I, on the other hand, lived in the world of the guilty. My past could not be deleted, and I couldn't see any future stretching out before me. I had walked a certain path and it had led me to someplace dark and airless. And so I had to pretend, to force myself to smile, to walk down to the inlet and dive in, hearing the everything-nothing of water in my ears, feeling the sting of salt in my eyes, pretending for a moment, with my head submerged, that I had somehow disappeared and managed at last to escape from myself.

I came out of the water before Peter that day, flopping down on the sand where Celeste was already sitting. She didn't want to swim. Too cold.

'You do know why he's here, don't you?' she said to me quietly.

'What do you mean?' I said, rubbing the chill out of my arms. 'Can't you just be nice to him for once?'

Celeste was silent for a moment. 'I'm looking out for you, Matilda,' she said at last. 'I'm trying to make sure you don't get hurt. You saw all the equipment he brought. He's here for the story. Nothing more.'

And then Peter was coming back out of the water towards us, dripping and shivering a little in the cold sunlight.

—

I brought it up with Peter that afternoon on the balcony, sitting in deckchairs, looking out towards the inlet. Celeste was at a doctor's appointment.

'I've already interviewed your mum,' he said. 'Before I left the city. She's really worried about you, you know. You should give her a call.'

'I thought Mum would come down here,' I said. 'I thought she'd want to look for Sem.'

Peter laughed at that. 'Tilly, it's been years. He's hardly her son anymore. What would her presence do except stir up trouble? You think she wants to go to the police and explain everything?'

I felt a bit uncomfortable when he said that. 'What do you mean by "everything"?' I asked.

'Everything from back then,' Peter said. 'From when you were younger. I told you, I already interviewed your mum.'

At this point, my head started to swim. I thought about what my mum would have told him. And I tried to remember what I had said to him myself. I recalled how once, when Peter asked me about Sem, I'd told him that I felt guilty for how he'd been taken away. I started to wonder: was Peter making a documentary about Sem's recent disappearance, or about what happened all those years ago, when he left our house? Was this the story of a missing man or a failed adoption? And what would the documentary say about me?

'What did Mum tell you?' I asked, trying to keep my voice casual, light.

'The truth, I hope,' he said. 'I've been waiting to ask you and Celeste if I could interview you too. About your time with Sem, and also, when you're ready, about what happened that night he disappeared.'

I nodded, trying to look unconcerned.

'A friend of mine, Mike, a great sound and production guy, lives just a few towns over. There are a bunch of really cool old film directors living around here, actually, that Mike's been working with. It's a great scene. I should show you this thing they made about local surfers. It's fantastic stuff. Anyway, I thought I could bring Mike over to help me set everything up.'

As I sat with Peter on the balcony, talking about his documentary, I had Celeste's warning on my mind. I think I wanted to prove her wrong. To show her that Peter wasn't just after the story, and that he really did care about me. So I think it was then, on the balcony, that I privately resolved to myself that I'd restart my relationship with Peter. Looking back now, I wonder if perhaps I was also trying to protect myself. Maybe I thought that if Peter and I were together, he might treat me better in his documentary. Celeste had told me that she valued my life above the truth: she said she'd got rid of Sem's body and lied to the police to protect me. Maybe I wanted something similar from Peter, with his documentary. I needed him to say that he'd put me above the truth. And I think part of me wanted Peter to know everything. I needed to get it all off my chest and share it with someone else. Maybe that's why, that day on the balcony, I told Peter everything I did.

I told Peter the story that Celeste had told me. What she said I had done. That I ran Sem over in our red car. And then I added something new, something of my own, that I hadn't planned to share. I said I was worried. I hadn't yet seen the interview with my mum, and so I didn't know what she had said about my childhood. I thought she'd probably told him something about what happened with me and Sem. So I said to Peter, 'I'm worried that maybe I *wanted* to kill Sem. That I ran him over as punishment for what he did to me when I was a child.'

I felt frightened when I said this last part. Peter's face, as I spoke, was impassive. But that was not what frightened me. It was my own voice, and my own face, which I could feel was equally placid. I hardly sounded concerned as I spoke about killing Sem. And I was disturbed to hear the way that I was talking, and how I framed it to Peter, as if it were an established fact that Sem had done something to me, when, in truth, I thought it most likely that Sem had never done anything at all. I was the one who had hurt him, by lying, which resulted in him being taken away. Listening to myself, I felt like I was moving even further into the nothing place. I felt empty. Remote. Cold.

When I had finished telling my story Peter was silent for a moment and then he leaned over and took my hand. 'It's going to be okay,' he said. And then he added, 'I'm going to give Mike a call, and when he comes over I want you to tell it again, exactly the way you did just now, and I'll still be here, and you can pretend the camera's not even on.'

After I'd said all that to Peter I felt tired. Too tired to do anything but just sit there and wait while he set his equipment up. Mike arrived, a tall muscular guy who responded to each of Peter's instructions with an ironic smile, but who nevertheless got everything together surprisingly quickly, and became serious and focused as we got ready to film. And then I told it all from the beginning again.

When I was finished, I said, 'What are we going to do?'

'Well,' Peter said, 'what else can we do other than try to figure out the truth?'

Later, when the documentary came out, I would see the interview that Peter did with Celeste at the beach house. I wasn't aware of it at the time, but he must have done it that same afternoon, right after I'd told him the story. I went to have a nap, and he must have found Celeste when she got home, and sat her down right where I had been sitting, with the camera running, to record her version of events.

I was a little surprised to find that she'd agreed to participate. My first thought was that Celeste wouldn't have been able to resist the attention. She would have relished the opportunity to get in front of the camera and tell her side of the story. Things like that didn't faze her. And she probably wanted to impress Mike. But later, I thought maybe it was also that she wanted to get ahead of things. She needed to substantiate our story at every opportunity. And maybe she thought that it might seem suspicious if she refused to be interviewed, like she had something to hide.

Celeste didn't tell Peter the story that she'd told me. Instead, she recited the version of events that we'd told the police. How, on the night of her birthday, after drinking down near the ocean, we went up to the house together and left Sem in the clearing. How she thought perhaps he'd caught a lift back to town or gone for a swim. 'Did Matilda tell you'—and was it my imagination, or did she falter a little over my name?—'did Matilda tell you how Sem liked to swim at the surf beach? It's dangerous out there. Once, some surfers came, and nearly drowned. Liam. You know Liam, right?'

When I saw Celeste's interview in the documentary, I thought back to the day that Liam was caught in the rip. After Celeste saved him and we took him back to the beach house, he'd tried to warn me about her. Looking at her calm face on the screen

I wondered again about the story she'd told me. Whether she was protecting me, or if something else was at play.

Peter let Celeste go on with her story of the night that Sem disappeared. She described how we went to bed, and how when we woke up in the morning it was raining and Sem wasn't around. She felt a little—'I wouldn't say *worried*, exactly,' she said, 'but I thought he must have been a bit miserable down in his swag in the rain. I thought about going down to see him, but I didn't want to go out in the rain myself, so I figured I'd just leave him to it. I think it was nearly dark by the time I started to wonder what he was doing and went down to look for him, but even then I wasn't all that surprised to find him gone; Sem was always coming and going from the beach house.'

It was almost as if Peter was playing with her. She told him everything and then, just when she was feeling comfortable, thinking that the interview was almost over and that it had gone so well, he sprung the other version of events on her: the story she'd told me.

'I thought you told Matilda that she was responsible?' Peter said. His voice was so even and emotionless, despite what he was saying and its consequences. 'Didn't you tell her that she ran him over in your car? Didn't you move the body?'

Celeste looked at Peter when he said that. He wasn't in the frame, but you can tell he must be standing just to the left of the mounted camera. She looked almost sick.

'Did Tilly tell you that?' she asked. Then she took a moment, and I could see that she was composing herself. 'That was just a joke.' She paused, and then her demeanour changed again, lightened. 'I was just joking around. Don't tell me Tilly took that at all seriously?'

'I think she did,' Peter said, his voice calm.

'I think she must have been pulling your leg,' Celeste said. 'Or she was being melodramatic. As if Tilly would have it in her to kill anyone. Like I said, we left him down there sleeping and haven't seen him since.'

I wanted to go to the police to confess. Now that I'd told Peter, I think I wanted to tell everyone else too. It felt good to get it off my chest. Almost like making a decision, or, out of the haziness that lay ahead of me, creating a future which, though dark, at least existed and offered me a way forwards. I wanted to greet my punishment, whatever it might be.

That evening, in bed, I told Peter that I wanted him to go with me to the police station the very next day. But Peter said no. He wouldn't let me.

'I think that would be a mistake,' he said. 'We don't know the full story yet. We need to get all the information and then decide what to do.'

It's curious: that night, Peter didn't tell me that he'd interviewed Celeste. If he'd said that he'd talked to her and doubted her motives, then I would have agreed that it was better to wait. But he said nothing. Perhaps he was worried it would spoil the process, ruin the film. Or maybe he thought that it would agitate me. Or maybe I didn't give him enough of a chance. I was so eager for him, reaching out to him in the bed, while he gently laughed and moved away.

But when I think back on those days, I do have the impression that Peter was anxious to keep Celeste and me apart, to avoid us spending much time together. Like that night, after he had dissuaded me from going to the police, I said I was going to go say goodnight to Celeste.

'Why bother? You'll see her tomorrow,' he said, and pulled me down against him in the bed. And I was so happy that he was reaching for me at last that I let any thought of Celeste drift out of my mind.

I find it unsettling now, when I think back to that night. Peter's sudden change in mood, when he pulled me to him in bed. At the time, I was happy, thinking he'd finally softened to my advances. But now I wonder if perhaps it was the documentary that was on his mind. If he reached for me as a way of ensuring my participation. Because when I woke up the next morning, he was already packing. 'We're going up north,' he said. 'I want to interview some of the people up there about Sem. I've spoken to Mike, and he's in. In fact, he left last night—he has family to see on the way, so we'll meet him there. He's bringing a cinematographer, too, James, who's great. You'll really like him, I think. You'll come, won't you?'

And of course I said yes. I was grateful. Grateful that Peter had taken me back, and grateful that he was taking me out of that house down by the beach. Without him, who knows how long I would have stayed. Peter was the one who was able to cut through Celeste's hold. Certainly, it felt that way to me, as we drove away. I was finally leaving it all behind: the green house between the beaches, the road that dropped away so steeply, the sleepy tourist town. And Celeste, standing on the balcony. All of them receding, while I moved on, trying to leave my past behind.

Chapter Fifteen

WE DROVE FROM THE SEA into the desert. Thinking of that drive brings back the stale smell of Peter's car. The rattle of old water bottles sliding around the floor in the back. Seats covered in piles of paper and film equipment. Outside, the land was vast. Everything seemed to stretch forever: the sky, the red sand, each day. Nothing moved. Like we were still, sitting in our car in the middle of the desert just waiting for the next town to come to us, to rise up from the horizon of sand.

We couldn't make the drive in one day, or even two. The first night we stopped at a motel, a low brick rectangle of rooms around a tarmac covered with a drifting layer of pale red sand. There was a road train parked off to the side, a beat-up car parked in front of one of the rooms, and a bicycle leaning by the door of another, but otherwise the place was deserted.

We parked out front, the sound of our car doors closing overpowered by the huge silence. The reception was a glass-walled office where a tall man with a long thin face showed us into the eating area-cum-pub out the back: a wooden bar and two tables pushed tight to the front glass where plastic venetians clattered.

A truckie was up at the bar getting stuck into a pie, and when we entered he turned and gave us a nod. At one of the tables sat a wiry man, balding on top, wearing a pair of wraparound sunnies propped up on his forehead. He was dressed entirely in lycra and wore cycling shoes.

'Riding across the desert,' the barman told us, nodding at the lycra-clad guy and whistling softly through his nose. He handed us each a plastic-covered menu and gestured for us to sit up at the counter. 'Crazy bastard.'

Peter took out his camera and started thumbing through the photos, flashing them up across the screen. Mum. Me. Celeste. When our parmas arrived, he finally put the camera down and began to eat. The truckie watched us from down the bar. He finished his beer, ordered another and then addressed us.

'Tourists, are you?' he asked.

'Here for work.' Peter, who was sitting closer, turned towards the truckie, so all I could see was his back.

'Ha,' the truckie said. 'Not cycling?'

'No.'

We went outside after dinner, when the sun had set, and beyond the glow of the lights above the car park the desert was opaque with darkness. The stars were shockingly real, so clear, and outer space really didn't seem so far away.

Next morning, when we came down for a greasy brekkie, the road train was already gone.

The second night, there was no motel to stop at, just endless desert stretching in all directions, so we slept in the car.

Welcome Well was hardly a town; it was just a pub and a petrol station on the side of the never-ending road. We drove up to the pub and Peter paused before he swung onto a dirt track, our wheels raising a cloud of red dust that hung around us as we drove past two or three small houses set back in wide red-dirt yards. And then: tents. It was getting dark, and so that first night we couldn't make out the extent of the camp, only the sound of voices, campfires flickering and torch beams darting. It was too dark for us to set up the tent we'd brought, so once again we put down the seats and slept in the car.

We woke with the sun blazing through the windows, cooking us. I opened the door, but there was no relief out there. It was hot. The camp seemed smaller in the morning, when the expanse of desert became visible again, stretching away in all directions as far as we could see, and all the human business of the camp somehow shrank. There were ten or maybe fifteen tents and a few caravans dotted about—all of them, Peter informed me, on the land of one guy, David Patrick, who had started up the whole thing and oversaw the goings-on in the camp from his trailer.

Mike and James arrived while we were eating breakfast, and so the four of us walked up to the trailer together, Peter deep in conversation with them, and me following behind.

It was still early morning but I was already coated in sweat. It was pouring out of me, drying before it could form rivers, so my whole body felt like a salt lake. Most of the campers were already awake, sitting outside their tents frying up breakfast, or in deckchairs under umbrellas, chilling out. A few had beers cracked open. A kid was running around with a nappy on, poking at the dirt with a stick, eyes staring brightly out of a sunburned face topped with crispy, curling blond hair.

Whatever I'd expected David Patrick to look like, it wasn't the guy who opened the trailer door for us: a man who looked more like a country accountant than a conspiracy theorist, down to his rectangular wire-rimmed glasses, pale blue shirt, and freckles reaching down to dust the edges of his lips.

'Come in,' he said. 'I've got a generator running so the air conditioning is on. You won't survive long out here without it.'

We came into a neat little room with a kitchenette down one end and a maroon curtain at the other, behind which I guessed David slept.

'Please sit,' he said, gesturing to a creased leather couch, and I took a seat while Peter, Mike and James set up the recording equipment. David sat opposite me in a matching armchair, his legs crossed. When they were ready to film, Peter came and sat down next to me, and David started to talk.

'I understand you're here to make a documentary,' he said into the camera that loomed over my shoulder. 'I suppose you'd like me to start by telling you the story of this place.' He sat back then, relaxing into the square brown cushion at the back of the chair. 'I first learned about Welcome Well from a friend.' He smiled. 'I owe her a great deal, but, as so many of these things go, we've fallen out of touch. Back then, when I first heard about this place, I was in a pretty bad spot, personally and financially—I won't bore you with the details, but I made a few bad investments—and my friend, well, she'd spent some time out here and she suggested that I buy up some land and try to make something out of it. She had connections with people in the area, and she helped me to find someone who was willing to sell at a reasonable price.'

'Did she see the UFO?' Peter asked, which elicited a thin smile from David.

'No,' he said. 'No, she didn't. She wasn't so much into that way of life as she was a good businesswoman. I built the hotel on her advice. Have you been there yet? It used to be something special. We had a theatre. I made a museum, with everything I could find about the extra-terrestrial sighting. But the hotel never really took off the way I'd hoped.' He laughed. 'Maybe she wasn't such a shrewd businesswoman after all. This camp has always been what drew people up here. The hotel couldn't compete. There are so many lost souls in the big cities, aren't there? Hell, I used to be one of them, going through the motions at a job I hated, the weekends just long enough for me to recover ahead of the next week. Some people realise they're lost, and they seek another way to live. So that's what I offer them with this place. I've heard people say that the vastness of the universe makes them feel small, but I think people come here because it's a place where the universe makes them feel big.' He had started speaking to us like he was in an advertisement, spinning out the New Age hype that drew people in.

He looked at me. 'You've come here looking for your brother, right? I remember him. Of course I do. I remember almost everyone who comes to the camp.'

I could feel Peter shifting on the couch next to me. Peter had been in touch with David by email and explained the purpose of our visit. Still, the way David announced it like that, it almost made it seem like he could read our minds. I think he probably thought that would look good for the documentary and in a way he was right. He seemed for a moment to be tapped into some bigger picture, despite his conservative appearance.

'You've come out here looking for your brother, and he came out here looking for you,' David went on.

'For me?' I asked.

'Well, not specifically for you. He came out here looking for a family, I think. Looking for connection. He wasn't alone in that. A lot of people come out here looking for someone else. I mean, they say they're looking for aliens, but really they're searching for something down here on Earth.' David smiled meaningfully at us and raised his eyebrows, and I couldn't quite tell if his expression was meant to underscore his words or undermine them. It was a clever look for the documentary, I guess, because it could play either way.

———

We spent nearly a week at Welcome Well. I was glad to be there. The place was so strange, and it had such a strong connection with Sem, that I could imagine that he was still around somewhere. There were only brief moments when reality snuck back in—when I saw a couple standing together and was reminded of Sem and Celeste, or one morning when a woman started yelling at a driver to be more careful as he reversed. But for the most part, the real world felt very far away. I suppose Celeste had felt that too, when she visited. And Sem. Welcome Well was a place where you could escape yourself. A place where the usual tethers of society couldn't reach.

Everything was long and flat around the camp. Long flat earth. Long flat sky. Long flat road trains rolling by, dragging forty metres of swaying cargo behind them. The first night, we sat on upturned buckets around a camp fire with a young couple who'd come up from Melbourne just a few weeks earlier. Mike and James were talking to each other in low voices as they handled all the complex equipment. When James shot me a quick smile, I realised I had been staring at them, watching their easy conversation, and I had to pull my eyes away. Look back to the young couple sitting opposite us, making dinner.

'You should have come sooner,' the man said. He was tanned and handsome, turning a sweating beer in his hands. His wife was quartering potatoes on a chopping board resting across her knees, her nipples visible beneath her thin cotton top.

'They've left now,' he said. 'Three girls from down south who said their friend was abducted.'

'What?' Peter asked.

'We only heard about it. Said their friend got sucked up into space. They described him just like you said: a tall guy with dark hair who came out here for a while. I'm sure it must be the same guy. Quite a few of the people still here knew him, if you want to ask them about it. They said he went missing in the bush down south but really it was up here. They reckon that it was extra-terrestrials and that the government is covering it up.'

The wife slid the potatoes into a pot of water that was simmering over the fire.

'Really nice guy, everyone said. He came up here often. A regular. Slept with his swag open so he'd be closer to the sky. Everyone said it seemed like he was waiting for something. Like he knew the secret.'

'The secret?' Peter prompted.

'If we could say, it wouldn't be a secret,' the wife said, smiling mysteriously.

James had a camera trained squarely on her face.

It upset me, hearing this conversation, and watching Peter capture it. It reminded me of the way Sem used to speak, but he never talked about abductions or anything like that. He was more interested in the reach of government control. It's hard for me to explain, but I felt angry, hearing the young couple suggest that Sem had been abducted. It somehow made his interest in those kinds of theories both more central to his life, and also more ridiculous, like he'd just been some guy who walked around waiting for aliens to suck him into the sky. But he really hadn't been like that at all. Maybe that's why I decided to cut the conversation short.

'I think we'd better get back and put up our tents,' I said, standing, interrupting the interview. Peter had been so busy filming all day that we hadn't set anything up. 'Peter, would you take me back to our camp?'

I could tell Peter wanted to get more footage. This was the stuff he would eventually use at the end of his story of Sem the Lost Boy. The idea that he might have gone into space. And again, at the very end of the film. Peter's little artistic gesture. The mystery of deep space, and what it means to disappear. That final shot of the starry night sky, taken from the camp out in the desert, with the credits rolling, as if to say: isn't everyone who is missing or dead up in the stars, in a way? But it was getting dark, so Mike and James said they'd be fine to pack everything up themselves, and Peter and I could go on to bed. We hugged the couple before we left. I could feel the wife's shoulder blades beneath my hands, her back firm and muscular. As we walked back to the car in the dark, I slid my arm through Peter's.

'I'm tired,' I said. I rested my head on his shoulder. 'Can we set up our tent tomorrow morning instead?'

I could tell that he was annoyed with me, but he didn't make a big deal about it. Instead, he said that would be fine, and so he slept that night in the front seat, while I lay in the back.

Next morning, I woke to the bounce of the car as Peter closed the boot, and when I opened the door I saw our tent already laid out on the ground, ready to be erected. Still groggy, I climbed out and picked up a corner, the slippery canvas fabric flapping in my hand, the wind tugging the material and making it sigh.

'Let me get the other side,' Peter said, but his voice sounded very small, and all I could feel was the slippery tent material between my fingers, and I could hear Celeste's voice in my ear, telling me about the swag, and how she'd used it to carry Sem's body down to the sea, and I felt my stomach flipping and rising up behind my teeth. I had to drop the tent and run to the bushes where I turned out the insides of my throat, chunks even making their way out of my nostrils, pale and bitter.

'Whoa, Tilly.' Peter was at my side, smoothing my hair back from my forehead. 'Jesus, are you okay?'

'It's the cold and the hot,' I said. 'The temperatures. I'm not used to it.'

I stood and went over to the car. Peter followed, finding me some water to swill around my mouth and spit into the dirt. After that, I didn't help Peter with the tent. I couldn't bear it, the slippery canvas, the sound it made when it whispered against itself. I sat in the car, sipping water, with my face turned away from him and the tent, watching the camp.

It doesn't make much sense, but I think part of me had been expecting to find Celeste at the camp, even though my rational mind knew that we'd left her down at the coast. Perhaps my feeling of expecting to see Celeste can be explained by remembering that we'd been together constantly for months. It must have been difficult for me to grasp that, suddenly, she could be so far away. She seemed so ever-present and powerful. And of course there was her performance with the conspiracy theory books. Maybe it was also that, with the cameras rolling,

I could imagine Celeste in her element, talking about the camp and Sem and what might be up there in the sky.

In fact, the camp was predominantly men. It was an almost even split between nerdy types with briefcases of alien detection gear and thick tomes on government cover-ups, and hippie types who went about the place half-naked, hoping to commune with some invisible spirit, imagining that something more was waiting for them out there beyond the oppressive heat. Most of the women were there with men. I talked with one of these women as she bathed her kid in a big tub of water.

'The government *wants* us to believe in aliens,' she said, as if reading from a script. 'It's part of a bigger plan. If they distract us with aliens, then we're not seeing what's really going on.'

The energy of the camp shifted overnight and throughout the day. In the evenings the place felt tranquil, slipping into something more eerie at night, but come morning all that peace was lost, and everyone seemed manic, revved up, furious to discover something up there in the long blue sky. They talked feverishly, white spittle collecting in the hot creases of their mouths, while their children watched with their fingers at their noses. All the while James held his camera steady with the big lens pointed at them, and Peter asked them questions, and more questions: What did aliens look like, had they ever met an alien before, did they know Sem, where did they think he was now?

'Yes,' they said, or, 'No.' 'In heaven,' they said, or, 'In hell.' 'In the sky.' 'Under the sea.' 'With that girl, what was her name, Celeste.'

And Peter blinked and said, 'Tell me more about Celeste.'

We heard so many stories about Celeste and Sem in the desert. How Sem arrived first, and Celeste came after him. How Sem had a little one-man swag that they slept in together, with the top unzipped so the starlight could come in. They said that he used drugs. 'Yes,' they said, 'he was in the desert trying to get away from all that for a while. Getting away from the worst of it.' They told us that Celeste was a great support, or that she was no use to him at all. They were a lovely young couple. They fought all the time. They woke the kids at night with their screaming. They told us how Celeste loved to fight, her voice echoing around the camp as she yelled at Sem. They were both so tempestuous, we were told, pulling this way and that. They couldn't control each other or themselves.

'Did it ever get violent?' Peter asked, and they said, 'No, not like that, just the yelling,' and they said, 'Yes, she threw things, she flailed her arms until he pinned them down.'

We heard how they were passionate. How they were crazy. How they loved each other and how they hated each other. And I thought of the broken vase, the shards swept up and put in the bin, and how I had stood on the stairs outside and hadn't gone into the room to see what had really gone on.

We stayed in Welcome Well for five days, gathering footage, and then we left.

———

'I want to talk to you about Celeste,' Peter said. It was two days after we left the camp. He had the tape recorder in the cup holder between us. Where once there had been only sand, we now saw trees and bushes out the window.

'Okay,' I said.

'Tell me, what was it like when they fought?'

'They hardly ever fought in front of me,' I said.

We could have left it at that. I didn't have to go on. But Peter's silence sounded like disappointment, as if I had let him down, like he really needed more, and I felt an obligation to fill the silence with something that would be useful to him.

'I came back from the beach one day and they were going at it. They were screaming at each other. I was coming up the stairs and I heard them yelling,' I said.

'Okay,' Peter said.

'I came up and I saw Celeste was holding this blue vase. She had totally lost it. She was screaming at Sem. She threw the vase at him. It smashed against the wall near his head.'

'What did you do?' Peter asked.

'They saw me and they stopped,' I said.

'Lucky you came when you did.'

'Yes,' I said. 'Lucky.'

And so, just like that, there was another blue vase, another day on the stairs. I managed, in this version, to save the day. As I sat with Peter in the car that day, after I'd told him about the vase, I felt pretty uncomfortable, thinking of how I'd lied. So, to reassure myself, I tried to think through the situation, and I decided that Celeste must have been the one to throw the vase, whether I saw it or not. After his fall from the bridge in which he broke his wrist, Sem had trouble properly throwing a ball. And Celeste was so strong, and so extreme sometimes. So she must have thrown the vase at him. I tried to tell myself that it didn't really matter if I'd been there to see it or not.

'Tell me again what you remember about the day Sem disappeared,' Peter said. I'd told him all this before, the day he interviewed me at the beach house, but I told him again in the car.

'It was Celeste's birthday,' I said. 'We went for drinks in town, in the pub, then down at the beach. In the morning, he was gone.'

'What about that night?' Peter asked. 'What about Sem and Celeste—what were they like?'

'Fighting,' I said. 'They were fighting. On the way home from the pub Celeste almost threw herself out of the car onto the road.'

'Were you with them all night?' Peter asked.

'I can't really remember,' I said. 'I don't think so. They were always going off together. They liked to have private time. I understood. It made sense.'

'Okay.'

'Celeste was having his baby. But he was never around. It was all a mess.'

Peter was quiet for a moment. And then he said, 'But you don't remember what happened that night?'

'I want to go to the police,' I said. 'I want to confess. It's gone on too long. It's too much.'

'But are you certain?' Peter asked. 'Do you actually remember running him over?'

My voice was very soft when I said, 'No.'

And Peter reached out and took my hand in his and squeezed it, still holding the steering wheel in his other hand. 'Don't go to the police yet,' he said. 'We've got to figure it out first. Why would Celeste tell you that story? That's what I want to understand. It seems so strange that you wouldn't remember any of what she described. What if she's lying to you? We've got to uncover the truth.'

Later that night, lying with Peter in the tent pitched by the side of the road, I could hear the sickening flap and slither of the canvas in the night wind, and I thought about Peter's words. I wanted to tell myself that he was trying to protect me by stopping me going to the police. But when I thought about what he'd actually said, he'd only said he was interested in the truth. I knew that documentaries sometimes figured things out before the police. There were plenty of documentary makers who got famous from breaking cases before the authorities. If I went to the police, I might spoil his scoop. And I thought of Celeste sitting on the beach, turning her face towards mine. 'He's here for the story. Nothing more.'

Part IV

Part IV

Chapter Sixteen

I'VE BEEN LIVING OUT HERE for about six months now, staying in a house that looks out over a wide lake forming part of a river system that eventually feeds out to the sea. The place is quite remote—about halfway between Sydney and the beach house where I spent that summer with Celeste and Sem. The house I'm living in is very simple: a single-storey structure with an open-plan living room and kitchen, and a small bedroom and bathroom off to the side. Out front is a paved area with a table and chairs, where I sit sometimes, and then there is a long stretch of grass that slopes down to a jetty, where there's a tinnie with an outboard motor that I'm renting along with the house.

I came out here just after the injunction was passed to suppress Peter's documentary. I think everyone thought it was for the best. Mum drove me down from Sydney, where we had moved for my trial, and I bought a bike to get around. The city wasn't doing me much good, especially with all the attention I was getting. Better to come out here for some peace and quiet. The lake house is about a twenty-minute drive inland from the coast and is only a few hours' drive from Sydney, when I have to go back for court dates. To pay the rent, I work five days a week at the local supermarket, which stands by the petrol station on the side of the road. And from time to time I cycle into the coastal town nearby. It's funny how all little seaside towns seem the same. This town has a wharf just like the one where Sem and Celeste and I fished. I've been there once or twice, but I spend most of my free time at the house, or out exploring in the tinnie.

The first few months I lived out here, I developed a habit of taking the boat out through the narrow passes between the lakes almost every morning and evening, and that was how I came to find the Hidden Place. The Hidden Place is an almost perfectly circular basin of water surrounded on all sides by tall white-trunked gum trees. There are no houses on this part of the lake. If you turn off the boat's motor, everything becomes still, apart from the occasional splash of a fish breaking the surface of the water. In the Hidden Place, nothing else exists. It's almost as if, here, there are no pasts and no futures, no consequences or obligations. There is no one and no reason to blame the fish for eating the worm, or the crabs for scuttling over the top of each other, or me, for pulling up a flathead and pressing my knife into its juicy neck. Things come and go, one thing occurs and then something else happens, and I can be in each second and then let it slip away.

In the Hidden Place, Celeste is the girl lying across my bed in the heat, with her hair spread out, driving with the windows down, splashing across the inlet, droplets glistening on her shoulders, loving me and loving Sem, screaming at him in the car, curling up with him on the couch. And Sem is the boy walking home with me in the rain and standing on the bridge and disappearing from the pool. He's the young man with the dimple in the top of his cheek, the thumbprint in his skinny chest, dancing on the balcony, drinking beer in the shadows of the pub, talking to me angrily with spittle in the corners of his lips, whispering warmly in my ear, his arm around my shoulders. In the Hidden Place, nothing is more than it is in the moment.

When I first came out here, the Hidden Place was almost the only place I could bear to be. I'll be working at the supermarket, or shopping in the little coastal town, and something will remind me of my past, and everything that happened with Celeste and Sem. I'll be standing at the register and a customer will look at me with a faint squint of recognition, and I imagine that they have seen the documentary and are replaying the scenes in their mind, understanding who I am and what I have done, and I will feel my hands go clammy against the milk or cigarettes or whatever it is I am scanning. Or I will be cycling along the headland road and the smell of the sea will make me think of Celeste on the beach with the wind in her hair, and then I will remember everything, and my stomach will slosh with the ocean waves. Even when I'm alone in the lake house, there are still moments when I will be reminded of the past.

I'll find a book on the shelves and think of Sem reading in one of the deckchairs on the balcony at the beach house. Or while cooking my dinner I will think of Celeste frying up sausages in the pan.

⎯

When I first went out to the Hidden Place, I always found comfort there. It was a place where I could feel truly alone. Time stopped running so relentlessly forwards. The past was not so powerful anymore, and instead everything spread out around me, as if time were as flat as the surface of the water, a disc where everything was connected in many directions, and nothing was solely responsible for anything else.

And then one morning, about a month ago, I took the tinnie out to the Hidden Place and cut off the motor and, for the first time, I found that I wasn't alone. As the vibrations from the motor died away, I heard a dog's bark. I looked around the circle of trees and there it was, down by the edge of the water: a brown dog with a long snout and its tail up in the air. When I met its eye, the dog barked again and wagged its tail.

At first I thought it didn't matter. That I could think of the dog as something that belonged to the place, like a fish, or a bird. But dogs are not like wild animals; they have been domesticated, and are aware of humans in a way birds and fish aren't. They understand things like love and guilt. And so, I could sense that the dog was watching me across the water. Even when I closed my eyes, I couldn't forget that he was there. When I opened them and looked at him, he turned in circles and wagged his tail, his mouth open, panting with excitement. The magic of the Hidden Place was lost. So, in the end, I turned on the motor and made my way home.

When I got back to the house, I found myself in one of my moods. Like a kind of mania, I am sometimes possessed by a furious determination to understand, at last, what happened. I will take out paper and pen and start writing everything down, as if I can somehow work it out, like a proof, and at the end will be able to draw a line and write under it 'guilty' or 'innocent'. It's when I'm in these moods that it's easiest for me to think that maybe I hated Sem, and perhaps that is the answer to everything. I imagine the hate to be like water, flowing in me, and if I can find just a trickle, then I can follow it downstream as it grows wider and deeper, until it is surging through me, breaking into white-capped waves, and searching for some ocean into which to empty itself.

It would be much easier if I hated Sem. I came to understand this, over the weeks and months after I left Celeste and the beach house. Time and time again I was shown that if I hated Sem, then the story of our lives made sense, and was neat and simple. And I agree. I think it's true, at least in as much as hating Sem would make this story easy to tell. I probably could have got through this whole account in just a few pages, rather than the long, drawn-out process it has taken to get us here. In fact, I probably wouldn't even need to tell the story at all, because you would already know it, that's how simple it would be. There would be nothing to explain.

You see, if I hated Sem, then other things would naturally follow: what Sem did to me and what I did to Sem. Our actions would have symmetry. Like the scales of justice, evenly weighted. I think that is why my lawyer tells me that revenge may be the story that the prosecutor will tell. And why Peter was able to tell it so convincingly in his documentary. The story of revenge is a way of taking everything that happened and making it coherent.

It's when I'm in this sort of mood that I almost wish it were true—not just the hatred, but all our actions too. I want it to be so simple: Sem hurt me and so I hurt Sem. I will pick up my pen and write 'Sem' at the top of the page and then make a list of all his failings and his crimes. Then, when I read over the list, I can believe that I did it, I killed him, it was deliberate, and it all makes a tragic kind of sense.

I think one of these moods had me in its grip the day I went to the police to give my statement. I find it difficult, now, to remember exactly what I said. My psychologist tells me that sometimes happens when you're full of adrenaline: your memory just cuts out.

I should probably explain that I now go to see a psychologist twice a week. Her name is Helen. She lives in the coastal town I told you about, a short ride from the lakes, in a dark old house that smells like salt and wood. Stress-related memory failure is just one of the things Helen has told me about during our quiet afternoon sessions in the study at her house. That study—I wish I could show it to you. If you're anything like your parents, I think you would love it. There is a wall of books that, in the afternoons, is illuminated by a shaft of light that comes through the window. The floor is covered with rugs that overlap and the three walls that are not full of books are hung with artworks and posters. There are pot plants on the windowsill and in all four corners of the room, and some hanging from the ceiling. More often than not, Helen is drinking ginger tea from a blue-glazed mug that she made herself on a pottery wheel. She always offers me a cup too, and sometimes, when I'm back at the lake house on my own and find myself lost in the past or gripped by an urgent desire to make sense of things, I instead make myself a cup of ginger tea and it helps me to calm down and start thinking a little more clearly again.

At the police station on the day of my confession, I was in a daze. When I try to remember the interview now, all I can see is myself as I appeared in Peter's documentary, when he began telling the second version of Sem's story—the story of revenge. There was a camera in the corner of the ceiling in the interview room at the police station, and Peter had somehow got the footage. I've wondered how he got a copy of the tape, and now I think perhaps it was my copy that he used. I think my mum might have given it to him during one of their later interviews, while I was out of the house. I remember my lawyer asking for it, and there was a bit of a scramble to find it again.

I went to the police station without Peter's knowledge, and certainly without his approval. He had told me to wait, while he worked at uncovering what he called the truth. I never got to find out how that would have gone, Peter's quest to discover what really happened. I guess I'll never know for certain whether, by telling me not to go to the police, he was protecting me or his story. Perhaps, as with most things, it was neither one nor the other but both. At the time, though, I didn't trust him enough to wait and find out.

———

When we returned from the desert, Peter dropped me off at the Angel Street house. I waved goodbye to him at the gate, and then walked up the front path. On the long drive back a feeling had been growing inside me. I wanted to sort out the truth at last. By the time we reached Melbourne, it was almost unbearably urgent. Peter was still sitting in his car, waiting to see me safely inside, so when I reached the door I turned and waved again, and he waved back then drove away. A sense of relief came over me when Peter's car finally turned the corner at the end of the street and disappeared from view. No Peter. No Celeste. It was as if all the strings holding me up had suddenly gone slack, and I wasn't sure if I was about to collapse or finally start moving on my own. I stood by the door a few seconds more. I almost turned the handle and went inside. But there was no one expecting me and no one to miss me. So, at last, the dam holding back the great urgent feeling inside me finally broke, and on trembling legs I turned and walked back down the path, along the street to the corner, and then I started running, my whole body pounding down through my feet against the bitumen, finally free, determined to find out the truth at last and face whatever it may bring, if I could just hold myself together long enough.

I can clearly picture the room where I waited to be interviewed at the police station. It was someone's office. There were little plastic toys on the windowsill and each toy—dog, cat, palm tree—was covered in a thick coat of dust that picked up the late afternoon light coming in through the window, so that I could see tiny mountains and valleys in the landscape of grime. I was still a little breathless, from running almost all the way there, and it was complicated, the way I was feeling, wanting to be honest but wanting to be safe, and burdened by terrible guilt and fear. The energy was starting to drain out of me now, replaced by an awareness of the empty space inside my head and chest, and the relentless throbbing of my heart.

'It was Celeste's birthday,' I say on the tape, the top of my head moving slightly as I speak. 'My friend Celeste. We were living together at the coast. You probably know all this already. This is what we already said. I mean, this early part of the story is the same. We drove to the pub. Sem drove us to the pub. We were drinking beers. Celeste, she wasn't drinking, because she was pregnant. Sorry. I probably should have started with that. Celeste was pregnant with Sem's kid. And so, they were fighting. Well, not because of the pregnancy. I don't really know why they were fighting. They used to fight all the time. Celeste said she'd throw herself out of the car. But she didn't mean it. She could just be like that sometimes. This was on the drive back home, after the pub. We had more beers in the car and we went down and drank in this clearing by the ocean. I don't remember much after that. I blacked out. I'm really not a good drinker. The next morning, when I woke up, I was in my bed. I went for a swim and when I came back Celeste told me about the night before. I didn't remember any of it. The last thing I remembered . . . I'm not even sure what it was. I just remembered drinking, and I remembered the ocean, and everything kind of faded out. Celeste said that I had wanted to move the car to shine the headlights out over the ocean. That Sem was sleeping in his swag in front of the car and I ran him over and he was killed. She said she wrapped his body inside the swag and carried him down to the rocks and dropped him into the sea. And we did have lots of cuts and scrapes the next morning, like we'd been down on the rocks, so it made sense, you see. Maybe I didn't remember what we did because it was too traumatic, and so I blanked it out. I think that can happen sometimes. I think maybe I did it out of revenge. Anyway, it was raining the next day, so when I went down to the clearing to look I couldn't see anything. But maybe the rain washed it away.'

I stop talking then, and the police officer looks up from the notes she is writing. 'Revenge?' she asks. Her voice is surprisingly soft and youthful.

'For what he did to me,' I say, 'when I was young.'

—

I felt queasy, when I watched my interview in the documentary. I had been let out on bail, and Peter had invited me to a special screening at an arthouse cinema in Sydney to celebrate the award his documentary had won. After I was remanded and released, Peter called incessantly at first, but I hadn't responded.

He even came up to Sydney to see me, but I wouldn't go to the door. I guess I felt that going to the police had been a kind of declaration. I'd gone against his wishes. I was, perhaps for the first time, doing things my own way now. Also, I think I was starting to have misgivings about the documentary. I was worried about what it would mean for me, especially now that I'd gone to the police. I wanted Peter to go away. And, after a week or two, the messages from Peter ceased. I didn't hear from him again until, months later, he sent me the invitation. He wanted me to sit up the front of the cinema with him, like part of the official crew, but I declined. I found a seat right up the very back, in darkness, and I made sure to leave the moment the film ended, before they had even turned up the lights.

Before the film began, Peter stood up to give an introduction, very self-possessed, his shadows fanning out around him like petals, and I found myself suddenly hating everything about him—the plummy confidence in his voice, his ridiculous little laugh.

Now, everyone says that Peter is developing a reputation for telling 'stories from the fringes'. Apparently he's already at work on something new, about survivors of sexual abuse in a cult. It suits him. He has always been so squarely in the centre, and it is probably only from there that you can see the edges and understand which people and stories are truly peripheral.

Watching my police interview replayed in Peter's documentary, I could hear the quickness of my voice, the eager, tumbling words, the questioning lilt. It was clear to me, as I watched it, that I was giving my story to the policewoman like an offering, for her approval. I was so ready to describe Celeste and Sem's fighting, because I thought that was the type of fact that might interest the police. I was quick to tell her how volatile Celeste could be. And I was right to think that those details were well suited to the ears of the police. In fact, those details have become very important now. Everyone seems to have a story about how manipulative and unpredictable Celeste could be, and about how she was with Sem, and the chaos of their relationship.

But I felt uneasy about the way I talked about Sem, and our history, in the interview. I expressed it with such certainty, saying 'what he did to me' and not 'what he might have done' or even 'what happened between us', as if everything was absolute and real, rather than the blurry mess of memories that existed inside my head, and my suspicion that I had invented it all. I think there was something about being in that interview room with the police officer taking notes so seriously, pausing from time to time to look at me with her frank brown eyes. I had this sense that I would have been wasting her time if I expressed uncertainty. It wouldn't have been right to come to her with unproven theories about my own past. I felt obligated to offer up as many cogent facts as I could. It was my life, after all—she'd expect me to know the truth about what had happened to me. So, I settled on the facts that I knew would make sense, a story that started with a motive: revenge. And after that, the other facts just followed naturally. Sem hurt me when we were younger, so I hurt him when we were grown up.

'So, Matilda, do you remember killing your brother?' the policewoman asks in the documentary.

You can see, in the footage from the security camera, my head move a little, and then I say, 'I think perhaps I do.'

⁓

The story that I told the police—the revenge story—was also a story that suited Peter's needs, which I'm sure is why he showed almost my entire interview in his film. Throughout the documentary, Peter presents different sequences of events in Sem's life, and each one is told as a string of facts, and each time Peter goes back to tell the story he simply introduces new truths and removes the ones that aren't useful to him anymore. This is how it has to be with documentaries, I suppose. They have to always be telling a story that you can call true, even if it's often changing and doesn't quite match with the things you were told before. It's almost better that way, for a documentary's popularity. People like to be presented with all this information, all these different stories, so that they think they are deciding for themselves what really happened. People are funny like that. Even if they weren't there, and don't know any of the people, and haven't ever experienced anything remotely similar themselves, somehow they still think they are capable of understanding better than anyone else what truly went on. It was startling to me, after the documentary was released, how certain the audience was that they had discerned the truth.

In telling the revenge story, Peter used my interview at the police station and also a long interview that he conducted with my father. When I watched the documentary for the first time in the stuffy cinema, I hadn't seen my dad in years. So it was then that I discovered, along with everyone else at the screening, that he was still living in a townhouse in Canberra, with his new wife, and that they'd had a third kid. Peter filmed my dad sitting in a spartan white kitchen, at a breakfast bar, with a glass of water. Sunlight was coming in through the kitchen window and hitting the glass to make a spot of glow in it. Watching the documentary made me remember, quite suddenly, something that I'd long forgotten.

When I was very small, before Sem came to live with us, my father used to do a trick with his watch, where he would let the sunlight hit the glass face and move his wrist to make the orb of reflected light dance around our concrete garden. He would tell me that this was a fairy come to visit. When I watched the documentary, and saw the orb of light in the water glass, I remembered that game my father used to play. It felt like a particularly significant memory to have discovered because my dad was so serious most of the time, and my mother was the whimsical one. It made me feel briefly happy, sitting in the theatre, despite everything, to know that there had been a time when my father had pretended fairies existed. But, of course, this was just a drop of happiness, absorbed quickly by the anxiety I was feeling watching my father onscreen.

The first thing that struck me was that my dad looked like an old man. His face was liver-spotted. His hair was grey and thin. He was smaller somehow. As soon as I saw that version of my father, my previous images of him were overwritten, and I couldn't remember what he had looked like back when I'd known him, those last few years when we lived with him in Canberra, before Mum took us away. Even now, I can only picture my father as he appeared in that documentary and as he looked in the back garden, conjuring a fairy with his watch. Everything in between has disappeared.

'I met Nancy, my first wife, at university,' my father says in the documentary. He taps his thumb against the countertop where he has rested his forearms and hands. He has adopted the tone of someone who is trying carefully to present facts. Like me in the police station, and Peter in his documentary, and even Celeste when she told me that terrible story the day after her birthday. As he is interviewed, my father doesn't speak with uncertainty, but presents each fact like a pebble that you can hold in your hand, an object with a weight that you could feel and measure. 'She was working in the university library, and I was studying literature, so I was often in there, checking out books. Nancy had these great purple glasses, and straight brown hair. She was a bit of a hippie, you could say, and I was very straitlaced, but that was a good combination back then. She loosened me up a little, and I helped get her life on track. We complemented each other.

'We got married, settled down, the usual story, and we wanted to have a decent-sized family. We both wanted three children, or even four. But it wasn't so easy. We tried for a long time to have Matilda, and after her Nancy had three miscarriages. At that point Nancy said she wanted to stop. It was too hard. We should be grateful for what we had, she said.

I disagreed. I hadn't given up hope. But we had been fighting about it for so long. Nancy hadn't wanted to try for the last baby, and then she went and put a stop to it all together, had the operation, and there was nothing I could do. I had to accept it, and so I did.

'You can imagine my surprise, then, when some ten years later, Nancy comes to me with the idea of fostering. After I've made my peace with everything and accepted it on her terms—no room even for discussion. She came to me wanting to turn our lives upside down. I said no. I was content with one child, I told her. But Nancy couldn't understand why I wasn't into the idea. Hadn't I always wanted another child? she kept saying. I felt like she was trying to trick me. It was like she was implying that I was a bad person for not wanting to foster. That it was wrong of me to prefer my own flesh and blood. It was as if I were obliged to want someone else's kid to come and live under my roof, with all his problems and complications. These kids are never simple to take on, and I don't hold that against them, they've been through a lot, but you have to be realistic about that when you're thinking about fostering. It just wasn't something that I wanted to do. And I think I was entitled to feel that way. But Nancy, so stubborn, she said she'd do it with me or without me. I wasn't ready to lose her then, and so suddenly there's this troubled young man in my house, slamming the doors and running off, and putting my family at risk.'

'At risk?' Peter asks, offscreen.

'Sem came to us with a list of behavioural issues. His own mother had found him too difficult to handle, and I know he'd been through other houses before us and things hadn't worked out. He just wasn't a good influence to have around Tilly. He was putting her in danger. I saw it with my own eyes. He was manipulative. She was under his spell. She'd do anything he said. And he was always taking her off into his room and closing the door. Nancy wouldn't allow me to insist he keep the door open. She said we had to trust him. But I didn't see why we should. We didn't know him. There were other changes in Tilly, too. She was suddenly interested in wearing a bikini. She made her mother take her shopping for one. She bought a miniskirt. Starting to wear clothes that showed off her developing figure. She was starting to have breasts.'

'Did your wife share your concerns?' Peter asks.

'Nancy was oblivious. About that and everything else. She's always been off with the fairies. That's why I had to step in and do something. By this stage, our marriage was essentially over. Nancy was living separately with the kids. I was so worried about what might be happening to Matilda without me there to keep an eye on her. Nancy just isn't a responsible person. She's not a capable parent. But no one believed me. The social workers all thought Nancy was great. I needed proof. I knew I had to get an outside opinion. So I took Tilly to a counsellor, and that's where it all came out. Tilly told the counsellor that Sem had been inappropriate.'

'What exactly did she say?'

'She said that he had touched her on the breast.'

'On her naked breast?' Peter asks.

'Yes,' my father says.

'How did she come to admit that?'

'Well, she was asked about it.'

'How was she asked?'

'The counsellor asked her if Sem had touched her.'

'And she said, "Yes, on my naked breast?"' You can hear the incredulity in Peter's voice.

'You're right, she didn't say that exactly. Of course not,' my father says. 'That's not what Tilly was like. No child is like that, really. Now that I think about it, I suspect Tilly was confused. So the counsellor pointed at different places on her own body, and said that Tilly could just say yes if he had touched her on that part.'

'And when she pointed to her breast, Tilly said yes?'

'That's right.'

'So how did you know it was naked?'

'The counsellor must have asked.'

'How?'

'I suppose she said something like, "Did he touch you on your naked breast?"'

'And Tilly said that he did?'

'I think she nodded, yes.' Here my father looks annoyed. 'Look, the counsellor agreed with me that there was clearly more to it than Matilda was prepared to say. She was such a quiet, introverted kid, she'd never volunteer much, but that doesn't mean things weren't going on. So I went to the social workers with the information and they said that they'd remove the boy from the family. As I said, by this stage, I was living separately from my wife. The strain of it all had become too much. And do you know what Nancy did? She came to me and asked if I would take Tilly, so that the boy could go on living with her. She said he was still recovering from his injuries—there'd been an incident, he'd jumped off a bridge—and it wasn't a good time for him to move. Can you imagine a mother like that, who would put a stranger above her own child? I said fine, I'd take Matilda, but there was no way I was going to let her keep looking after that boy. He was clearly not coping in her care. To be completely frank, he'd tried to kill himself on that bridge. He wasn't doing well. He needed a more stable environment and, heaven knows, Nancy wasn't capable of providing that. I recommended to the social workers that the boy be assigned to a new family, regardless of whether Matilda lived with her mother or me. Afterwards, I went around to the house to see if the boy was still there, in which case I was going to take Matilda away. But he was gone.

'I think it was at that point I realised I just couldn't have anything to do with Nancy anymore. She wasn't the person I thought she was. And I knew it would just be another painful, drawn-out process trying to keep Matilda in my life, because Nancy wanted full custody. The lawyers said we'd have to go back through everything that happened with Sem in the custody proceedings. That I'd have to prove Nancy's household was an unsafe environment if I wanted Tilly with me full time. What would that have been like for Matilda? Honestly, I just couldn't take it. Not any of it anymore. I had to let them go. I moved on. And, ultimately, I think I did the right thing. I'm happy now.'

Watching this part of the documentary, Mrs Rose's office had never seemed so far away. I had no memory of saying anything about Sem touching me on my breast. I was thirteen years old. I wasn't sure I even had breasts back then. If anything, it made me feel more certain that nothing had happened between us. Hearing my dad talk about it made me feel sad. I don't know if he truly believed I was in danger, or if he was more interested in proving that he was right and Mum was wrong, that he was the good parent and she the bad.

Even though the idea of Sem touching my breast did not seem credible to me when I heard my father talk about it, the incident was presented almost as if it were fact. So this interview with my father, and the details of what I said Sem had done to me, was at the heart of Peter's story of revenge. The way Peter told it, when we were younger, Sem and I had a sexual relationship. Peter suggests that it might have been compli- cated. Perhaps I had been the one driving it. Had I, perhaps, been besotted with Sem, so that the relationship, although inappropriate, was also consensual? Maybe I had encouraged it or, at the very least, been a willing participant. But perhaps the relationship hadn't gone the way I wanted. Maybe Sem had rejected me, or I'd found it all too confusing and decided that Sem was to blame. Peter skirts the issue of my mother's responsibility and the tension between my parents. After all, that would probably only make the story more murky, and at this stage Peter was trying to construct a narrative that was clear: a simple revenge story. So Peter turned his attention to me. In particular, me as a young adult: withdrawn, mysterious, strange. The type of girl who might be a secret killer, planning to take revenge on her pre-teen love.

In order to tell this part of the story, Peter had to draw my character in a particular light. To do so, he used fragments from interviews with people who knew me: my parents, Celeste and her mother Christina, Liam and even Noah.

'She's a funny kid,' Liam told the camera, sitting at the strawberry farm, outside, in the sun. 'A quiet one. You can never tell what is going on in that head of hers.'

'Never had a boyfriend,' my mother said. 'Well, aside from you. I'm not even sure if she's really interested in boys. She certainly never came to me with any crushes, or anything like that. I always tried to foster open communication with her, but she was all clammed up.'

'She's a bit of a freak,' Celeste said. 'I think she was kind of in love with Sem, in this demented way, because she also thought he was her brother, and so it was wrong. Thoughts like that are the kind that would just about explode Tilly's head. She's too black and white about everything. So unable to express anything of what she's really feeling.'

'She was obsessed with him,' my father said. 'It wasn't healthy. Maybe for some kids, having an older boyfriend at a young age wouldn't be a big deal. But I could see it would be damaging for Tilly. She wasn't cut out for that kind of thing. And especially living in the same house as him. It wasn't appropriate. Honestly, it wouldn't have been good for the boy either.

I discussed it with the social workers. The power dynamics were all mixed up. So it was for the best. We really had to have him taken away.'

And, finally, Peter. One of the only times in the documentary where he becomes the subject, facing the camera. I'm not sure if it's just me, but when I saw the documentary, I thought that he'd managed to capture an attractive side of himself. Face slightly angled, messy dark hair, a wide, honest-seeming mouth, unfashionably sensible-looking glasses. 'It can be a complicated thing,' he says, smiling self-effacingly, 'to make a documentary about people who are close to you. I'm not sure what my relationship with Matilda says about me, or how I fit into this story.' He sighs. 'Initially, I embraced the complexity. Or at least, that's what I thought. But now, facing the revelation that my former partner may be a killer, I find myself in uncharted waters.' His voice, at this point, has become almost ridiculously grave. 'I'm finding myself in a position where I think I have to seriously ask: if Matilda killed a former lover, might I be next? I think I have to look at this documentary and how it might seem to her . . .' Here, some clever footage of Mike and James filming Peter as he talks. 'Consider if this very documentary might provoke another act of violence. I'd been prepared for challenges in this journey. Moments where I knew I might have to confront my distance from the subject matter, my impartiality and my role as a filmmaker. But I did not, until now, think I might also have to seriously consider the threat to my life.'

The police arrested me immediately after I had given my interview. The inquiry had been ongoing at the coast, but it had been a month since they'd started looking for Sem, and by this stage their efforts had shifted more towards searching for his body. Their inquiry hadn't been entirely fruitless. They'd found Sem's shirt washed up on the next beach and also his shoe in a nearby cove. But, in truth, I suspect the search had petered out a little by the time I went to the police. So I think my confession might have reinvigorated things, because a few days later, they found some canvas material matching Sem's swag in the clearing by the surf beach and also about ten metres away, down on the rocks.

I wasn't thinking about it at the time, but of course my confession implicated Celeste too. It's a crime to conceal and dispose of a body. But I was just waiting for the relief to come, now that I'd finally got it all off my chest. That feeling never came. They arrested me, but Sem was still missing, Celeste was still Celeste and Peter was still Peter and I was still me. The seconds and minutes rolled into hours and days in the same unbearable way they had before. It reminded me of that day at Rita's Pizza. I had confessed, but it didn't bring me the absolution I thought it would. It didn't take me long to start to understand the consequences of going to the police and saying what I said, and begin to regret what I had done.

Chapter Seventeen

AFTER I WAS ARRESTED I was taken before a magistrate and extradited to New South Wales, where they held me for three weeks on remand. Then I went before another magistrate in Sydney and was granted bail, with my mother providing the surety. Later, I asked her how she'd found the money, and she said that she'd put up the Angel Street property, which, without my knowing, she'd purchased a few years back with some money she unexpectedly inherited from her aunt's de facto partner when he passed away. The Angel Street house was Mum's main source of income. Mum said she'd already spoken with the Legal Aid people, and it would be easier for us if we stayed in New South Wales. So she'd rented out our rooms at Angel Street and found a place for us in Sydney, living with a quiet young couple from Germany and a woman named Sky, who had two rambunctious young sons. I had to sleep on the couch, falling into the routine of the place, the people coming and going, the noise, the rising and falling of the light.

During the day I walked the cold streets or I sat in slow, foggy buses that hissed through the rain, later trudging home with shoes full of water, drying out on the couch with an old book. I took my résumé around to a few places, in a half-hearted effort to find a job. When I think back to those first few weeks after I was let out, I remember Mum as calm and serious. She made me call Legal Aid, to talk about my options, and then found a lawyer we could afford. She put up a calendar in the kitchen with my court dates in permanent marker. We didn't really talk about Sem, or what I had done. I got the sense that in some ways that conversation wouldn't change anything. Perhaps that's what unconditional love means. Mum was focused on working out what needed to be done next.

I thought about Peter. Even though I had ignored his attempts to make contact, I was still half-expecting him to turn up anyway, to seek me out as he always had, so that I could once again let him back into my life. But he was back in Melbourne, and weeks and then months passed and he didn't come. I suppose he was off making his documentary. And besides, I'd pushed him away.

How did I come to terms with Sem's absence, and what I had done, over those grey days? I'm not sure that I ever really did. There were court sessions, but I tried to push those from my mind too. I wanted to forget about the harried lawyer my mum had found for me, all the money it was costing, even with the assistance of Legal Aid. Erase those days with

Celeste at the beach house, pretend that Sem was somewhere else, the places where he had gone as a boy, or where he had spent those years after Carlisle Road, or the places he went to from the beach house. Maybe he was out in the desert, staring up into the sky. Maybe he was *in* the sky, floating above us, or in some parallel place we weren't able to see. Among the stars or swimming in some distant sea. It felt good to let that feeling settle over me. It was easier than facing the question of where he really was. It was easier than trying to understand that now he might be truly gone, and examining what role I had played.

I was reading on the couch about six weeks after my committal mention, when Mum came in and sat on one of the big armchairs.

I looked up from my book. Her hair was completely grey now, her face shrunken beneath her softly sagging skin.

'How are you feeling?' she asked.

'The same,' I said.

'You waited a long time to go to the police.'

'I was confused,' I said. 'I thought maybe he'd show up sooner or later, like he always does.'

'Maybe for someone else,' she said, 'but you know Sem. It wasn't like that with Sem.'

'He left all the time, Mum. He was always coming and going.'

'He was haunted,' Mum said, and shook her head.

'He was fine,' I said. 'He was always fine.'

'You know that's not true.'

I said nothing.

'You think you knew your brother?' Her eyes were hard. 'The things he went through? You didn't know him at all. I think none of us did.'

'What if I killed him?' I said. I started to cry. 'What if I didn't go to the police earlier because I couldn't face what I had done?'

———

Looking back, I can see that my mother always had a quality that set her apart from the rest of the world. She never entirely fit in. Perhaps we are similar like that. The best way I can put it is that my mother didn't understand stories in the same way as everyone else. For example, she was never really persuaded by the revenge story, despite its neat symmetry. She didn't feel the need to seek explanations, or to link everything together into a cohesive narrative. Mum wasn't really interested in that. She didn't believe that a troubled childhood led to a troubled adulthood, or that a confession or a motive equated to guilt. And I always had the feeling that she was sceptical of facts that you could hold like a pebble in your hand. She thought that people who held out these kinds of facts and encouraged you to feel the weight of them and see how together they formed a certain shape, or how they could be laid out in a trail so one led to the next and then the next, were actually playing a game and could never fully be trusted. My father, I think, was one of those people Mum couldn't trust. But he wasn't unusual in that way. Most people like the comfort of a familiar story. It was Mum who was the odd one out. In a way, I think it was her great gift, though one I failed to appreciate when I was young.

I can see now, for example, that my mum couldn't understand the familiar story of the family: mother, father, children all living together as a unit in a neat little house. That story made no sense to her. Worse, she was suspicious of it. I remember once, in our early days in the Angel Street house, I told her, furious, that she was no kind of mother to me, leaving me alone for such long stretches in a house full of strangers.

She said, 'I trust these people.'

I think she must have been very unhappy all those years living with my father, quietly strangled by the story of family life that to her was strange and brought no real joy. Mum's happiness came from choosing the people that she lived with and cared for: Sem and Christina, Liam and the people who came and went from the Angel Street house. And she loved nature. Those were the things she understood and that made sense to her. And, in her own way, she loved me. Despite all the tension, and our history with Sem, she's the person who's been there for me the most. Even when I confessed to killing Sem, whom she had loved, she still had a place for me in her home.

About a week after our conversation in the living room, Mum shook me awake one morning and said we were going on a trip. I felt a little anxious when she said this, because the rules of my bail forbade me from staying at a different address without prior approval—like I did later, when I moved out to the house on the lake—and I knew that although those rules wouldn't mean much to my mother, there would be serious consequences for me if we broke them, and probably for her too, with the house on the line. But as it turned out, Mum didn't have such big plans for us that day. We were only going out into the bush, not so far from home.

Mum had borrowed Sky's car, which was long and low and blue and smelled like mothballs. Mum drove us erratically through the city, and it reminded me why I'd never liked getting in the car with her. She was a terrible driver.

'I studied a map beforehand,' she said, 'and I've chosen the route with the fewest right-hand turns.'

Still, a chorus of horns followed us through the city, and it was only once we started to rise into the mountains that the horns gave way to cool air and the sound of birds through the open windows, and a sickening rush as Mum careened around each hairpin bend, her hands clenching the wheel.

'I don't often drive,' she said, after one particularly sharp bend, 'but I thought it would be nice to do something together, just me and you.'

She drove us to a place where the trees were thick-trunked and old, and we got out and walked among them. Mum spread out a tartan picnic blanket she had brought. I recognised it from our days back at Carlisle Road. It was one of the rugs we'd lain on in the garden, after the pool, drinking cordial in the sun.

'We've come out here to meditate,' Mum said. 'I think it will be good for you.'

That day that I meditated with my mother, the first person who came into my mind was Celeste. I could never keep her out. Sitting with my mother among the old trees, I thought of the first time I saw Celeste: a glimpse through an open door. Her bare foot, as she lay in bed with her white headphones on. And the last time I'd seen her was at the house near Eden, through the early morning mist, as she came out onto the deck. That morning I was already sitting in Peter's car, so I last saw Celeste through the speckling of dried rain on the windscreen as Peter put the car into gear and we drove away. I thought about this as I meditated with my mother. Both times, I had caught Celeste off guard. She hadn't expected me to peer into her bedroom, and she hadn't known that I was leaving, sneaking away with Peter in the half-light that preceded the dawn.

It gives me a pain in my stomach now if I think too much about Celeste. Peter painted such a negative portrait of her in his documentary. If you've seen it, I worry that it shows your mother in such a bad light. I wonder, too, what the future will hold for you both. Our fates are still linked. Legally, of course, the outcome of my case affects hers. But in other ways too, I think we're bound together, with Sem. I don't think anything can undo that. So, part of the reason I'm telling you all this, I think, is because I don't want Peter's account to be the only story of your mother you hear, if things turn out badly for us both and you end up staying with your grandmother for a while. I want you to make up your own mind. You have to see that your mother is more than a character in a story told to you by a documentary. It's much more complicated than that.

When he began telling Sem's story for the third and final time, Peter devoted a lot of attention to Celeste, and her character. He used snippets from an interview he had done with my mother, where she is sitting in the garden of the Sydney house. She talks about the day at the pool when the little boy was knocked down and split his head on the tiles. 'Celeste pushed him,' my mum says. She looks away from the camera.

'But it wasn't just that day. Celeste was known for her temper, and for this way she had of trying to control people. She was manipulative, I suppose you would say. But that makes it sound like something that's entirely bad. With Celeste, it was more than that. She had this ability to persuade people, to make them do things her way, and that's not inherently such an awful thing. Only when it's used for the wrong reasons.

'One time, for instance, she was suspended from school for making her geology teacher cry, but it had something to do with studying South America, and that the geology teacher had got something wrong, and Celeste had embarrassed her in front of the class by tricking her into admitting it. And she had terrible fights with her mother about going out to parties on the weekend. Celeste would use this circular kind of logic, so that in the end Christina would come upstairs to where we were living and I'd have to give her an aspirin and a cup of tea. And one time Celeste cut all her mother's nice clothes into shreds. This was when we were all living together on Carlisle Road.

I had to lend Christina something to wear to her own opening that night.

'Celeste even used to fight with Sem. They'd have these huge arguments—God knows what they were about. Teenagers. But Celeste was like a dog with a bone. They'd argue for hours and afterwards Sem would come away looking so tired and defeated, and Celeste wouldn't even seem to understand his point of view at all, she'd just ask him why he was so determined to disagree with her.'

Peter used footage from up north, too. Bits of interviews he did up in Welcome Well: people talking about how Celeste and Sem had fought. One woman recalled that when Celeste had arrived, Sem hadn't looked too pleased to see her, and they'd hardly spoken at all for the first few days, until Sem had finally given in and acknowledged her. The woman had a little smile on her face as she said this, as if it were something she was pleased to report.

As I watched the documentary, I wondered what Peter had done with all the other parts of these interviews. The parts where people had described the magical closeness between Celeste and Sem. How they'd stay up late talking. How they slept together in his swag. How Celeste would read to Sem in the evenings from old books she had brought with her. I had been there with Peter and heard these stories myself, but they didn't make it into his documentary.

And Peter used parts of his interviews with me to construct a picture of Celeste's character. My voice can be heard describing the fights Celeste and Sem had at the beach house, how she threatened to throw herself out of the car the night of her birthday. And the blue vase. I say, in a voice that never falters, that I saw her throw it at him. As I am talking, the scenes are re-enacted onscreen. The face of the actor who plays Celeste is always obscured or turned away.

'How would you describe the relationship between Sem and Celeste?' Peter asks, and I say, 'Volatile.' This was when Peter and I were driving down to Melbourne from Welcome Well. I must have felt guilty for talking about them like this, though, because I added, 'But she really loved him, I think.'

'Okay,' Peter said. 'And what about Sem?'

'You mean, did he love her?'

'Yes, sure, that's one question.'

'I honestly don't know.'

There was so much about Sem I wasn't sure about. I've been asked so many questions about him: where he went, what he got up to, was he depressed, was he addicted, was he suicidal, did he know how to swim? And in the back of my mind Celeste is always there, her face lighting up at the sound of the tyres on gravel that signalled his arrival, and then quickly trying to hide her eagerness, not wanting to show how vulnerable she was in her love for him.

When he began to tell Sem's story the third time, Peter painted a particular picture of Celeste, and he also took great care to show a certain side of her relationship with me. Some of this was based around details that I'd shared. How, when the house water got contaminated, Celeste gave me beer to drink until I was too woozy to think straight. How, when I was first dating Peter, Celeste told me he was too boring, and I had stopped returning his calls. How Celeste was the one who encouraged me to reconnect with Sem, to accompany them back to his house from the pool when I hadn't wanted to. And how she didn't tell me Sem was going to join us at the coast, and how I'd felt confused when he just turned up. When those things were revealed in the documentary, my voice telling Peter how things had been, I felt a little self-conscious, because it didn't necessarily portray me in the best light. I was embarrassed about how I came across: meek and persuadable. Someone who couldn't stand up for herself or make any decisions of her own, and then turned around and got indignant about it, like I thought it was somehow Celeste's fault that I didn't have any opinions of my own. It was unflattering. The way I seemed to expect her to look after me, like I couldn't take any responsibility for myself, let alone for her or for Sem when they might have needed me. It reminded me of the time at Eden when Celeste implied that I was self-involved. Watching the documentary, it seemed she was right.

I also remember feeling surprised by the other interviews Peter had done. It was unpleasant to hear everyone talking about me, sharing things that they'd observed that they'd never told me to my face, things I had no idea they thought or felt or even knew about.

For example, Peter had done an interview with Liam at the strawberry farm where he had worked with Sem. Liam is sitting on a log and, in the distance, you can see the greenhouses where the berries are grown. Through their translucent walls, it's almost possible to make out the shadows of figures moving around: the current workers tending the crop.

'Celeste dated my little brother for a moment, in Melbourne,' Liam says. 'My half-brother, I should say. Noah. Noah has a habit of choosing women that bring trouble. Celeste was no exception, but, at the start, Noah couldn't see it at all. Celeste was always around—and I mean *always* around—but Noah just thought it was nice. Slowly, things turned sour. Noah was always apologising to Celeste, even when she was the one who'd gone through his personal email, or totally lost it at him for just looking at another woman in the street. When they broke up it was absolutely toxic. She would call up and scream at him down the phone. But then, she changed tactic, and suddenly she was all sweet, saying they should just be friends. Noah, of course, fell for it. They're still friends now. That's Noah for you. He'll forgive anyone. Not so for me. But it's pretty difficult. I mean, I'm sure you've heard how she pulled me out of that rip. It sounds petty to be so critical of someone after they saved your life. I probably sound like a monster. You must be wondering why I'm not grateful. But you met Celeste, didn't you? You must understand.

'It took me a while to realise that Celeste was also involved with Sem. I met Sem independently. Nancy—my ex, Matilda's mother and Sem's old foster mum—told me that he wanted to come down to pick fruit, and so I helped set him up with a job. And then I found out there was also a connection between him and Celeste.'

Liam rubbed his hands on his knees, as if to warm them, before going on.

'When I found out that Celeste and Matilda were staying at that place by the beach, well, I was concerned. Because of my relationship with her mum, I felt a bit protective of Tilly. Not like a father, but not *not* like a father, if you can understand that. So I wasn't too happy to find her living out here with Celeste—especially knowing the way Tilly can be. I mean, you know Tilly: she's so . . . persuadable. That expression she gets sometimes, kind of a blank look, but you know that underneath the cogs are whirring away, drawing some conclusion. When I saw her down here, I just thought she should watch out. I tried to tell her as much. She needed to look out for herself. She wouldn't stand a chance against Celeste.'

That day when I meditated among the trees with my mum, I hadn't seen the documentary yet. I wasn't yet aware of how persuadable I appeared, or how Celeste was shown in such a bad light. So, when I thought about Celeste, I thought about the ways that I had caught her off guard. I was the one who had left her out there at the beach house, without a word of explanation. I remembered all the ways she'd been good to me. Looking after me when I couldn't get out of bed, trying to guard me from Peter and taking me down to the coast and lending me her clothes and hanging out with me when no one else had ever really bothered. She was my only friend. And I had snuck away without even telling her I was leaving. And then I had gone to the police, and implicated her in a crime, when it was possible that she'd done the opposite for me— protecting me from punishment for the awful mistake I'd made. I could picture her at the police station, sticking valiantly to the story we had told them from the start: how we had gone back up to the house together to sleep and woken to find that Sem wasn't there. I imagined her telling the police this story and them looking at her and seeing the belly that was full of baby, and her transparent efforts to charm them: the widening of her grey eyes, perhaps the shoulder of her jacket slipped down as if by accident. They would see all these things and think that she was trying to con them, that we had killed Sem, and that she'd dragged his body down to the sea, that she was guilty too. Sitting among the trees with my mother, it seemed so possible that she had been trying to protect me this whole time, and I had turned against her and betrayed her again and again. Sem had trusted and loved her, but that wasn't good enough for me.

I guess, like Mum, I too am sceptical of these neat stories we tell about people. How if Celeste was manipulative or loud or hard to control, then those big elements of her personality are the ones that define her rather than all the ways in which she was decent. Like with Liam. It troubles me now, recalling how Liam spoke about Celeste in the documentary. How cold he was towards her, even after she'd saved his life that day at the beach. It's funny how something like that could count for so little, really. How, in the end, it was the drama with his brother that defined her in his mind.

———

It was after my day out with Mum that I started having trouble getting out of bed again. We arrived home and I lay down on the couch and could barely get up for the next three days. Mum brought around a friend who was a nurse, who arranged for me to do some blood tests, but everything came back negative and inconclusive. There were surveys to fill out too, about my mental health, but I didn't want to do those, and selected the answers at random. In the end, the friend thought it was probably brought on by stress. Mum got me up and onto a bus out to a clinic, where they gave me white pills that made me feel even duller and drowsier and which after a while I refused to take. Mum and I lived in this uneasy way for almost four months, and I just let the days run past me, lying on the couch. Peter's documentary was released, but I didn't attend the initial screenings. I couldn't face it. It was only when it won the award that I finally forced myself to go.

It was shortly after this that I went back to court, and it was confirmed that the case would go to trial. My lawyer called police officers to give evidence, including Sergeant McIntyre and the woman I had spoken to in Melbourne when I confessed. They talked about how Celeste and I had waited to report Sem missing. They made a big deal of my confession. There was other evidence too. My lawyer had discussed this with me before we arrived, but even so I wasn't prepared for how different it would feel to hear it all laid out in the courtroom. They went through all the things that had turned up in the search. Some fabric fibres, found in the clearing and down on the rocks, that matched descriptions of Sem's swag. A white flip-flop, like the ones Sem used to wear, had been found on a beach a bit further up the coast. The checked shirt Sem had been wearing that night we went to the pub had washed up on the next beach over. And my fingerprints were on the wheel and gearstick of the red car, despite the fact that I didn't have my licence. My lawyer had told me ahead of the hearing that I should plead not guilty, despite my confession, because I'd been drinking and didn't properly remember the events of that night, and Sem's body hadn't been found. He thought we could easily explain away the evidence the prosecution planned to present. We were the ones calling the witnesses, to test the strength of the prosecution's case. But in the courtroom I felt uncertain. The case against me sounded so convincing. And when the magistrate looked at me, I couldn't see any hint of leniency or forgiveness in her gaze. She looked at me with calm calculation, weighing up the details on a set of scales deep in her mind.

As I mentioned before, it was around the same time as my hearing that Peter's documentary was picked up by a new streaming service. And that's when everything blew up: the ODPP stepping in to prevent the documentary's wider release, the story about freedom of expression and justice. Suddenly my face was in the newspapers and magazines, and overnight

I became the centre of attention. I couldn't even go out for milk without being recognised. It became clear that I couldn't keep on going in the way I was. I needed to get away.

Unexpectedly, Mum came to my aid. She helped me apply to the court for permission to move down to the lakes. She even paid my first two months of rent. And when I got here, I discovered that I did feel better, well enough to get the job at the supermarket and pay my own way, at least until the trial comes around.

I suppose the documentary didn't bring only bad attention. It was because of Peter's documentary that a new lawyer contacted me and offered to handle my case pro bono. Alison emailed me before I moved to the coast, and I went back to court and told them I wanted to change representation. And then, after I was living at the lakes, she drove all the way out to meet with me, and helped me find my psychologist. The first thing she said in her email to me was: 'I saw the documentary about you, and I think you might have a very strong case.' It was Peter's third and final retelling that gave her the idea. She—like everyone else—had somehow seen the documentary that no one was meant to have seen. When I asked her about it, her reply was vague. Alison was interested in the story Peter told about my father, and the story about Celeste, and what that might mean for me.

Chapter Eighteen

YOU WOULD THINK THAT, WITH the trial fast approaching, my legal defence would have been my primary concern these last few months. But the truth is I've been more preoccupied with the dog at the Hidden Place. After I first saw the dog, I thought maybe it was just a one-time thing and the next time I went it'd be gone. And so, about three days later, I returned. When I arrived at the Hidden Place, there was no sign of the dog, and I was alone again with only the sun on the water and the whispering trees and the punctuation of a fish splash. But no sooner had I cast out my line than I heard, echoing across the water, the dog's whine breaking into a bark. When I looked up, there it was, on the far bank. Seeing it again made me wonder if its owner might not be far behind. Maybe they would come down to the water's edge, looking for the dog, and find me, in my boat, and I would see the recognition dawning on their face: *You're the girl from the papers, from the documentary about the young man who disappeared.* So I pulled in my line and started the boat's motor. I was relieved when the vibrations of the engine replaced the trembling in my hand as I steered through the muddy passes.

The next time I went back, and the time after that, the dog was already standing on the bank waiting for me, and so I didn't even shut off the motor. I just turned and left immediately. Even so, the damage was done. The dog had a reach that extended far beyond the Hidden Place. I found myself thinking of it as I made lunch, or while I was sitting out on the sloping lawn reading a book. I caught myself wondering if it had an owner, or if it was lost and, if so, where it was finding food and water. Sometimes I even thought that I should get in the boat and go out to the Hidden Place to see if it was still there, and take it a bone and some fresh water to drink. But then I imagined the dog's owner turning up, and that look of recognition. So I didn't go to see the dog, and instead I thought about it, and when I wasn't thinking about the dog, I'd think of Sem.

I often think about Sem and how he could use words, even really formal words, completely without pretention. He'd find some new word and then would start using it all the time—almost testing it out—with this pure enthusiasm. A kind of raw love for the word itself. No one else I've ever met has used language like that. I wish, back when we were younger, I hadn't always been so quick to tell him that he was wrong. Now, when I have some time to myself at the lake house, sometimes I will sit and remember Sem delighting in a certain word, and then remind myself that I was the one who shut him down.

In his documentary, Peter breaks up the interviews he did with my mum about Sem. Peter does this with a lot of the interviews, returning to them to add new layers to the story as he retells it again and again. He never plays an interview straight through from start to end, but presents them piecemeal, and mixes different interviews together, so it's not clear in what order things were said, or what point really led into the next.

In her interview, Mum was sitting at the kitchen table at Angel Street, in one of her hessian outfits, her hair—grey now—swept back from her face. As she spoke, her hands rested on the table, and she never lifted or moved them, not even when she became emotional. It's not till near the end of the documentary that you see my mother talking about adopting Sem.

'My ex-husband and I fostered Sem when he was a kid. Semyon is his full name. It means "listening". It means "God is heard". I thought that was very beautiful. Don't you think so? It kind of fits with fostering. God is heard.

'He was thirteen when he came to us. Very quiet at first. Attachment difficulties. Behavioural problems. He was always running away. Sem's mother wasn't very reliable. She'd miss visits with him, sometimes fail to turn up without any notice. They say if a child doesn't properly bond to his mother as soon as he's born, he will always have difficulty forming strong relationships. I don't know if that's true, but I do know that Sem didn't think he could trust us. Sometimes it seemed like he hated us. God. He was probably right to, in a way.'

'Right to hate you or right not to trust you?' Peter asked.

'Both, I guess,' Mum said, with a short laugh. 'I'll be honest. It was embarrassing, sometimes, how he was always running away. I just felt like a bit of a fool. I'd told everyone I was taking this child into my house and then he didn't even want the house or me. He didn't want a mother, even if he needed one. Or maybe he already had a mother, and I just couldn't see that.

'And people didn't understand what he'd been through. It was natural for him to reject us. It didn't mean that we'd done anything wrong. But I knew what they were thinking. They thought there must be something wrong with us. That there was something about us that made him want to flee.

'It put a strain on our marriage, but things hadn't been that great between me and Andrew for a while. Maybe since the very beginning. Andrew was always very dominant. Very possessive. Perhaps that's just men.

'It was my idea to bring Sem into the family. Andrew was against it from the start. And so, because it was my idea, when our marriage was breaking down I think Andrew knew instinctively that it was something he could use against me. He got this idea into his head that if I was harming my daughter through my insistence on fostering, then it would be clear I wasn't a good mother and he would be allowed to take Tilly away. Take them both away. He hated me, I think. I really believe that, by the end, he just wanted to punish me. He wanted to prove that I was an unfit mother. He wanted to take Tilly and start a new life that had nothing to do with me. Actually, I don't think he even really wanted Tilly, because in the end he let me have her. It was more that he knew that I loved her, and so he wanted to hurt me by threatening to take her away.

'So Andrew took Tilly to this counsellor, and made her say these things. But kids can be coached and encouraged to say things and remember things that aren't true. And even if Matilda was a bit old to be completely misled—I think she was what, thirteen?—even at that age, kids can still be encouraged to say things and even believe things that aren't real. Matilda didn't have an easy time at school, you know. She struggled to make friends and fit in. And I know she found it difficult when her father and I separated. She was desperate for his approval. So if she thought it was what he wanted, she might have gone ahead and made accusations about Sem whether he had really done anything or not. Worst of all, Tilly said that I knew about it, but wasn't stepping in.

Andrew and this counsellor had tapes of the interviews, and they shared them with the social workers and the lawyers— by this stage the separation had got pretty ugly—and it was clear that Andrew was going to use it all as evidence to try to take my children away. I went to Andrew and I begged him not to do it. I even offered to let him have Tilly for a bit so I could look after Sem, just until he was ready for the move to another home, but Andrew was adamant. He was determined that Sem had to be removed from the house right away.

'So what choice did I have? I think it almost killed Sem. To have me appear to give up on him like that, after everything. He was distraught. It was terrible.'

These words of my mother's were used in Peter's third version of Sem's story. The final retelling, a story of manipulation. This is the story that caught my lawyer's attention.

I should tell you, probably, about my meeting with Alison. I feel a little treacherous doing so, because she stressed to me at our first meeting that everything between us was confidential—it was called lawyer–client privilege, she explained—and it would be in my own best interests to avoid discussing with anyone what we were planning for the trial. But by the time you're old enough to read this, the trial will be long over, things will have gone one way or the other, and this information won't really have much power anymore. I suppose it is possible that you may want to open things back up, if you can, or have the case retried, and you might find what I'm about to tell you useful for that. Well, that is your right. And I would rather that everything was clear and known. So, I am happy to tell you this.

My new lawyer arrived at the lake house in a sleek silver car. She was wearing a pencil skirt and grey jacket, and flat shoes. Her hair was straight and blonde. She had the air of someone who was just starting to become rich, but who was serious, and self-made. I think I admired her in a way, but I was also suspicious. To become self-made you have to find the ways to make yourself. Alison reminded me of Peter. I had the sense that, like him, she was looking for footholds in the world, and I might just be another one.

'As soon as I saw the documentary,' she said, sitting calmly opposite me at the kitchen table, 'I thought that I could help you. My background is in family law, so I was intrigued by the details of your parents' separation. Your mother's allegation that your father may have used you, may have wittingly or unwittingly coerced allegations of sexual contact from you about your foster brother, Semyon. I've seen cases like that before.

'I'm not here to demonise your father. Please don't think that. It's possible that he may not have even realised that he was manipulating you. Most likely, he honestly believed the allegations that you made, and thought that Semyon and your mother were making the home an unsafe place for you. Sometimes, when things get very acrimonious, a parent can lose sight of the harm they may be causing to their child in their determination to hurt their spouse.

'Another thing that stood out to me pertains to your temperament. I hope you'll forgive me for being direct. The documentary went to some pains to depict you as particularly reserved. Unconfident. That you had difficulty engaging with your peers. A need for approval from your father. A very intense friendship with Celeste. That you spent a lot of time ruminating on things. I'd like to have you evaluated. I wonder if perhaps you're particularly susceptible to manipulations like the one your mother accused your father of. For people who don't have the clearest sense of their identity, who have high emotional dependency, or need for approval, those things can make you more susceptible to being manipulated. Over-intellectualisation, too. Overthinking things. People like that can be more easily persuaded.

'I'm not saying this to open up past wounds. But I'm thinking of your upcoming trial. When I saw the documentary, I started to think there was a strong possibility that you were particularly disposed to believe what Celeste told you, even if it wasn't true.'

I interrupted her at this point. 'I've thought about what Celeste told me, and I've doubted it myself,' I said. 'But why would she lie? It doesn't really make sense.'

'You're right,' said Alison, 'in a way.' She smiled at me. 'Don't get me wrong, I understand that people sometimes do things for no reason, and just because we can't understand *why* Celeste might have lied to you, it doesn't mean that she didn't. It would be very difficult to argue that in court, though. We need to have a story we can tell that might explain why Celeste would try to convince you that you killed Semyon. That's why I've come down here today to talk with you. I already have some ideas from my research and, of course, the documentary, but I'd like to hear from you about everything that happened with Semyon. Together, I think we will be able to come up with quite a convincing explanation.'

I have to confess, I had a little trouble keeping up with the lawyer as she outlined her plans. I felt a kind of buzzing in my head. A return of that terrible tired feeling, which I'd had a respite from since I had been living down at the lakes.

'There are a few things that I think you should do ahead of the trial,' Alison told me, reaching over and opening her briefcase. 'First, I think you should start seeing a counsellor or a psychologist. I'll try to find someone local who specialises in identity issues and emotional dependency. The sooner you can start seeing her, the stronger her evidence will be at trial. The prosecution may want you to see an independent psychologist too, but it will be helpful if we could connect you with someone who can start treating you immediately, and who will be able to attest to your mental state and your vulnerability to persuasion.

'And I'd like you to tell me more about Celeste. Were there any reasons why she might have resented you, or wanted to implicate you in Semyon's disappearance? Based on the evidence, the shoe and the shirt, I think we can assume that Semyon's body is in the sea. So I think we need to think about that, about what you remember yourself from that night, and what Celeste's role in all this might be. Was Celeste the type of person who might have hurt Sem, intentionally or otherwise?'

Alison stopped then, and smiled at me. 'I know this is rather a lot to assimilate. I'll let you think on it, gather your thoughts, and perhaps we can meet again tomorrow? I've booked a room at the hotel on the headland for the rest of the week, so we have some time.'

I remember nodding and shaking the lawyer's hand. I remember her explaining that she would be able to represent me pro bono, because of the nature of the case and how it had been so much in the media. And all the while, I was thinking of Celeste and Sem. I was remembering them at the beach. The two of them in the water, Sem's arms wrapped around Celeste's waist, Celeste shrieking and twisting, their laughter floating in the hot air. The two of them out on the balcony in the evening, with the chimes of the bellbirds echoing across the water, her resting in his arms, just chatting about things. And, of course, all the private moments between them that I didn't see. All the time they spent together before I saw Celeste at Noah's party. The emails when they were younger. How they'd got back together again so much later. All that time they had together, without me.

———

Before I'd left the beach house, I asked Celeste about the blue vase. 'Did you throw it at him?' I asked. We were in the kitchen, and I remember she looked at me in disbelief.

'I was the one who broke it, yes, but I never *threw* it,' she said. 'That was what set off our fight that day. I knocked it to the floor and it smashed. Sem was always going on at me about how clumsy I was. And that was the day I discovered I was pregnant—not that I'd told Sem yet. But I just wasn't in the mood for his shit.'

I can't remember if I replied, but I must have been looking at her strangely, because she said, 'You thought I threw the vase at Sem?' She laughed. 'Jesus, you're deluded. You think that if you can tell yourself I threw the vase, it will make you less guilty? Is that it?'

I thought about the blue vase after the lawyer left. Whether I believed Celeste or not, I had lied to Peter about the vase. I had told him I saw Celeste throw it. I'd lied to him about other things too. About what happened between Sem and me when we were younger. Even when I was talking to the police, there were times when I had lied. When I presented things as facts, though I didn't believe they were true. And I had a similar temptation when it came to the lawyer, Alison. Already, I could feel stories emerging in my mind, ways of presenting things that I knew would please her. Maybe, I thought, I was more like my father than I'd realised. Looking for ways to convince other people of things. If I said that Celeste threw the vase, that made her violent, and instead of hesitating on the stairs, I became someone who had entered the room to bear witness. If I said that Sem had touched me when we were younger, then it seemed like I had a reason to hurt him when we were adults. Just like my dad had tried to convince the social workers and the lawyers that if my mum allowed me to live in an unsafe environment, then she was a bad mother. Maybe I was trying to convince people of things too. Weaving my own stories, creating my own version of events. Maybe that's what I've been doing for you all along. Telling this story, so that in the end you will look at me with your innocent baby eyes and give me your verdict: innocent or guilty, right or wrong, forgiven or condemned.

Chapter Nineteen

WHEN I FIRST CAME OUT to the lakes, I looked up the distance from here to the house near Eden, where I had lived with Celeste and Sem. I had no plans to travel there. I wasn't looking at the map with any view to actually going. It was almost the opposite. Living at the lake house and cycling to the little coastal town nearby reminded me so much of that summer with Celeste and Sem that I got out the map to reassure myself that I was far enough away from the beach house, and of the distance between then and now.

I pressed my finger on the spot where the beach house would be, then traced a line back to the house on the lake, almost caressing the distance between the two places. As I did so, I cast my eyes over the names of the places that disappeared and reappeared under my fingertip. One of these was the town near the berry farm where Sem had worked. I took my finger from the map and looked at the region more closely. I could see where the farm was located. It was a few hours' drive away, along a road that cut through the flat land without a single bend, as there were no hills or mountains to work around. I knew there were buses that ran along the coast, and I'd be able to catch one that would take me close to the farm. Once I understood this, I was overcome by a feeling of inevitability. It was not a question of whether I would go to the farm but when. It was a temptation too great to resist. I guess I thought that if I could see the farm for myself I might understand something about what had happened to Sem. Sometimes it feels like I've spent my whole life in this way, alternately trying to hide from or seek out my past and Sem's place in it. Filled either with endless empty dread or furious insatiable hope.

As my court date approaches, the dog at the Hidden Place has been on my mind more and more. It has got to the stage that, no matter where I am, I think I can hear it barking. And that's why, about a week ago now, I had to take all the knives out of the cutlery drawer and put them at the bottom of the pantry, under a towel. I'm not sure, really, how I got it into my mind that I might kill the dog. The best way I can explain it is that I had almost the opposite thought. I'd been worrying about the dog, and whether it had access to food and water, and what if it died, and then I just moved on naturally to the next thought: How terrible would it be if I went and slit that dog's throat to drive him out of my mind? And once I had thought it, the idea kind of got stuck to the inside of my brain, so that I couldn't think of the dog without thinking of killing him, and I was thinking of the dog almost all the time. In the end, I got so fixated on the thought that hiding the knives seemed like a sensible thing to do. A way of protecting me from myself. But it only made things worse, because now I had the memory of the knives in my hands, so I could almost believe that I had already killed the dog, and when I went out in the boat I couldn't take it anywhere near the Hidden Place, because I was so afraid of what I might do or what I might have done already, until it got to a point where I couldn't bear to take the boat out at all, and started spending my days lying in bed, getting up only to go to work at the supermarket—though increasingly I could barely face that, and started calling in sick—or to visit my psychologist, Helen.

I like going to Helen's house, and I like Helen. Of all the people who are in my life these days—and there aren't very many—Helen is one of the few I think I can trust. I never really get the sense that Helen wants anything from me. She seemed content enough with her life when I entered it. She's not looking for me to further her own ambitions in any way. So we can talk freely. Just recently, I've started talking with Helen about stories, and why we tell them. Mostly, Helen just listens. She hasn't tried to tell me what she thinks, or what I ought to believe. I even told her that, since I came out to the lakes, I'd started writing everything down for you, so that you could understand what happened, and she didn't tell me to stop, and she didn't encourage me either. She just nodded her head and sipped her tea.

'I know what you're thinking,' I said. 'You're thinking I'm a big hypocrite. Saying how much trouble I have with everyone telling stories, only to write my own. But it's not like that. I'm putting it all down to try to make sense of things.'

'What would it look like,' Helen asked me, 'if it all made sense?'

I didn't really have an answer to that. So instead, I told her about the dog, and how I was afraid of myself around it, and I was surprised that this time Helen had some concrete advice to offer.

'Let's try an exercise,' she suggested. 'When you get home, I'd like you to take the knives out of the pantry and put them back where they belong. And then,' she said, 'you should take your boat around to that lake to visit the dog. You could think of it as your friend.'

I felt uncomfortable when she said that. It made me squirm a little in my chair. I tried to keep my voice deliberately light and carefree as I replied, 'I'm not so sure about that!' and I even gave a little laugh that sounded awful and hollow to my ears.

'You might be surprised,' Helen said. And then she put her hands on her knees meaningfully and said, 'I think that's probably where we should leave things for today.'

———

When I got home, I did take the knives out of the pantry, like Helen had suggested. I was still feeling unsettled by the idea of visiting the dog, but moving the knives was something I thought I could do. I had already driven myself so crazy with them; now just thinking about them made me feel exhausted. I guess they had lost some of their power over me. After I had taken the knives from the pantry and returned them to the cutlery drawer, I finally decided to go out to the berry farm. I think I needed something to do, and I wasn't ready to think about taking the boat out to see the dog. Maybe also it was because, without the knives to worry about, there was nothing for my anxiety to stick on to. I needed to find somewhere new to pin my thoughts.

So I gathered up a jacket and my wallet and cycled into town to look at the bus routes. There was one that left the next morning, returning later the same day.

I got to the bus stop early the next morning. It was a few hours' journey, and I sat quietly, letting my tension dissipate, to be replaced by calm. In this moment, at least, I had a purpose. A hope that the answers I needed were waiting for me at the farm.

The farm was down the end of a dirt track, marked on the main road by a hand-painted sign saying FRESH FRUITS AND BERRIES. I walked up slowly towards the greenhouses. It was a cold day, and the sky overhead was grey. The lawn on either side of the track had been mown, and kangaroos stood, eating and flicking their ears. Beyond were the greenhouses, standing against the grey sky.

At the end of the track was a low orange-brick house. When I went up to the flywire door, I saw that the front room had been turned into a small shop. I guessed that the owners lived in the rest of the house, and perhaps some of the workers too, though there were other buildings at the rear of the property, so perhaps some people were housed back there. I entered the shop, where jars of strawberry jam and tomato relishes and packets of homemade biscuits had been arranged on a table, behind which stood an older woman wearing a dark green apron.

The woman must have known that I was the girl from the documentary—Sem's disappearance was big news in the area—but at first she didn't give any hint of recognition. She simply welcomed me and stood smiling as I walked up and down in front of the table, looking at the products she had set out. There were no fresh berries, only preserves, and I figured it was because I'd come at the wrong time of year. It was only when I had finally selected a jar of strawberry jam and took out my wallet to pay for it that I said, 'My brother worked here a while ago—perhaps you knew him?' My voice, as I said this, sounded ridiculously casual. But if the woman noticed, she responded only with kindness.

'Oh, my dear,' she said, and put her hand on my arm gently. 'I remember him well.' Her fingertips felt dry and light. 'Please,' she said, after a moment, 'wait here. I have something I think I should give to you.'

I waited while the woman went through a door into the main house. After a few minutes she came back with a white envelope, unsealed. I opened it in front of her. Inside was a photo of Sem, standing in one of the greenhouses, barefoot, with a crate by his left foot that was full of punnets overflowing with strawberries. He was thin, like I remembered he was towards the end, and wearing shorts and a loose grey long-sleeved t-shirt. He was smiling.

'Not the most reliable worker,' the woman said. 'But he had a good soul. Lost, I suppose. He seemed a little lost. But who isn't at that age?' And she gave me a smile. 'He had a good heart.'

It's funny, because when the woman handed me that photo, I looked at Sem and it was almost as though I didn't recognise him. I've spent my life meeting Sem and then meeting him again as an entirely new person. But what the woman said at the greenhouse that day, and the fact she'd kept that photograph, makes me think that perhaps one of Sem's most central and unchanging qualities was the way that he made people like him, almost without fail. It made me sad. All I really know about Sem is how *I* felt about him—nothing to do with Sem's feelings, or who he was, or what he really thought about anything at all.

'Don't you worry,' the woman said. 'Some people think you did it and others think that you didn't. But at the end of the day, even if you did, well, wasn't it just a terrible accident, anyway? My darling, if you did do it, well, my heart goes out to you even more.'

I must have had an awful expression on my face when she said this, because she immediately began apologising. Telling me that she didn't know what had possessed her to say those things. That it wasn't any of her business and that it was terrible of her to have brought it up like that. But I wasn't even really thinking about what she'd said. I was thinking about Sem. The stranger in the picture. I saw that perhaps I hadn't ever really known him. Never made the effort to understand him. In a way, I was just like all the others, like Peter and the lawyer: just another person wanting a foothold to climb into the adult world. Not wanting to understand Sem as another person, climbing on a journey of his own.

I don't remember paying for my jam, or how I left the farm. The next thing I knew I was on the bus, heading home. In my lap, I had the jar of jam and the picture of Sem. From time to time I took out the photo and looked at it, before sliding it back into its envelope.

—

This morning, Celeste came out to the lake house to visit me. This was in violation of the terms of my bail, and hers too, I guess. But still, she showed up, uninvited. I heard her pull up, the sound of the wheels jerking me out of my dazed state on the couch. I went to the window and drew aside the gauzy blind and there she was, getting out of an unfamiliar green car. I pulled on a jacket and went out to meet her in the drive, before she could come up the path and knock on the door. I could feel my heartbeat in my fingers. In truth, I was strangely excited to see her, despite everything. I felt like she'd come back for me. Like when she'd brought me flowers at the house on Angel Street, nearly two years ago now. But then, as I stepped onto the front porch, I thought of how I'd left her at the beach house, and how I'd betrayed her by going to the police. Maybe she'd come out here to berate me. To punish me in some way for what I had done. What could I possibly say to her, given everything we'd been through?

Celeste was standing by the car. 'I probably shouldn't be here,' she said, looking around at the driveway, my blue bike, the wattle trees. 'Nice place.' She looked different. Shorter, somehow. Diminished.

'Thanks,' I said. My throat felt dry.

She then went to the back of the car, opened the door and bent to look inside. I clenched and released my hands. Tried to be calm.

Still half in the car, she looked over her shoulder at me. 'Can I come inside, or should we just do this out here?' She was reaching into the car, fiddling about, and when she straightened, it was with you in her arms, cuddled against her chest.

'Out here is fine,' I said.

She stood next to the car, the door still open. You were wriggling a bit in her arms. Dressed in a pink onesie.

'You brought the baby,' I said.

'Yes.' She looked down at the ground and then back up at me. 'I wanted you to know that I'm sorry for how everything went,' she said. 'I honestly thought I was doing the right thing. It wasn't your fault.'

'Okay,' I said. I was hardly listening to her. Instead, I was transfixed by you. It reminded me of how I had been with Sem. All that time spent dreaming about him. Imagining the ways things could have been between us. In my mind, I've been creating all these versions of you. I've been telling you all these stories about your parents and about me. All this time asking myself: Am I guilty or innocent? All this time pretending that I've been writing this account for you, so that you can know what is true, when really, in my heart, I've been hoping that at the end of it you will somehow turn to me and say, 'You're innocent,' or perhaps just, 'I forgive you.'

So it was then, seeing Celeste holding you, that I started to understand how deluded I'd been. Because you were only a baby. A real baby, squirming in your mother's arms. But maybe that was part of it. You were still so pure. If you could pardon me, then maybe, I thought, I could somehow forgive myself.

'But that's not why I came out here,' Celeste said. 'Actually, I wanted to give you this.' She held out a small book. Sem's notebook.

'I can't take that,' I said.

'You should,' Celeste said. She came and put it down on the bottom step to the porch, bringing you closer to me, so I caught a glimpse of your little face, your big eyes drinking everything in. Then she turned and took you back to the car. She put you in your seat, closed the door, and went and got into the driver's side. She started the engine and, after a moment, reversed away, the car tyres crunching gravel, both your faces obscured behind the darkened windows.

I watched until the car was gone. Then I picked up Sem's notebook and took it into the house. I put it in the drawer under the television. I didn't want to look at it. I went into my bedroom and lay on the bed and waited to cry, but no tears came.

All that time spent going back over the past. Searching for a story that would exonerate me. A story that would make me feel good. 'It wasn't your fault.' Celeste's words echoed in my head. Weren't they the words I'd been hoping to hear?

Yet when she said them, I'd hardly even been able to listen. I was thinking instead about you. Understanding, for the first time, that you're real.

———

I stayed in bed for hours. I was exhausted. All the adrenaline that had pumped through me when I saw Celeste in the driveway had evaporated, leaving me feeling brittle and empty. And into that empty space, all my thoughts came seeping in. Again, the events of that summer with Celeste and Sem. The night of Celeste's birthday, down at the clearing. And also, the last time I'd seen her, at the house near Eden. How I'd left her there, standing on the balcony. I tried to remember the expression on her face. Had she been hurt to see me go? I thought about all the ways that Celeste had been good to me, and then all the ways that she had felt suffocating. How sometimes she seemed like the only person I could trust, but other times she was the one person I couldn't rely on at all.

Outside my window, the shadows shortened and then began to lengthen again over the grass slope that ran down to the lake. I started thinking about what had happened to Celeste since I left the beach house that day with Peter. How she had given birth to you. What that meant. And then I started thinking about the trial. It was those thoughts that eventually got me out of bed.

I went to the kitchen for a piece of paper and a pen and started to write notes. I made a list of things I needed to talk to my lawyer about. Questions I had. I found myself suddenly seized by panic that I might be too late. All the months I had wasted, lying around, so uninterested, hung over me. I felt almost dizzy, and had to take a deep breath. Pour myself a glass of water. I didn't have time to regret those lost days. I had to move forwards. Had to think about what could still be done. What I should do, and what that would mean for us all. What the best outcome might be. I had to really think about you.

In the late afternoon, when I couldn't think anymore, I went down to the boat. It had rained overnight, and the bottom was full of brackish water, so I took out the bung and let it drain onto the muddy bank. Then I pushed out into the reeds, closed the choke, pulled the cord, and began to wend my way to the Hidden Place, my ears full of the pulsing song of the motor. I knew the route so well, by now. I sat up and let the wind rush into my face, cold even with my jumper zipped up to my neck.

When I arrived, the Hidden Place was just as I remembered it. The tall trees still stood in thick ranks on the banks, their white trunks gleaming. The sky above was the same blue. The light still caught the surface of the water in the same way. There was no sign of the dog.

I cut the motor and sat for a while in the quiet until I heard the echoing splash of a fish. I lay down across the narrow seats of the boat and closed my eyes and felt the cold sun on my face. I opened my eyes and looked into the sky. Waited for the feeling of calm to return, now that the dog was gone and the place was all mine again. But, strangely, the peaceful feeling was gone. I suppose the best way I can put it is that I felt a little lonely there, in the Hidden Place, without the dog. Contrary to all my thoughts over the past weeks, I found myself unexpectedly thinking fondly of him. I thought of that funny excited expression he had on his face when he saw me.

I continued staring up into the sky. I've been taking a lot of comfort in the sky, recently. I've been telling myself that no matter what happens, or where I go, I will always have the sky. If I can just get outside for an hour, or look out the window, there will be solace up there. Today, lying in the boat at the Hidden Place, I looked up into the sky and imagined Sem looking up at the same clear blue expanse, as if that might connect us. But I knew that if he was looking up into the sky, it was not this one. I tried to imagine that all his conspiracy theories were true. That there was life in space. Maybe the sky had taken Sem, and he was up there, looking down on me. I tried to imagine it. But I couldn't feel him. I was alone.

The trial is less than a month away now. I will go into the courtroom and the lawyers will tell their stories about me and Celeste and Sem. And no matter what happens, and wherever I go, I will have the sky. That's what I've been telling myself. But now, looking up at that expanse of pale and hardened blue, I think I'm seeing for the first time just how distant and empty the sky can be.

It's getting dark now. The evening comes early here, with no city lights to keep it at bay. I know I'll have to sit up soon and take my boat back to the house before it's too dark to see the way. Just one last moment here, in my circle of water. And that's when I hear it. Echoing across the water. A dog's bark.

Sitting up, I see the dog standing on the bank in the evening's last light, wagging his tail at me.

'Hello, dog,' I call out, and he opens his mouth and pants. It looks almost like a smile. I take the boat and run it close to the shore. The dog turns in a circle, excited to see me.

'Hello, dog,' I call out to him again, and he barks, once, then sits on the bank. I keep the boat there, idling, for a few moments more. I can smell the eucalyptus. The air is crisp and cold. I know I have to leave. It's getting dark. I do one more loop with the boat, and it bumps against the small waves made by its own passage, before I make my way back to the narrow channel away from the Hidden Place. In the growing darkness, scuttling crabs make the mudbanks look alive. My hand vibrates with the motor. The cold wind has my face feeling sharp. I think maybe tonight I will take Sem's notebook out of the drawer. Hear his voice. Finally start reading his poetry.

Acknowledgements

THANK YOU TO EVERYONE AT Allen & Unwin. With warmth and wisdom, Annette Barlow was instrumental in helping me realise this book—thank you. Christa Munns was there every step of the way, and Ali Lavau's insightful edits were invaluable. I'm grateful to Aziza Kuypers for her thoughtful proofreading, and to Ali Hampton and Laura Benson for all their work. Thank you also to Jennifer Thurgate for her assistance. I'm so lucky to work with you all.

I'm very grateful to Alan Stevns and the Stevns family, *The Australian* and Allen & Unwin for *The Australian*/Vogel's Literary Award, which has provided me with incredible support. Thank you to Caroline Overington, Hsu-Ming Teo and Kate Adams for selecting my manuscript.

Luis Jaramillo and Helen Schulman at The New School— thank you for teaching me to write. The team at Sterling Lord Literistic taught me about publishing, especially Flip Brophy,

Jim Rutman and Martha Millard. My parents, Mark and Margaret Pierce, showed me how to love books and, with Mimi Pierce, read early drafts of this manuscript. Mary Krienke helped transform this manuscript into the book it is now. Thank you to Shirley and Wanghua Chu for all their support. And thank you also to Manny Brennan for your legal insights.

Finally, and most importantly, thank you, Mark. This book is dedicated to you because without you it wouldn't exist. Thank you for encouraging me to write, giving me the courage to move across the world for books, talking with me about writing craft, teaching me what you knew even when I was a difficult student, helping me find the time to write each day, and reading this manuscript so many times and always with such care. Thank you for teaching me about love, showing me parts of the world I wouldn't have discovered without you, being so generous, and making me laugh. I love you.